# DEVIL'S REDEMPTION

## THE DEVIL'S PAWN DUET BOOK 2

### NATASHA KNIGHT

## ABOUT THIS BOOK

**Isabelle**

Just when I was beginning to trust my husband, he betrayed me.

Just when I thought I was falling in love he showed me the beast he truly is.

I understand his thirst for revenge. But I don't want to play this game of pawn and puppet master.

No matter how his hands make my heart race and my body crave his devil's touch, I won't give in.

I love his daughter.

But I can't let myself fall in love with her father.

**Jericho**

I have exactly what I want. Revenge.

Soon everything the Bishops have will be mine.

But it will cost me more than I bargained.

Isabelle Bishop hates me. As she should.

I know what I am. And now she does too.

But falling in love with my wife was never part of my plan.


*Devil's Redemption is Book 2 of The Devil's Pawn Duet.*
*You'll want to read book 1, Devil's Pawn first.*

# 1

## JERICHO

"What did you do?" Isabelle hisses. She's naked, on her feet pounding small fists into my chest. She has no energy, though. Her strength is zapped from days of not being able to keep any food down and probably weeks worth of frustration.

To look at her now, I've gotten what I wanted. The beginnings of it at least. A Bishop in my clutches. Weak to the point she can barely stand. My baby in her belly.

My future should be bright. I'm well on my way to burying Carlton Bishop. But it doesn't feel very bright right now. In fact, I don't feel anything but a creeping darkness as I take her in my arms trying not to bruise her. Not to hurt her.

What I accused my brother of—his weakness when it comes to the suffering of this particular

Bishop—have I become so weak? Has she worn me down as much as I've worn her down?

"What's happening?" comes a little voice from the hallway.

"Get her out of here!" I yell to anyone who is listening. "Get Angelique out!" She will not witness this. I won't allow her to see Isabelle in this state. See me in this state. She cannot know what I've done.

My mother's soothing voice comes over Isabelle's accusations and a moment later I hear the door click closed. My mother was the one who alerted me to Isabelle's 'bug'. She knew, I'm sure, that it was no bug.

"Lay her down. I'll give her something to relax her," Dr. Barnes says.

"Get your hands off me!" Isabelle protests as I wrap a towel around her, lift her, cradling her against my chest. "Let me go you bastard! You lying bastard!"

"I never lied to you," I clarify calmly as I carry her to the bed. She struggles. Doesn't she know yet I won't let her go? Especially now. But her struggles don't matter much. They only cause the towel to drop to the floor.

Dr. Barnes has the blanket pulled back, but I shake my head. "I want her in my bed," I tell him and let him follow me through the connecting door to my room.

"No! Let me go!" She's half sobbing, half fighting now.

"No, Isabelle," I say, voice low and steady. "I'll never let you go." I lay her down and sit beside her, keeping both of her wrists in one of my hands with just enough pressure on her to keep her down. "Stop fighting me."

"I will never stop fighting you," she cries out, her voice catching as tears stream from her eyes. Her gaze moves beyond me and her panic is renewed. A glance over my shoulder tells me it's Dr. Barnes approaching with a needle.

"It won't hurt them?" I ask.

"No. If there's a baby this won't hurt mother or child."

I nod.

"No! Please!" Isabelle thrashes, kicking her legs. I have her arms pinned to her chest. I turn her onto her side and trap her legs with my free arm as Dr. Barnes swabs an alcohol prep over her hip then pushes the needle in.

She whines as he does it but the effect is almost instantaneous. I feel her legs and arms go weak, her body grow limp.

I loosen my grip and roll her onto her back. When I release her, her limbs relax. She tries once to slap at me, but it doesn't work. She can barely lift her arm a few inches.

"Why did you do it?" she asks, her words beginning to slur as she struggles to keep her eyes open. "Why would you do this to me?"

Guilt grips me in a way it never has before. Not when Kimberly died. Not when I took Isabelle. Not since and not ever before. This, what I'm doing now, I am actively doing.

I am doing the damage.

Causing the harm.

I am consciously destroying this life.

It's a choice.

*You always have a choice. All of life is a choice.* My own words haunt me. When I spoke them to her they were over something so inconsequential. Now, this? It's the opposite.

I swallow the guilt down. Harden my heart. I make myself think about Kimberly. How she died in my arms. But something has shifted. Something has changed. And all I see is Isabelle's face. Hear her desperation. The defeat in her voice.

"Why?" she asks weakly one last time, eyes closing as her head lolls to the side.

I'm saved from answering because she's gone now. Asleep. I draw the blankets up over her and brush wet hair off her face. I look at her here in my bed. Small and vulnerable. So vulnerable. And innocent.

I know the monster I am. I've always known it. I've just never cared. Until now.

"I'm sorry," I say so quietly no one could have heard me.

Dr. Barnes clears his throat. I collect myself and stand. I draw a second blanket to her chin.

"Will she dream?" I ask the doctor without taking my eyes off her.

"Pardon?"

I turn to the man who I'd guess to be in his late forties. He's one of the new Society doctors. He'll do exactly what I need him to do. I think about that. About how I've planned every detail of this.

"Dream. Will she dream?" I ask, my tone shorter than I intend.

"No."

"Good." Because I don't want her trapped in that hell she dreamt the night of our wedding.

I draw a deep breath. "Do what you need to do. I need confirmation she's pregnant. How far along. She's been sick. Lost a few pounds." How had I not seen how thin she was getting? "She'll need something so she can keep food down. And vitamins. She's a vegetarian," I add, surprising myself because the only thing that should matter should be the baby. "Whatever you can give her now, do it."

He puts a hand on my shoulder. "She'll be all right. Go wait outside while I see to your wife."

I shake my head. "I'm staying."

"It's better—"

"I'm staying."

He shuts his mouth and nods. I'm sure any doctor who wasn't employed by The Society would question what the hell was going on, but Barnes won't do that. Another benefit of my status within The Society. Thanks dad.

Dad. Fuck. I need to get on a plane to Austria tomorrow. I can't leave her like this. Not until I'm sure she's okay. Not until I'm sure she won't harm herself or the baby. Although she won't do the latter. I know enough about Isabelle to know she's not capable of that.

I take a seat on the armchair and watch the doctor do his work. He draws several vials of blood and I want to ask if he should take it easy. She's so small. He examines her, taking care to cover her so she's never fully exposed. After what feels like an eternity, he gives her a shot of vitamins and sets two containers on the nightstand.

I get to my feet.

"I'll write out a prescription you can refill as you need, but try the vitamins first. They should help with the nausea. If she still can't keep anything down, you can give her these."

"They're safe for her and the baby?"

"Yes. Although the nausea should go away on its own in time. I'll have my office email you some pamphlets. She is quite thin."

I glance at the slight form beneath the blankets and nod. Is it because of the pregnancy though or had I already started the process of breaking her down the moment I'd brought her into this house and made her my prisoner?

"We'll keep an eye on her. You just make sure to give her what she can stomach. Plain foods. Lots of snacks rather than big meals."

"Okay."

"I'd like to see her in my office soon. This week."

I nod. "When will you know the results of the pregnancy test?"

"Within a few hours. I'll let you know as soon as I hear."

"Thank you, Dr. Barnes."

"Of course, Mr. St. James."

A knock comes on the door then. It's my mother. She glances at Isabelle then at the doctor and me.

"Can you walk Dr. Barnes out?" I ask her. "I'd like to stay with my wife." *My wife.* How strange it sounds. How off course life has gone in five years' time.

"Of course, Jericho. This way, Dr. Barnes."

They leave and the door closes behind them. When it does, I walk to Isabelle's bedroom to get a pair of panties and from under her pillow I find that ratty T-shirt she likes to wear to bed. I carefully dress her before laying her back down. I notice how cold her feet are so I go back into her room and find a pair of fuzzy socks. I slip those on as well before I tuck her in. Her breathing is quiet and calm, so

opposite how she was just a little while ago. I look at
her for a long, long minute before leaning down to
kiss her forehead.

The door opens just as I'm doing it. I school my
features and turn, expecting to find my mother. But
it's not her. It's Angelique. I can see she's been crying
and her eyes grow wide when they settle on Isabelle.

"Is she hurt?" she asks, a sob breaking the
sentence, her lip trembling.

I go to her, lifting her up to carry her to her bed.
"No, she'll be fine. She just hasn't been feeling well
so Dr. Barnes gave her something to help her sleep."

"When will she wake up?"

"In a little while, sweetheart," I say, brushing her
hair back from her face. She inherited Kimberly's
wild curls.

"I saw you kissing her." She smiles but her eyes
are still sad.

I don't say anything but smile back.

She touches my cheek. "You're bleeding, daddy."

I look at her little thumb, see the smear of red. I
wipe off her finger. Isabelle must have scratched me
when she was struggling.

"It's nothing. Just cut myself shaving." I watch
Angelique. "She isn't your mommy. You know that
right?"

Her eyes flit to Isabelle again and she nods.
"Why don't I have a mommy?"

Fuck.

She's asked this before and it never ever gets any fucking easier.

*Because Isabelle's brother murdered her. That's why.*

"Your mommy died before you were born, sweetheart. I know she was sad not to be with you. She loved you very much. I can tell you that. She was so excited to meet you."

"But she couldn't." She knows these answers. This conversation never changes.

I nod. My throat is closing up. It's the look in her eyes. Her young mind unable to process. To understand something so unnatural. So wrong.

"Why did she die?"

"I don't know," I lie. "Let's go fix your book, okay? I know Isabelle would want to do it but since she can't, I'll help you. If you'll let me," I add.

"Why were you fighting?" she asks, eyes so much like mine it's as if they see right to my core. Does she see the monster there?

"How is she?" my mother asks from the door saving me from having to answer.

"She'll be all right."

My mother looks at me a bit longer but knows not to ask the question we all want confirmed. Is Isabelle pregnant?

I turn to Angelique again. "What do you say? Let's go get your book and we'll fix it. That way when Isabelle wakes up, we can show it to her."

"Will you read me the story after?"

"Yes."

"Okay. But leave the door open a crack in case Belle needs us," Angelique says as I carry her out into the hallway, leaving the door open a crack just in case.

# 2

## ISABELLE

I wake slowly my vision fuzzy as I take in the light filtered by drawn curtains. On the nightstand is a book. I can't read the title on the spine. It's too creased. There's a jacket hanging on the back of a chair. Beyond it is a door.

The door that connects my room to my husband's.

It's open. My towel lies on the floor. And I remember why, just as my gaze lands on the man sitting across the room in the large leather wingback chair.

Jericho St. James.

My husband.

My devil.

The liar.

I shift to sit up and he sets his reading material aside. I notice it's my notebook.

"What are you doing with that?" I ask even though there are about a thousand more important questions that need answering.

He walks over to me. "You write your own music," he says. It's not a question. "Why aren't you in school?"

"I'm slow, remember?"

"It's good." He shoves his hands into his pockets and I see the line of worry between his eyebrows. He looks different than he has before. Is it guilt I see in his features? In his stance?

No. A man like Jericho St. James wouldn't feel guilt. It's not in his DNA.

"My music is none of your business," I tell him.

"I'd like to hear you play."

The blanket falls away as I sit up. I notice I'm wearing Christian's shirt.

Jericho moves to adjust the pillows behind my back and although I'd like to tell him to fuck off, I don't. I need to conserve my strength. I'm going to need it if what I suspect is true.

"How do you feel?" he asks.

I look up at him. That usual cockiness isn't there and he's handsomer for it. His features somehow gentler.

No. I banish the thought. This man is not gentle. He is a devil. A liar. He is my enemy.

Julia knew all along. I'd told her it wasn't true. I

had my birth control pills, after all. He hadn't taken those away. God. What a fool I am.

"I feel like shit. Like I've been lied to. Deceived in the worst possible way. Shall I go on?"

Someone knocks on the door and Jericho calls out for them to come in. It's Leontine carrying a tray. When I smell the comforting scent of soup, my stomach growls. I am starving.

"Isabelle," she says with a smile as Jericho takes the tray from her, setting it on the nightstand. "I'm glad to see you awake."

"Did you know?" I ask her.

She's silent and therein lies her answer.

"Did you know that he was swapping out my pills?" I say the words aloud, accusing them both. Hearing them makes the betrayal uglier. More monstrous. I glance at Jericho who doesn't make a sound. Doesn't deny it. Nothing. He just watches me.

She looks to her son. "Go," he tells her without taking his eyes off me. "Make sure we're not disturbed."

She nods and without another look in my direction, leaves.

"You've got everyone under your thumb, don't you?"

He sits on the edge of the bed, reaching to adjust the blankets.

"Don't touch me!"

He stops, not commenting, but doesn't touch me.

I draw my feet up, see the fuzzy pink socks with their white polka dots. Did he dress me? I was naked when they knocked me out. I'd just come out of the shower.

It doesn't matter, though.

"You need to eat, Isabelle. I'm going to feed you."

"I can feed myself."

"You're weak."

"I'll manage."

"Do I need to tie you to the bed to do it?"

"You'd do that, wouldn't you? Is there anything you won't do? Any line you won't cross? Or is human decency beyond your comprehension? Not really your concern?"

"Do I need to bind you?" he asks again.

"No," I tell him because truth is, I am weak. In so many ways.

He picks up the bowl. I see a clear broth with small dumplings inside it.

"It's homemade and vegetarian," he says. "Catherine made it for you."

"I'll just throw it up."

"We'll go slow. The doctor gave you some vitamins. The B vitamins especially should help with the nausea. He left other medication if you can't keep food down."

I glance at the nightstand, seeing two containers. I'm flooded with emotion suddenly. I press the heels of my hands into my eye sockets. They come away wet.

"Is it confirmed then? I'm pregnant?" My voice sounds strange. Thick and full of emotion I'm trying too hard to suppress.

He nods. "We'll go to the doctor's office in a few days and find out more then."

"I'm nineteen years old." Tears fill my eyes and a lump makes my throat close. "This isn't what I wanted." What I expected. Hoped for.

Jericho puts the bowl aside and takes hold of my arms. His jaw is tense and his grip isn't hard, but it is solid. "I'm going to take care of you, Isabelle. I promise."

I want to shove him away, but it feels good having him hold me. He's like an anchor. Someone stronger than me I can lean on. It feels good because I haven't had someone hold me in so, so long. Not like this. Not like they might care.

But then I remember he doesn't care. Not about me. He cares about his baby. He's a monster. A beast. So I shrug out of his grasp.

"You swapped out the pills. Julia found them. The real ones."

He's silent.

"If she hadn't would you have lied? Told me it must be an accident?"

"I haven't lied to you once, Isabelle."

"No, you've done far worse."

He picks up the soup and readies a spoonful of broth. "Open."

I look at it, hungry. I open and he's careful as he brings the hot liquid to my mouth. It's bland but hot and good. Simple. How I like soup.

*I'm pregnant.*

I take another spoonful of broth, taste the salt of a tear that slides to my lip.

*I am pregnant with Jericho St. James's baby.*

He wipes my chin then feeds me another bite, this one with a dumpling. They're good too, doughy, and salty. I eat in silence. He's patient, not rushing me.

When the bowl is empty, he sets it down and picks up the plate of thick-sliced buttered white bread. "Salt?" he asks, picking up the shaker.

He remembers from the other night.

I nod, watching him as I eat the bread he feeds me. I think about how much I am under this man's control. How he is the dictator of my life. I am in his house. In his bed. His hand is the one that feeds me. Literally. His mark is etched into my skin. He can lock me in that cellar if he wants. Keep me there until the baby is born and take the child from me. He can leave me there to die. Bury my body along-side Nellie Bishop's and no one would know. And if they did, no one would help me. Angelique may remember me but I'm sure he could spin a story to distract her until she forgets about me, too. Would anyone even care? Julia? Carlton? Matty maybe.

"I need to know one thing," he finally says as he sets the empty plate aside. I swallow the last mouthful.

"I'm all ears," I say in a mock upbeat fashion. Inside something is twisting me up and tears just keep flowing.

He looks squarely at me, eyes searching mine. "Are you going to try to harm my baby?"

I flinch. And it takes me a full minute to dissect his words.

Am I going to try to harm his baby?

*Harm* a baby.

*His* baby.

"Will you chain me to your bed if I say yes?"

He nods as if it's a no-brainer. An obvious answer. A normal one.

"Do you know how fucked up you are?"

"Believe me, I know exactly what I am."

His comment takes me by surprise.

"Answer me, Isabelle," he says.

I feel stronger. It's the soup and bread and probably the vitamins.

"I'm not like you, Jericho St. James. I'm not someone who can harm another human being."

It's his turn to flinch. Good.

He nods. Stands.

"We won't tell Angelique until you're farther along just in case."

"There's no we. There's you and there's me."

He ignores that. "I don't want to get her hopes up."

"Well, that's probably the one thing you and I agree on."

"Good. You'll sleep in my bed going forward. And your priority will be your health. The health of my child."

"Not pleasing you? That's not my priority any longer?" I ask, my tone mocking.

"Isabelle—"

"It's why you did it." I don't know why this knowledge hurts. It's not really breaking news. And on some level, I had to know. It's not as though he has any affection for me. The horned devil who saved me from those men in that chapel has proven himself to be more villain than hero. Many times over. I doubt he ever wanted to be the hero, though. That night for one moment I'd thought it. My knight in shining armor. A stranger come to sweep me off my feet and carry me away.

Away where? I ask myself now. Away to what? The last three years have been a sort of hell. Losing my parents was bad. But losing Christian? And the way I lost him? That broke me. The three years I've been living in the Bishop house with a man who is blood, my half-brother, I've only ever felt alone and cold. Even with Julia. Only with Matty was there some affection. Some physical contact. And human beings need that. We need touch. We need gentleness. Need to feel wanted. Loved.

I shake my head. Jesus. I'm pathetic.

He takes a deep breath in and waits, looking down from his great height. I wonder how I look to him.

"Julia was right." He knows about the phone. No sense in trying to hide how I know from him. "She told me how the Bishop inheritance works. That Carlton needs to produce an heir to keep control of the family fortune."

"Your brother is unable to produce any heirs."

"He has a year. I'm sure—"

"His wives have miscarried every single time."

I know that.

"I'm not worried about Carlton Bishop magically producing an heir in the eleventh hour. You, being blood, are next in line to inherit. Once the child is born, your place is sealed. And so is his."

"And as Head of Household, so is yours. You'll take control of the inheritance."

"Correct. Upon the child's birth, I will take control. It should coincide nicely with Carlton's fiftieth."

"You're a terrible human being, do you know that?"

His eyes narrow and there's a menacing tilt to his head. "You don't know the things he's done."

"You mean the things you accuse him of. They're only things you would do, Jericho St. James." I push the blanket off feeling stronger and get to my feet. I step closer, getting to within an inch of him. "Things only a monster like you is capable of."

A darkness descends over his features, a grin making something wicked out of his mouth. He walks me backward until I hit the wall. "Shall I tell you more, Isabelle?"

"I wouldn't believe a word you say so save your breath."

"Shall I tell you exactly how he decided your destiny before you even became aware of his existence?"

His words confuse me but before I can answer, he takes my arms, slips them behind my back and grips both wrists with one hand.

"No. I'll spare you that. I'll tell you something else instead." His eyes flicker to my mouth, lower to the exposed part of my chest. "You are my wife. You carry my child. You belong to me, Isabelle St. James."

Isabelle York. Isabelle Bishop. Isabelle St. James. I've come a long way in three years.

I open my mouth to protest, to curse him to hell because he won't hurt me. Not now. Not while I'm carrying his child. But before I can, I hear the unbuckling of his belt, the sound of his zipper. I swallow, glancing down then back up at him.

The wicked set of his mouth is different now. Dirty. His gaze darkly erotic.

"And what's more, wife, you want to belong to me," he says, releasing my wrists and gripping my hips to lift me off the ground. I have no choice but to wrap my legs around his middle as he balances me between himself and the wall. I feel his fingers at the crotch of my panties, pushing them aside. And as much as I hate it, I'm aroused.

"I don't," I tell him even as I feel him at my entrance, even as my body prepares to welcome him. "I don't." My arms are around his shoulders, hands gripping handfuls of hair and tugging. Hurting.

"You're a liar too, wife," he says as he thrusts inside me.

I grunt, taking the full length of him, my passage too tight, the intrusion too fast.

"Kiss me," he says, thrusting again, hands cupping my ass.

"You want a kiss?" I ask, taking another hard thrust, my clit rubbing against him, my body doing exactly what he said. Wanting him. Wanting to belong to him.

"A bloody kiss. I'll give you that," he says. "Do your worst."

I sink my teeth into his lower lip and taste the copper of blood. His thrusts come faster and I'm not sure it's his moan or my own as I suck on his lip and bleed him.

When I come, I cling tight to him, arms on his shoulders, legs locked around his hips. He bounces me on his cock, spearing me again and again, growing thicker. I pant my release, his name on my lips, my body throbbing, vision blurring, nipples tight and too sensitive against my shirt, every sensation heightened. When he comes, I hear my name on his breath, feel the press of his chest against mine as he pins me to the wall and stills. Our eyes are locked, lip bloody, each of us hating the other. Me with a secret vow to destroy him. To take from him all he plans to take from me. I do have some power over him.

Sex.

He wants me as much as I want him. I will use that to bring Jericho St. James to his knees.

## 3

## JERICHO

The jet to Austria leaves in just over an hour but it gives me enough time to drop in on the Bishops. Even though our properties back up to one another, it's a fifteen-minute drive around to their front entrance. The gate opens as we pull up. Carlton must be expecting me.

"Want me to come in with you, boss?" Dex asks when we pull up to the double front doors.

"No. I'll just be a minute."

He nods.

I take in the state of the place. The Bishop house was once grand. I have the blueprints at home. Know the nooks and crannies. I wonder if Carlton Bishop has ever bothered to study them. If he knows the weak points of the wall between our properties.

The gardens are unkempt. Leaves need to be swept, bushes trimmed. The roses that have crept over the wall need to be cut back, dead flowers cleared. I know financially Bishop is hurting. He may have the house and the properties, but he isn't liquid. He needs to sell off some of his land. The apartment in Paris he'd purchased for his wife. He needs cash.

I step out of the Rolls Royce once it comes to a stop, adjust my jacket, and look up at the façade of the stone mansion. It's built much like ours with its French chateau design, large windows, ornate wooden shutters. If you don't look too closely, you won't notice how the paint is peeling here or there, how a shutter is hanging just off center.

The door opens before I reach it but it's not who I'm expecting. Not a butler or housekeeper. Not even Carlton Bishop. No. It's his cousin, Julia.

She stops with her hand on the doorknob. No smile on her face today. She's wearing a pair of running pants and sports bra that leaves her stomach exposed. She's toned and tanned like she works on it.

"Ms. Bishop," I say as I step up the stone stairs toward the door.

"Mr. St. James," she says, her gaze moving over my shoulders and chest, then back up to my eyes. "I was just about to go on a run when I saw you drive up," she says.

I get the feeling she wasn't about to go on a run

at all. That her being here, being the one to open the door, is a calculated move.

She steps aside, gesturing for me to enter. I do. Her breasts brush against my arm. I want to say it's because the entry isn't wide enough to accommodate us both, but something tells me even that is calculated.

She closes the door and a silence descends over the large house. From here I can see the stairs curving to the floor above, the living room, and dining room. It's so quiet I wonder if there's anyone else in the house.

I turn to her. She's about the same height as Isabelle and when she looks up at me with the pale blue eyes of most of the Bishops, I notice she's wearing full makeup to go for her run. Heavy eyeliner, lipstick, perfume, the works.

She smiles but stands just a little closer than would be appropriate. I don't move as she raises her arms, stomach muscles flexing. She pulls her long blonde hair into a ponytail at the top of her head. She works it into an elastic with long, polished fingernails combing through it, then drags her hand slowly over the length of it to set it over her shoulder.

"Carlton isn't here," she says and I understand something. I think I do, at least.

"No?"

She shakes her head. "I'm sure I can help you

with whatever you need. Come into my office. Would you like coffee?"

"No, thank you."

She smiles, turns, and walks ahead of me down the hall shaking her curvy ass the whole way. It's something to look at in her tight running pants. I'm sure that's by design. I wonder how close she and Isabelle are. How much Isabelle knows about Julia. And I make a mental note to learn more myself.

She opens the door to a study but I wouldn't say it's a woman's office. It's old, dark wood at every turn. Very masculine. But maybe that's me assigning gender roles.

"You sure this isn't your cousin's office. Doesn't look like furnishings for a woman to choose."

"No? Not pink enough?"

I look down at her. Take in her too-red lipstick. Julia Bishop arrived in New Orleans a single mom about four years ago. She moved in with Carlton right around the time Monique moved out. That's all I know about this woman who I'm beginning to think I've underestimated.

I reach into my pocket and take out Isabelle's phone. I set it on the desk. The SIM card is in my office at home.

"I'm guessing you slipped that to my wife the night I found you two in the chapel."

She glances at it, turns a surprised face to me. "I

thought it had been forgotten by the man who collected her things. You know how it is to be without a cell phone these days. Can't survive, really." She smiles casually.

"I'm sure you had only the best intentions for Isabelle."

"Of course. How is my cousin?"

"I think you know."

She blinks, gives nothing of what she's thinking away. "Do I owe the happy couple a congratulations?"

I only smile, neither confirming nor denying. Isabelle's pregnancy won't remain a secret for long but if I could have it my way, no one would know until the baby is safely in my arms.

"You stand to lose quite a bit if she's pregnant, don't you?"

For the first time, on the few occasions I've interacted with or seen Julia Bishop, her mask drops, her expression giving away her thoughts and making her usually attractive face ugly. At least momentarily. And I wonder just how much in control Carlton Bishop is of the Bishop house.

"The inheritance was never mine. My father was the younger brother. It's like the monarchy. An heir and a spare. He was the spare and me, well, I'm barely that, aren't I?"

"Does that upset you?"

Her eyebrows knit together.

"The fact that Isabelle exists. That she ranks higher than you."

She swallows. "Of course not. I love my cousin."

"Hm. Where is Carlton anyway?"

She shrugs a shoulder. "Didn't come home last night. Probably at the Cat House."

I don't know why that surprises me, but it does, at least momentarily. "Does it bother you?" I ask, testing.

"Excuse me?"

"Does it bother you that he's at the Cat House. Fucking other women."

Her face flushes red. "We're not... He's... We're cousins. That's all."

"I had a cousin once," I lie, letting one side of my mouth curve upward.

"That's not us!"

"My mistake," I say. I walk around the office, take a seat on the couch, and lean back, folding my ankle over the opposite knee. She remains where she is, still flustered. "You were here when Isabelle's brother was killed and she almost died. When Carlton took her in."

She nods, folds her arms across her chest defensively.

"How long did you know of Isabelle's existence? That she was a blood relation?"

"Sorry?"

"How long did you know about her? Carlton

would have learned about his half-sister at the reading of his father's will where the old man claimed paternity. A DNA test was done, without Isabelle's knowledge by the way, years before she came to live in this house. Carlton knew about her for a long time. My question is how long did you know?"

"Only when she moved in."

"Is that so?"

"What are you getting at, Jericho?"

*Jericho.*

I stand. Walk toward her. "We are not friends, you and I. Mr. St. James will do."

She looks up, flipping her ridiculous ponytail off her shoulder. I don't like her. In fact, I feel such an aversion to her it's almost physical. There is something so calculated about her. So cold. But she's a Bishop and my hate for all things Bishop runs deep.

But then I think of the Bishop at my house and that feels different. Maybe it's the fact that she's carrying my child. Maybe it's that she sleeps in my bed. That I've seen her at her most vulnerable and that she depends on me for everything. My hand is the hand that feeds her.

I don't know. All I know is she's not like this one.

"Stay away from my wife. Am I clear?"

"She's my cousin and my friend. I'm guessing she needs one of those these days."

I lean toward her. "Stay. Away."

She swallows hard and steps backward.

Satisfied, I walk to the door. I have my hand on the doorknob when she speaks.

"What will you do to her once the baby's born?"

My jaw tenses. I turn.

She must see some weakness in my expression, my posture, because she stands up taller. An ugly grin appears on her too-perfectly made-up face.

"Bury her like you did your fiancée? Like your ancestor buried Nellie Bishop?"

I snort. Walking back into the room, I'm pleased when she hurries to back away from me. "Stay away from my wife and my family or I'll come for yours."

Low blow. I know it. To threaten her kid.

Her face pales. Her mouth moves but she doesn't say anything. Or if she does, I don't hear it because I walk out of that office, out of that house, feeling like I want to scrub my skin raw to get the poison that is Julia Bishop off me.

# 4

## JERICHO

I fly alone to Austria. I'd have taken Dex with me but given the turn in circumstances, I want him home to watch over Isabelle and Angelique. He'll also be interviewing three men who will possibly guard Isabelle. I know I can't keep her locked away in the house forever. It's not good for her or the baby. But she won't go anywhere without a personal guard, especially now after my visit with Julia Bishop.

My gut feeling about people is always right. Always has been. The one time I didn't listen to it led to Kimberly's murder. I'd felt the same way toward Felix Pérez that I do Julia. But I'd shoved it aside. I was doing business. Necessary business that had been left unfinished and needed to be finished. That was all.

But that wasn't all.

No one apart from Dex knows about my trip to Austria. And Zeke can't know. Because after my meeting with Santiago I am more curious than ever about what he and Zeke aren't telling me.

My father was on a ski holiday in Austria when he died. I know he'd met with some men on that trip regarding business that wasn't exactly above board. But from what I've been able to learn, those meetings had gone well. Those men wouldn't have had cause to harm him. The opposite.

He'd also been with one of his mistresses. I'm glad now that he'd taken that woman and not my mother or she'd be dead too.

The accident had taken place late at night. They were on their way back to the chalet after dinner. It was late and dark, and a fresh snow was falling. All things that could lead to a man inexperienced driving in those conditions to veer off the road.

But my father wasn't inexperienced. He lived in New Orleans for the second half of his life, but he was born and raised in Colorado. A ski junkie who spent winters for much of his youth and early twenties in the mountains. He was a good driver. Solid.

Their SUV had gone off the road at a hairpin turn coming down the mountain just five minutes from the chalet where the guardrail was already damaged. It had been slated to be repaired the following week. By the time the police got there, snow was coming down hard. Any evidence on the road like skid marks or animal prints or anything that would give a reason as to why it happened were gone. They blamed icy conditions, but it wasn't icy. It was snow and my father could handle snow.

The car itself had exploded upon impact once it had gone over the cliff causing a minor avalanche. There was nothing left of driver or passenger but charred bones.

The thought turns my stomach.

My father wasn't a good man. I know that. He was abusive toward our mother. Toward us sometimes—more Zeke than me. But he was my father.

I make a point to drive past the chalet we sold after the accident. It looks the same, just older. I park outside and look at it. The place holds no memories for me. We never came here. Only our parents, mostly our father. I don't think he brought mom more than a handful of times.

A light goes on inside and someone pulls the curtain back to look out onto the road. It's a quiet road. No reason to be here unless you're going to the restaurant at the top of the mountain and the restaurant is closed in the off season.

I put the SUV into drive and make a three-point turn to head back to the hotel. I don't drive the five minutes it would take me to see the place where their car went over the guardrail. Maybe I will after. But I have an appointment with the manager of Hotel Petterhof.

The hotel is large with over five hundred rooms. It's just one step above a hostel. A place for someone to get lost in. To be overlooked. I park the SUV in the lot—no valet here—and walk inside. It's run down with fixtures and furniture that are cheap knock offs that needed to be updated about thirty years ago. It's very different to the usual sort of place Zeke would stay.

There's a pit in my stomach as I make my way to the front desk where a young woman looks up and smiles as I approach.

"Good evening, sir. How can I help you?"

"I'm here to see Mr. Spencer. Mitch Spencer."

I don't give her my name.

"Yes, he said he was expecting someone. I'll call him. Just have a seat."

"Thank you."

I've sent a sizable deposit to Mr. Spencer for the work he's done. I expect discretion in return. Discretion and information. Because I found something in Santiago's files. Something he may not have intended for me to see.

The guest list from this hotel contained a name I recognized. Jack J. Z. Wilder. He was my brother's best friend when we were in high school. It's too coincidental that his name would be on the overnight guest list.

Santiago had gone so far as to gather the names of all the guests in the nearby hotels and chalets.

The out-of-town renters. The locals. He was thorough. And Jack's name caught my eye. It was the middle initials. That's what Jack went by in school.

When I contacted Mr. Spencer, who has been working here for fifteen years, he was kind enough, after some financial encouragement, to share with me that there is a camera recording the comings and goings of the lobby, the front entrance, the side doors, and the staff entrances and exits. Normal security measures. But Hotel Petterhof never got rid of any of the old recordings. He was able to find the one from the week of my father's death. The week Jack J. Z. Wilder supposedly spent skiing in Austria.

Except, Jack had been killed in a motorcycle accident the summer after graduation. I attended his funeral.

The camera footage, although grainy, shows a clear enough image of the tall, dark-haired man posing as Jack.

My brother.

My brother was in Austria the night my father's car went off the road.

My brother was in a hotel room not half an hour away.

And I had no idea he'd even left the country.

"Mr. St. James. It's good to meet you. I'm Mitch Spencer."

I blink, clear my head, and drag myself out of my reverie to meet Mitch Spencer. He's a short, thickly built man in his late fifties. He extends a hand and I notice how his suit is worn at the wrist.

"Mr. Spencer," I say, shaking his hand. "Thank you for making time for me on such short notice."

"This way." We walk in silence down a corridor where the carpet is frayed, and the smells of food, stale cigarettes and weed permeate the walls. Zeke would hate this place.

I walk behind Spencer into a small office over-crowded by large ledgers and books, stacks of video-tapes, a desk that's seen better days, and a chair behind it that tilts to one side.

The one thing it has going for it is the view from the window behind the desk. It is spectacular.

"The office isn't much but watching the sun set nightly is something else," Spencer says, as if reading my mind.

"I bet."

He gestures to a seat. I take it while he slips into the chair behind the desk. He turns the laptop around and without preamble, hits play. I watch the footage. I saw screenshots of it just days ago. I watch Zeke enter the lobby, a baseball cap pulled low over his face. He also wears a heavy, bulky coat zipped up to his neck, and walks to the elevator. I check the date of the footage. The night of my father's accident.

I bite back any emotion, any thought.

Spencer pushes a few keys to play another scene.

Zeke again, this time dressed in a suit and wool coat not for skiing.

"He checked out early. His reservation was for two nights but he left after one."

I look at the date and time stamp. "Just an hour after he came in. Play them again."

He does. And I watch Zeke come into the lobby in the cap and oversized coat. Spencer kindly pauses to expand the image and although grainy, I can make out his expression. At least a little. It's determined. Hurried.

But when he checks out his hair is wet. He must have showered and changed.

"There's one more," Spencer says. "A curious one."

He turns the laptop around, punches some keys then angles it so I can see the screen. Zeke, walking out of the hotel, dumps his full duffel bag into a trash can near the entrance before climbing into a taxi and leaving the property.

"You've made a copy?" I ask, wanting to give nothing away.

"Of course." He opens the drawer, takes out a flash drive and hands it to me.

"Thank you." I take out my cell phone, log into my banking app and make a second transfer. I stand as his phone dings with a message. He looks at it, then up at me, and smiles.

"Thank you. Thank you so much," Spencer says.

"Discretion, Mr. Spencer. I'll expect that footage to disappear."

He pushes a button on his laptop. "Already done."

"Goodnight."

I walk out of the cheap hotel on wooden legs. I climb into my rented SUV and drive back to the small, private airport from where I'll fly home tonight. No one the wiser about my trip halfway across the world.

# 5

## ISABELLE

"Daddy!" Angelique calls out. I turn to find Jericho walking into her room looking like he hasn't slept in the twenty-four hours since I've seen him. For some reason I expected he'd be at my side constantly. Keeping an eye on me. Watching to make sure I eat. Making sure I don't hurt his baby. But after the day he fed me soup, I didn't see him again. When I woke, his side of the bed hadn't been slept in.

"Morning, sweetheart," he says, catching Angelique in his arms when she runs to him, lifting her in a bear hug.

It's still shocking for me to see him like this. He is so completely different with his daughter than he is with me. With anyone. Like a man I don't know. The one I wish I did.

I touch my stomach. Will he be like this with our

baby? Or will he hate him or her because of the Bishop blood?

"Nana said you probably had a lot of meetings," she says. "I didn't even get to see you at dinner."

"It was a long day," he replies, setting her back on the floor and, still holding her hand, walks toward her desk. He glances at Angelique's book, lying open. It's a children's book about music. Specifically, about a bear who has a gift for the violin. It was one of my favorites when I was younger. When I asked Leontine if we could buy it for Angelique, she had it and several others delivered to the house within just a few hours.

This all happened before, though. I'm now using Before and After as demarcations of time. Of my life. Before, when I knew Jericho St. James was evil, but I didn't know how evil. Now, in the After, I know.

"Isabelle," he says, setting a heavy hand on my shoulder. "How are you feeling?"

"She's much better," Angelique says. "Aren't you, Belle?"

"I am, sweetheart." I smile to her, then fix my face when I turn it to him. I want to be sure he gets the message but not cause any harm to Angelique in the process.

"You're eating?" he asks.

"Yes."

"Good."

I stand up. "I'll go," I say, assuming he wants time with his daughter and step toward the door.

"What are you reading?" he asks, picking up the book, glancing at the title then a few pages of the interior.

"It's about a bear who can play the violin even when he's little," Angelique says. "See?" she takes the book and turns a few pages. "Belle is going to teach me to play too but I'm still too young."

Jericho looks at me. "That's very good. Maybe she'll play for us later today. What do you think, Angelique?"

"Oh, she's very good, daddy. You should hear her."

I feel myself flush and turn away from Jericho. "I'd love to hear her. Later today then," he says to me.

"If I'm not too tired." I try to move my lips into a smile.

A knock comes on the door and Leontine steps inside. "Time for lunch," she says.

"Then we can go?" Angelique asks her.

"Go?" Jericho asks, eyebrows arching.

"Your mother and I are taking Angelique to a local bookstore," I say, feeling rebellious. Like I want to challenge him.

Jericho's eyebrows now disappear into his hair-line. "You're what?"

"A bookstore. You know, where they sell books?

They host a story time after lunch for kids Angelique's age. We're going to take her to story time and then we're going to eat cake."

"It's a special place, daddy. Cotton Candy. Belle showed me pictures. Everything is pink and looks like cotton candy and they even have—"

"Who said you could do this?" Jericho asks, cutting her off, glaring at me.

I smile wide. "I had a craving for cake."

He wraps a hand around the back of my neck and squeezes a warning. "Catherine can bake you a cake."

"No. It's a very particular cake they have only at Cotton Candy. You don't want me to ignore a craving, do you?"

"Please daddy? You can even come with us." He looks down at Angelique, opening his mouth, but she continues. "Uncle Zeke said he'd have cake for lunch! I'd like cake for lunch, but Nana said I have to have lunch first."

"Zeke's coming?" he asks.

"He is," I say, my smile widening. "Isn't he sweet to take time out of his busy day for us?"

Something twitches in Jericho's temple. "Fine," he says through clenched teeth.

"You'll come?" Angelique asks excitedly jumping up and down.

"Yes."

"Well, I'm glad to hear that," Leontine says,

looking surprised and satisfied. "That's settled then. Do you think I need to change the reservation, Isabelle?" Leontine asks me.

"No, it'll be fine to add one more chair. And if not, Jericho can always sit on his own." That last part is directed at him.

"Belle knows the owner," Angelique says. "She's friends with her. She's a pastry chef. She's baking us something special."

"I bet."

"Maybe I'll even ask her to put something extra special in yours," I tell Jericho.

He shifts his gaze to me. It turns to a glare.

"Come, Angelique," Leontine says. I wonder if she senses the tension building.

"Belle aren't you going to have lunch?" Angelique asks.

"Of course." I take a step toward them, but Jericho catches my arm.

"We'll be down in a few minutes."

Angelique looks at us but Leontine ushers her out of the room.

As soon as they're gone, I tug free of Jericho's grip and walk out into the hallway. I get as far as my bedroom but just as I put my hand on the doorknob, Jericho closes his hand over mine.

"You were craving cake?" he asks, words clipped.

His proximity makes something flutter in my stomach. Makes the hair on the back of my neck stand on end. I shift my gaze from our joined hands to his eyes without turning my head.

"A day ago, you couldn't keep food down, wife of mine."

"I guess the vitamins really worked." I have been feeling better but honestly all I've eaten has been more of that soup. I'm not sure I'll be able to stomach cake, but I was dying to get out of the house, and this was the way to do it. Knowing I'm pregnant has made me braver. Given me a backbone.

"Hm."

He opens the door and gestures for me to enter. When I pass him, I notice a familiar scent on him. I can't quite place it but it doesn't belong on him. Doesn't belong here in this house.

"Where were you?" I ask when he closes the door.

"Did you miss me?"

"I was just wondering because the nausea going away coincided so nicely with your absence, I just wondered if it would be best if you stayed away for the next nine months. Or forever. Either works for me. Or better yet, let me go home."

Home. That's when I realize what the smell is.

I lean toward him and sniff his collar.

"What are you doing?" he asks.

I step back. "That's Julia's perfume." It's faint and maybe it's the pregnancy that has amped up my sense of smell but, I'm sure. And something about it gets my hackles up.

He seems surprised by my comment and it takes him a minute to reply. "I ran into her when I returned your phone." He walks around me to the door that connects our rooms, moves into his.

I follow him. "What do you mean you ran into her?"

He strips off his jacket and undoes his tie, tossing it aside. He unbuttons the top buttons and cuffs of his shirt before pulling it out of his pants and over his head. He tosses that onto the bed too, slips off his shoes and walks toward the bathroom.

"I mean, I went to return your phone and tell your brother there would be no more contact between you and them. But he wasn't home. She was." He switches on the shower and undoes his belt, turning to me. "You're not jealous, are you? Is there lipstick on my collar?"

"Why would there be lipstick on your collar?" I sound defensive and angry. Or maybe that's jealousy. I realize my arms are folded across my chest so I drop them.

He grins, satisfied.

I shake my head. "You dick. I'm not jealous. I just don't understand why her perfume would be clinging to you."

He raises his eyebrows and steps toward me,

wrapping an arm around my waist. "She's not my type. You don't need to worry."

"I'm not... Jesus! What is wrong with you?" I shove at his chest, but he tightens his grip.

"Besides, you're my type. And you're my wife. Not to mention you are carrying my child. You're the only woman I'm interested in fucking."

I shove again. "You're welcome to go fuck every woman at the Cat House if that's what you want. Just as long as you leave me alone!"

"I don't think you mean that."

"Oh, I do."

"Shall I prove it?"

"Fuck off!"

He grins and, keeping his arm around my waist, reaches into the shower to switch off the water. He lifts me, carrying me into the bedroom where he deposits me on the edge of the bed. With a nudge of two fingers on my chest he has me on my back. He pushes my dress up and slips my panties off.

"What are you doing?" I sit up as he crouches down, his face at my sex.

"Eating your pussy," he replies and before I can open my mouth to protest, he tugs me to the very edge of the bed, his mouth finds my center and I can't think. All I can do is feel his wet, hot tongue expertly licking my clit. His hands spread my thighs wider as he slips two fingers inside, then closes his mouth over the swelling nub and sucks.

"Oh. God."

He pauses to look up at me. "Jericho will do." He grins, then nudges me back so I'm lying down again, lifting my thighs over his shoulders. It's only moments before I'm gasping for breath. Before my fingers are knotted in his hair and I'm coming.

I'm limp by the time it's over. He stands, looks down at me, and wipes his mouth with the back of his hand. He strips off the rest of his clothes and I can see how hard he is. He sets one knee on the bed and takes his cock in hand, leaning over me, jerking himself off.

"See what I mean?" he asks, kissing me then pulling back, eyes moving over my body.

"I hate you," I tell him.

"If only you meant that."

With his free hand he shoves my dress up to expose my breasts clad in a lace bra. He's rough when he takes first my right breast out of the cup and then the left, letting the lace collect beneath my tender, swollen breasts.

"Come here," he says, cupping the back of my head. He lifts me to sit, coming close enough that I know what he wants. Or I think I do, until his fingers tighten in my hair and he's tugging my head back. "Who invited Zeke?"

"What?"

"Who invited Zeke for cake?"

"I... Angelique."

"It wasn't you?"

I try to shake my head but can't because of his grip in my hair.

"Are you sure?"

"Yes." He loosens his hold.

"Good. Because you're not his. You're mine. The sooner you understand that, the better."

He releases me and I drop to my elbows. He draws back, looks at my spread legs. At my sex. I'm dripping because I want more than his mouth. I want him inside me.

"You want to come again, don't you?" he asks.

I bite my lip in answer. I want to tell him I hate him, but I don't. There's time enough for that. Right now, I want to come.

He grins, grips my thighs and when he pushes his cock inside me, I grab hold of his shoulders, nails digging into flesh. The way he moves inside me, the way he makes me feel, I can't think when he's looking at me like this. When he's fucking me like this.

"Come, Isabelle. Come on my cock so I can come all over you."

I do. I hate myself for it, but I do right on command. He watches and he's still hard, thrusting, so when my body goes limp, he pulls out, grips his cock and thrusts twice more in the palm of his hand before he comes. I watch it happen. Watch how all the muscles in his face and body tense before I shift my gaze to the tight grip on his cock. I can't drag my eyes away as he marks me, my stomach, my chest, my breasts. He places one hand on the bed as he bends over me, squeezing out the last of his orgasm, his breathing ragged, eyes closed. When he's finished, he opens his eyes, straightens, and looks at the mess he's made. He sets the flat of one hand on my stomach and rubs his come into my skin, over my breasts, down to the V between my legs.

I watch him do this, watch him cover me with it, his scent, him. He's marking me. As if the tattoo on my back isn't enough. When he's finished, he looks down at me. At what he's done. He nods once and turns to walk back into the bathroom. A moment later I hear the shower turn on.

I lift to my elbows and look at myself. I'm his. His in every way. I get to my feet, my legs wobbly. I strip off my dress and follow him into the bathroom. He's not surprised when I step into the shower. When I step right up to him.

He cocks his head to the side, studies me for a long moment before wrapping a hand around the back of my skull and kissing me.

There's nothing tender in that kiss. It's another marking. His. I'm his. And I want to leave my mark too. When I dig my nails into his back and drag them down, his body tenses momentarily but then he tugs me closer. He kisses me harder. When we're done, when he's done kissing me, when I'm done scratching my nails down his back, he washes us both and then switches off the water. He wraps me in a towel, then himself and without a word we walk out of the bathroom and get dressed. It's like this strange moment didn't happen when we go downstairs to have lunch and get ready to take Angelique to story-time at the bookstore, and then to a cake shop.

Like we're a family. A family where my husband wraps his hand around the nape of my neck to remind me he is in control. To keep me within arm's reach. As if I could ever forget that I'm his.

# 6
———

## JERICHO

For the first time in her life, we take Angelique to story time at a bookstore. Angelique sits on the carpet, Baby Bear on her lap, forming a circle with a dozen other kids. They're all roughly her age. We're in the children's book section of a small bookshop. A Thomas the Tank Engine table stacked with toy trains in a village sits in the corner. We're surrounded by the vibrant colors of stuffed animals, toys and books as well as an elaborate mural of a fairy tale world along the far wall. The children's section is in the back of the bookstore. I hover at the arched entry between it and the rest of the shop. My mother and Isabelle sit near Angelique and listen to the woman reading the story.

All I can do is watch my daughter's face. She's smiling, happy, clapping her hands and singing along as much as she can. She doesn't know the words to the songs the other children seem to know by heart. When she falters she watches the others. I think she's trying to mimic them, to fit in. It twists something inside me. I don't like that she has to do that.

Dex comes to stand beside me. "She's enjoying herself." Dex has been here for most of Angelique's life. At some point, she took it upon herself to call him Uncle Dex. I never corrected her.

"Yeah." She is.

"How was your meeting?" he asks after a long minute as a song finishes and Angelique catches my eye. She gives me a happy little wave.

I smile back and wave, but the smile is mechanic. "I found what I was looking for." Found what I wish I hadn't.

He doesn't comment. He knows why I went to Austria.

I take a breath and exhale, turn to him. "Now to understand why."

He nods.

The kids start to rise, mothers pushing strollers loaded with younger siblings walking over to collect their children. Angelique beelines to Isabelle, who takes her hand and ushers her over to a bookshelf. They spend the next ten minutes choosing books. My mother, witnessing this, walks toward Dex and I.

"She's just the shiny new thing," I tell her, not

wanting her to feel hurt over Angelique's obvious preference for Isabelle.

"Oh, I'm not hurt, Jericho," she says, patting my hand. "Isabelle is good for her."

I watch them too. She is. I can see it from here.

"But she's not her father," my mother adds.

I smile. "I'm not hurt either," I tell her, realizing it's not quite true as I speak the words.

"Well, if you were, it would be natural."

I grit my teeth because my mom knows me well.

"Can we buy these, daddy?" Angelique asks, carrying a stack of books. Isabelle follows behind.

"Aren't they a bit difficult for her?" my mother asks Isabelle after looking through them.

"I don't think so. Angelique is quite a good reader already."

"And I want a notebook like Belle's please," Angelique says.

I raise my eyebrows and look at my wife.

"For music," Isabelle says and turns to Angelique. "I usually make my own. If you have an empty notebook, we can make—"

"Buy what you need. For yourself too."

Isabelle looks up at me like she wants to say something but then she takes Angelique's hand, leading her to what I guess is the music section. We follow them and a few minutes later, Angelique has two more books, a notebook, and a new stuffed animal. She is exhilarated. I see it in the brightness of her eyes. The flush of her cheeks. She's looking everywhere, at everything, and beaming.

"Can you take care of this?" I ask Dex, handing him my credit card.

"Sure. Come on, kid," he says. "Piggyback?"

"I'm getting too old for piggyback rides, Uncle Dex," she says, but hops on excitedly anyway.

My mother follows them and when Isabelle tries to pass me, I touch her arm, halting her. She looks at me. "What?" Any sweetness she has in her voice for Angelique is gone.

"Why do you make your own notebooks?"

"Why do you care?"

"Isn't it easier to just buy them?"

"*Just buy them*. That's what people with money do, right? Just buy things. Anything they want. Including people."

"Is it money?" Her cheeks flush and her gaze wavers. I know it is. She's embarrassed. "Is that also why you're not in school?"

She folds her arms in front of her. "I have a music group I study with. Or I used to."

"Not a music school?"

"Again, why do you care?"

I shrug a shoulder. "Just curious."

"No, not a school. I didn't have money for school, so I found a group I could afford to study with. I used the meager allowance Carlton gave me. Satisfied? I won't be humiliated for not having money. For not being *allowed* to have a job or go to school."

"I'm not asking to shame you, Isabelle. I really do want to know. Now show me what you need."

"I'm fine."

"For my daughter then. Show me what you need to teach her."

She grits her teeth. Stubborn. Then her expression changes. Her eyes brighten. And I swear I can almost see a lightbulb go on over her head.

"I've missed a bunch of violin lessons. I'd like to go again. And I'd like a job."

"We've talked about a job. That's a no."

"But the lessons?" she asks. I realize, given the speed of her response, she knew the job would be a no. She asked so she could have something to bargain.

Angelique comes running to us then, her bag in hand. "We're done! Let's get cake!"

We both smile at her, and I wait until Isabelle looks at me again. "Get what you need to teach my daughter and we'll discuss your lessons later."

"Later when?"

"We'll see."

"Not good enough. Today."

I sigh. "Fine, today."

She smiles and it's a smile I haven't seen before. "Okay. I'll be quick," she tells Angelique and hurries to choose a few things from the shelves. She then hands them to me and again, I see a flush on her cheeks.

I take the books and lead her toward the cash register.

"I hate this," she says as we wait in line.

"What?"

"That you're paying. I want a job, Jericho. I want to earn my own money."

"I will pay you to teach my daughter," I say, the idea taking shape then and there.

From the look on her face, she's intrigued but skeptical.

"I'll deduct these from your first check," I tell her as I set the books on the counter and look at her. "Deal?"

"Really?"

I nod.

She studies me. I raise my eyebrows.

"Okay," she says. "Deal."

"Good." I thank the cashier, take the bag, and lean toward my wife. "Now let's go get you that cake you've been craving, little liar."

She smiles victoriously.

I can give her this.

## 7

## ISABELLE

Cotton Candy is as busy as ever but since I know Megs, I snagged us the best table at the back. Zeke's already there when we arrive and Angelique runs to show him all her new books. I wave to Megs and take a step toward the counter. Jericho, ever suspicious, grabs my arm.

"Where are you going?"

I look from his hand to his eyes. "I'm going to say hello to my friend." I make a point of stopping, cocking my head at him in false concern. "Do you need me to define what a friend is?"

He looks around the busy café, glancing at Dex standing at the door like some goon. He then finds his brother who I notice is watching him over Angelique's head. "I'll come with you."

"What do you think I'm going to do exactly? I

will literally be five feet from you. I promise not to make a break for it."

"It's not that, Isabelle. I have enemies."

"Well, that doesn't surprise me to be honest—"

"You have enemies too."

That makes me stop. Makes something inside me go cold. I think about the night of the break in. About Christian surprising the intruder, dragging him off me. About Christian getting himself killed when he told me to run.

The anniversary is coming. It's just around the corner. I hate this time of year.

But I shake my head. Clear the thought. That man is in prison. He was caught and tried and convicted. He can't hurt me or anyone else.

I open my mouth to tell him he's wrong, but he leans toward me. "Now that you're pregnant, you're even more of a threat to your brother and cousin than you were before."

"I'm not a threat to them. They're my family. It's not—"

"I don't want you hurt, Isabelle."

*I don't want you hurt.*

I blink, confused by those words. The tenderness in them.

But no, I need to keep a clear head. Jericho St. James has one goal in mind. Bring my brother down no matter the cost. He doesn't care about me. He doesn't want me hurt because I am growing something of his inside me. That's it. I shouldn't be fooled. Shouldn't let myself think up a false reality.

"I'm not a threat. A baby isn't a threat."

"Not to someone like you maybe but—"

"Someone like me? What does that mean?"

"You're not devious, Isabelle. But you're the exception."

I am taken aback. Is that some sort of compliment? But then I look at his hand around my arm, feel his grip. It's not tight but it's clear I'm not going anywhere without his permission.

"You're not afraid of something happening to me, just the baby."

"Like I said, I wouldn't want to see you hurt."

"No, because that would compromise the baby. Please don't pretend to care about me. Just say it like it is, Jericho." A moment of silence passes and there's a part of me that wants him to tell me I'm wrong. That he does care about me, too. But he doesn't. He just stands there silent and hard as a brick wall. "Look, I just want to say hi to my friend whom I haven't seen since you took me. Please just let me say hello." That last part is said through gritted teeth.

"I'm not stopping you. I'm just coming with you."

He doesn't give me a chance to argue but walks us toward the counter.

"Hey stranger," Megs says, coming around to meet us. She's smiling at me, casting a curious glance toward Jericho. She's been watching that little display play out. I wonder what she makes of it. "It's so great to see you." She wraps me in a giant hug forcing Jericho to release me. "You good?" she whispers in my ear.

"Yeah," I tell her, hugging her back, loving the warmth of her. The last time I saw her was at violin lessons more than two months ago. Megs is a single mom in her early forties and one of the kindest, warmest people I know. She has sworn off men forever. She jokes about it, saying cake is better than sex, but I know underneath that light façade is damage. Something bad happened to her.

"Julia was in here just last week," she says, drawing back. "Stunk up the place with her perfume but Matty was as sweet as can be." Megs does not like Julia and makes no secret of it. "Told me the happy news." She studies Jericho, obviously not intimidated by the hulking man glaring down at her. "You must be the lucky groom. How did you snag this one?" she asks him, pointing her thumb at me.

It takes him a moment to reply, but he extends his hand. "Jericho St. James. Good to meet one of Isabelle's friends."

"He with you?" she asks, gesturing toward Dex.

Jericho nods.

"You think we can ask him to take a seat? He's going to scare off customers."

Jericho draws in a deep breath. Looks at me and

nods, then actually leaves me alone to go talk to Dex. I'm shocked.

"He's intense," Megs says.

"Tell me about it," I say, surprised he let go of me at all. I turn back to Megs. "How have you been? How's Janie?"

"She's good. You know. Busy with school and pre-teen angst." She rolls her eyes. "So." She glances to the table. "You a mommy now?" It takes me a moment to realize she's talking about Angelique. She doesn't know about the pregnancy.

"I don't know what I am, honestly. Come meet Angelique. She's a sweetheart."

She touches my arm to stop me. "Julia was strange when she came in. Stranger than usual."

"Why don't you like her?"

"There's something about her. I don't know what, but I do know one thing. I know to trust my instincts and they send up red flags whenever that woman's around."

"Maybe she just doesn't like cake?"

"Anyone who doesn't like cake cannot be trusted," she says with a wink. "That bitch is too skinny for her own good. Anyway, she wasn't exactly sharing happy news. Dropped in with an older guy and Matty. Matty was talking up a storm while the two of them sat brooding." She rolls her eyes. "Didn't even order anything for themselves. Like my food isn't good enough for them."

"Who was she with? Carlton?"

"Don't know." I remember she's never met Carlton. "Middle-aged. Balding. Unremarkable."

Sounds like Carlton. "Weird."

Jericho joins us just as we get to the table. I introduce Megs and she takes everyone's order, making a fuss over Angelique. Angelique loves this and hates it at once. She's a shy girl and doesn't like attention drawn to her. But she's also just beaming and full of energy today. It's the outing, the excitement of it all. This is how a five-year-old should always be. Happy. Excited. Enjoying life.

There's a strange vibe between Ezekiel and Jericho. I study them, curious what it is, but Megs is quick with cake, tea and coffee. Having Angelique here eases the tension a little. At least it has everyone pretending there isn't any. I take a few bites of cake hoping not to throw it back up but feel the nausea before I've finished a quarter of my slice.

Megs come by as we're getting ready to leave. "So, I'll see you Wednesday night?" she asks.

I put a hand to my stomach hoping to settle it. Wednesday night is the night we meet for violin lessons.

"I hope so," I say.

"Text me and let me know. I may need a ride. The potato is giving me a headache lately." The potato is her car. It's her dad's. The beloved Mustang is over twenty years old and is always giving her a headache.

I look at Jericho who is watching us as he helps Angelique stuff the books back into her bag.

"You need to get a car you can rely on," I tell her, standing.

"I'm attached. What can I say?"

We hug. "It was really good to see you," I tell her, aware of my stomach pressing against hers. Knowing she can't feel anything. Nothing shows just yet. But it will soon.

"You too. Don't be a stranger." Tears sting my eyes. She has no clue about my new life. Doesn't know this is the first time I've left that house, apart from Jericho taking me to those Society events.

A wave of nausea has me clutching the back of the chair.

"Hey, are you okay?" Megs asks, wrapping an arm around me.

"Yeah, fine. I'm just going to run to the bathroom." I go before she can say anything else. I can feel the cake making its way back up as I push through the bathroom door. I'm grateful no one's in the stalls and drag my hair back as I reach the first one. I just make it to the toilet before the cake makes an unwelcome reappearance.

Throwing up is gross.

Throwing up at a public bathroom? It takes that gross factor up several notches.

I heave and feel a hand at my back. Feel my hair lifted as the next wave passes. I'm left empty, drained, my eyes watery. I stay where I am and reach up to flush the toilet.

"Okay?" Jericho asks.

I get to my feet, shoving past him to the sink, remembering my hope in the bookstore. That he'd allow me to go back to my lessons. That he'd pay me to teach Angelique which is the closest thing to a real job I'm going to get. I remember that hope. That stupid, idiotic hope.

"No, not really," I tell him as I rinse my mouth and splash my face with cold water. I reach for paper towels, but he's already got them. He cups the back of my head to wipe my face.

"It'll pass," he says. "Stick to soup for a few more days."

"Are you a doctor now? It's because of you I'm sick. Get away from me."

He grits his teeth but allows me to take the paper towels from him, while standing there as I finish wiping my face. I try to ignore him, throwing the paper towels away and exiting the bathroom. Jericho stays on my heels.

"Isabelle," he says as I walk through the café. Everyone's already left. I give Megs a wave and hope she can't see the tears I'm trying hard not to shed. She's busy, so I'm glad I don't have to talk to her although I see the questions in her eyes. I get to the door and open it, grateful for the cooler air outside. Feeling better for it.

"Belle!" Angelique calls out from across the street. The sports car Ezekiel is driving is pulling away as she waves from the window. We came in two cars since we all couldn't fit in one. I was hoping to ride back with her, but I guess that's not happening.

I force a smile and wave. I take a step, but Jericho's hand falls heavy on my shoulder.

"Dex is pulling the car around."

"I don't want to be with you right now," I tell him, shrugging him off. "I'll walk. I need some air."

"For fuck's sake," he starts but I walk away. The traffic light changes and someone honks their horn. I glance left and feel Jericho's presence at my back like a great, hulking shadow. I don't know why it matters that I get away from him right now, but it does. As traffic clears, I take a step toward the street. Just as I do, my heel catches in a crack in the sidewalk. I stumble forward, simultaneously hearing the screech of tires and someone shouting my name as a van takes the turn too fast and too tight, bouncing over the curb. It's the last thing I see because it comes too fast for me to even scream.

# 8

## JERICHO

I call out her name, grabbing her arm. I'm pulling her back into my chest and out of the way of the van half on the sidewalk, half off. It runs the red light and speeds away. I'm not sure if that's my heart or hers thudding between us as I hold her to me. I smell her shampoo as I stare over her head, searching for the beaten-up vehicle with its windows blacked out by garbage bags taped to them. It's moving too fast for me to get more than a couple digits of the license plate. When I feel Isabelle begin to shake in my arms, I turn my attention to her.

She looks up at me, deep sapphire eyes wide with panic, the whites, pink, the skin around them wet.

"Are you okay?" I ask her.

She stares up at me.

"Isabelle." I squeeze her arms.

She blinks, her eyes coming into focus. And a moment later, her knees give out. I wrap my arms around her as she grabs hold of me.

"It's all right. You're safe," I tell her, pulling her to me again and looking for Dex. He comes to a screeching halt at the curb seconds later.

"Fuck!" he says, jumping out of the car. "Is she all right?"

I shake my head, not sure she's quite all right.

"Fuck."

"Did you get the license plate?" I ask.

"Just the first few digits." He looks down at Isabelle, then up at me.

"Me too. Let me get her in the car," I tell him, glad she doesn't fight me when I put her into the back seat. She leans forward, face in her hands. I wonder if she isn't going to be sick again.

"He was waiting," Dex says, voice lowered. "He got here a few minutes after everyone went into the cafe. I noticed the van. It's too out of place here."

I look left but there's no trace of the van. Not that I expected there to be.

"All right. Let's get her home."

He nods and I climb in beside Isabelle. I rub her back and she straightens, looks out the window.

"You're safe, Isabelle," I tell her, my voice thick. If I hadn't grabbed her in time...no. I don't let myself go down that road. "Isabelle?"

She turns to me, wipes her eyes but tears keep coming. "I didn't see him."

I nod, wrap an arm over her shoulders and pull her to my side. She doesn't resist and I don't tell her it doesn't matter whether she saw him or not. Because he saw her.

"My heel got caught," she says. She takes one sandal off. Sure enough, the heel is damaged where she must have caught it in the pavement. She turns to me. "Thank you for saving me."

I study her. I realize she doesn't know it wasn't an accident. It wasn't her stumbling or the driver going too fast and losing control of the vehicle. He didn't lose control at all.

"You're never going to let me out of the house again, are you? I see it on your face."

"I just want you safe, Isabelle."

"It was an accident. I am safe."

"Let's get home."

"Please. I need... I can't live locked up in that house. I need to see my friends. I need space. Freedom. You have to give me something."

"You were almost killed just now. Do you think you can give me a minute to think?"

"I didn't—"

I raise my eyebrows and it stops her. "You would have survived being run down by a van? Because if I hadn't pulled you out of the way..." I stop. No need to say more.

She opens her mouth, closes it. "Please, Jericho. Please," she asks. Begs. Her voice is earnest. No mockery, no hate. Just desperation.

And I can't ignore it. Can't deny her.

I take a deep breath and exhale as we near the house. The gates are still open so Dex pulls through.

"Please," she says again, eyes filling with tears.

I take another deep breath, exhaling slowly. "You'll have your violin lesson at the house this week."

She looks up at me.

"That's the best I can do. Take it or leave it."

"I'll take it."

"Good. Wednesday night, was it?"

"Yes."

"All right. Wednesday night. I'll need the names of everyone who will be at the house."

"You want social security numbers too?"

I grin, glad to hear her quick remark. "If you have them, it'll save me time."

She shakes her head, but she's satisfied for now even though she's still wiping rogue tears. "Thank you."

I nod in acknowledgement.

When we get inside, she gives me the names of the students who attend the lesson with her, as well as her teacher. When I tell her to go upstairs and take a nap, strangely, she doesn't argue with me. She nods and goes up to her room to lay down.

It's a testament to the toll the day's outing had on her. Or a testament to what almost being killed will do to you. I wonder if subconsciously she realizes what happened wasn't an accident.

That afternoon I get people searching for the van that almost ran down my wife. I'm tempted to confront the Bishops, but I don't. I'm just glad Angelique didn't witness what happened. Zeke had turned the corner just before.

Which brings me back to Zeke.

He'd dropped everyone off then left right away and it's late when he gets home. I wonder if he's trying to avoid me.

"Brother." I call out from the shadows of the living room. I lit a fire and am having some whiskey as I watch the flames, listen to the pop of damp wood.

Zeke turns, tucks his phone into his pocket.

"Didn't get to talk much during the afternoon's outing," I say. "Whiskey?"

It takes him a moment to nod, walk to the fire and take the chair beside mine. He pours himself a tumbler of whiskey from the bottle on the table between our chairs.

"Isabelle's okay?" he asks. Dex filled him in on what happened after he left.

I nod. "She thinks it was an accident."

"But you're sure it wasn't." It's not a question.

"Dex saw the man drive up while we were in the café. He was waiting for her."

"You're sure she was the target?"

I grit my teeth. I know where this is coming from.

"Maybe it was you. Isn't that more likely?" he asks.

I sip my whiskey and watch the fire. "Not this time."

It's silent for a long minute.

"Did you ever wonder why Zoë didn't leave a note?" I ask him, not ready to talk about dad. About what I learned in Austria.

He clears his throat, looks to the fire when I shift my gaze to him. "Yeah. Of course."

"If she'd said why..."

A shadow crosses his face, he looks down at his lap and swirls the whiskey around. They were twins so I'm not sure how different that is than being a sibling. Does he feel her loss more acutely? Does he feel it still? It's been more than a decade.

"She'd still be dead," he finally says.

"But if we knew why—"

"It wouldn't matter," he snaps, eyes hard on me. "She'd still be dead."

"I heard you the first time."

"Did you?"

"What were you doing in Austria the day our father was killed?"

It's too dark for me to read his features but I

swear I see a flash of surprise in the way his mouth opens then closes. He snort-laughs, bringing the glass to his lips, and swallows the rest of his whiskey. He pours himself another. Swallows that too. His movements are reckless suddenly.

"Is that where you were?"

I nod, never taking my eyes off him.

"What did you do, Zeke?"

He shakes his head. "You didn't see her like that, did you? Just me and mom."

I turn away, guilty. I know he's referring to Zoë. To when he found her. I wasn't home that night. I didn't hear what had happened until two days later when I turned my phone back on. I had a habit of disappearing. Taking trips and vanishing. I was always good at it. When things got shitty at home, I left. When dad drank, I took off. Zeke and Zoë were stuck, though. Sixteen. Too young to get away. They put up with our father's dark moods. His punishments. They and our mother.

"Do you know what a person who's been hanging for a few hours looks like?"

I swallow the contents of my glass over the lump in my throat.

"I won't describe it. I don't want you to see that in your nightmares."

I turn to him. "I should have been here," I say, voice thick. "I should have been the one to find her. Or dad should have."

"No. Not dad." A darkness more complete than anything else morphs his face into something different. Something monstrous. Or maybe it's the fire playing a trick on me.

"Then me."

He shakes his head. "It had to be me. There's a reason for it. Maybe she planned it. I don't know." He looks to the fire again. "She tried to tell me you know. If I think back on it, she tried."

"Tried to tell you what?"

"Me finding her was my punishment."

"What the fuck are you talking about?"

He leans the back of his head against the chair and looks up at the ceiling. "Dad deserved what happened to him. Zoë didn't." He stands, turns to me. "As far as Austria goes, I took care of what needed to be taken care of. Just as I don't get to question your motives with Isabelle, you don't get to question mine where Zoë is concerned. You weren't here. You didn't see her. You didn't cut her down. You didn't know what she endured. So, if you want to play detective in Austria, be my fucking guest. But know that I'm no different than you, brother."

## 9

## ISABELLE

Jericho stumbles into the bedroom long after I've fallen asleep, waking me when he knocks into something. I open my eyes and see the shadow of him in the dark room. I don't move but watch as he strips off his clothes, muttering something under his breath. He's drunk. I can see it in the way he moves. When he climbs into bed a moment later, I smell it.

"I know you're awake," he says.

I roll onto my side to face him. "You were gone overnight," I say.

He stares up at the ceiling, blinks without comment. I'm not sure he's listening to me. He seems distracted.

"Were you with Julia?" I don't know why I ask it. I don't really believe he was. But her perfume clinging to him, I don't know, I didn't like it. I remember how she acted when he walked in on us talking at the chapel. Remember her asking about the sex. And I just don't like it.

He turns to me. "You think I'd sleep with Julia Bishop?"

I don't like how that sounds. The words out there like that. "Did you?"

"Don't be ridiculous, Isabelle. Go to sleep."

I sit up on one elbow when he rolls onto his side away from me. "It's not so ridiculous. She's a beautiful woman. Closer to your age. More sophisticated than me. More experienced. More—"

I don't get to finish because he rolls back, grabs my arms, and has me on my back, straddling me.

"That woman is a pariah. The only part of what you said that's true is that she's closer to my age and it wouldn't take much to be more experienced than you, would it?"

"Why do you always have to be a jerk?"

"The rest is bullshit. You? You're honest. You bring light. You are light. It's what this house needs. What I...what Angelique needs."

I blink, watch his expression change as if he just processed what he said. I don't know who is more surprised, him or me. But then he ruins it.

"You said you weren't jealous," he taunts sounding like his usual dick self. "Were you lying?"

"I just—"

"Don't tell me you want me all to yourself, Isabelle."

"If you're fucking someone else I need to know. It's to protect myself. That's all."

He lowers himself to his elbows on either side of my face and rests one hand on top of my head.

"You're my wife. I'm only fucking you. I have no interest in fucking anyone but you. And speaking of..." he trails off, dips his head closer and brushes the scruff of his jaw over my cheek. Nudging my head a little so his mouth is at my ear.

"You're drunk," I manage weakly. I'm already aroused.

"Not that drunk," he says and licks the shell of my ear as he slides one hand over my stomach, into my panties, and cups my sex. "Not so drunk I can't make you come. Because you know what I love?"

"What?" I ask on a breath. He's doing that thing with his fingers that drives me crazy.

"I love watching your face when you come. I love hearing you breathe my name and bite your lip when you come."

I close my eyes and bite my lip. Do I always do that?

"Yeah. Like that," he says and pushes my top aside to take a nipple into his mouth.

I cry out as soon as he does it, teeth and lips and tongue wet and hard and soft all at once. When he draws my nipple out and curls his fingers inside me.

I find myself panting, clinging to him, wrapping an arm around his neck to pull him closer. I hold onto him when the wave of orgasm begins to take me under.

My anchor.

"One more, sweetheart," he says when I can breathe again. "Turn over." He doesn't wait for me to do it. He lifts himself up just enough to roll me onto my stomach. His hands are on my hips and he's on his knees, drawing me up to mine.

I arch my back as he settles between my spread legs and splays me open.

"You're fucking beautiful, you know that?" he says. I look over my shoulder to find him looking at me, a raw hunger in his eyes. "Perfect," he adds and dips his head to run the flat of his tongue over my sex and then my ass, before straightening to draw me to him, entering me in one long, deep stride.

I suck in an audible breath. It feels so good to have him inside me. To be stretched by him. For him.

"Are you going to watch me fuck you?" he asks, breathing ragged as he moves inside me.

I nod, resting my cheek on the bed, mouth slack.

"Good. Don't look away. I need to see your face. Your eyes," he says. A moment later, as he thrusts into me, I feel him at my back hole, pushing a finger inside me.

I moan.

He hooks his finger, pulling me up a little, his other hand tight on my hip as he thrusts harder, faster. Sweat drips down his face onto my back and I rise onto my elbows to brace myself for his thrusts.

I like this. Him taking me like this. I shouldn't. I should hate him. But when he slides one hand between my legs I stop thinking about that. Stop thinking altogether. I need this. I need him like this. And I let myself have this moment, this reprieve from reality.

I'm his. And there are moments I want to be his. Even after everything. To let him be my anchor. To let go and give myself to him.

# 10

## ISABELLE

When I wake several hours later, I'm alone in the bed.

"Jericho?" I ask but he's not in the bedroom or bathroom. I push the blankets off, pull on the shirt he discarded earlier and open the door. The hallway is dark. It's the middle of the night. I creep downstairs barefoot, buttoning two of the buttons on his shirt and wrapping my arms around myself to keep warm. The house always feels cold inside. It must be the marble.

Inside the large fireplace in the living room are the remnants of a dying fire. I smell it and can see the deep red glow as I walk past. If he was here, he's not anymore.

"Jericho?" I try again quietly. Nothing.

I walk through the rooms on the first floor, but still don't find him until I get to that heavy steel door leading to the cellar. It stands open and I can see the dim light from a single, naked lightbulb downstairs. He's left his key in the lock. It's not like him. Too careless. He wouldn't risk Angelique coming down here. Especially at night.

Although he was drunk earlier. Maybe he got up and drank some more. What do I know?

I take the first step hugging myself tighter as I descend into the cellar, the memory of the night I spent down here making me shiver. I should call out to him. Let him know I'm coming. But I don't make a sound, my steps careful.

I recall the other time I was down here. How he threatened to leave me in that room or bring me back to punish me. I remember the man I'd met that first night. My horned devil. I remember him stripping me naked but giving me his shirt to wear. But I also remember him locking the door and walking away when he knew I'd be terrified.

That was the point. I shouldn't forget it.

"What are you hiding?" I hear him say just as I near the bottom of the stairs. The way the stairs are walled in you can't see in either direction of the corridor until you're properly in the cellar. The light overhead blinks but the hall to the right is dark. That's the side I'd been on. I remember the other side. How dark it was.

I wish I'd put on shoes, or socks at least, as I take a step toward that other corridor. It's several degrees colder down here and the only dim light is from the open door of a room at the very end.

"Jericho?" I say, my voice too quiet to be heard.

Nothing.

Nothing but a noise behind me that makes me jump. Makes my heart fall to my stomach.

Just the house settling. It's an old house. That's all it is.

I keep going. I know he's in the room at the end. I hear his mumblings. See his shadow fall across the hall as he walks from one side of the room to the other. And I find myself hurrying, too far from the stairs to run back up, too terrified to stay where I am. Because we're not alone down here. I feel it. Feel the icy presence with us.

But when I get to the door of the room, I stop. I see him inside, his back to me. He's wearing nothing but a pair of sweats so I have a full view of the twin dragon tattoo. It's huge and spectacular but that's not what has caught my eye. For the first time since I've known Jericho St. James, I see him at a loss.

He hasn't noticed me yet. He's sitting on a wrought iron bed that must be a hundred years old. Older. It makes the one in the room I was locked in look brand new. The mattress on it is modern though and it doesn't quite fit it. It hangs over the side a few inches. An almost empty bottle of whiskey is on the nightstand. I've seen him drunk before. It's not pretty. But tonight is different. There's a darkness to him. A shadow. A sadness.

I realize what's different. Missing. His anger. Something about it, how he's sitting there alone and a little lost, it makes my heart twist. Makes it hurt.

He's looking through a box, an old wooden box that must have been painted pink once. From inside, he's taking out folded sheet of paper after folded sheet of paper.

"Where is it?" he asks. "Where did you leave it?"

I look around the room and smell the stale, old scent of cigarette smoke from years past. I see the doll house. Barbie. I had a similar one growing up but this one's a little older. Not too much though. There's a small table in the corner, the once-colorful mosaic design on top now just old and broken. It looks like something that belongs outside in a garden. Beside it is a simple wooden chair.

"Where?" he says again.

I step into the room. "Jericho?"

He looks at me and is on his feet in an instant. I realize it takes him a minute to realize it's me because his expression is different in that moment.

"You shouldn't be down here. Go back upstairs," he says, voice like gravel.

I look around the room, see a crucifix hanging crooked from a nail. I also notice a picture on the far wall. Whatever was framed inside, now yellowed and faded.

"Whose room is this?" I ask.

"No one. Go upstairs." He sits back down, takes a drink from the bottle then opens the nightstand drawer, beginning to rifle through it.

"What are you looking for?" I ask, taking a few steps toward him. Unsure what to make of him like this.

"Nothing," he says.

He closes the drawer and looks at the box again. It's open, the pieces of paper scattered on the bed. He starts to load them back into the box but when he's done, instead of closing it and putting it away, he picks it up, and, as if suddenly furious, he hurls it across the room.

I let out a scream, jumping back.

It crashes into the single frame on the wall. The box drops to the ground, frame swinging on a single nail.

"This is where they did it. Both of them." He shakes his head, looks up and points. "The hanging beam."

I look up too and shudder when I see the ancient wooden beam that stretches from wall to wall.

"Hanging beam?" I ask.

"That's the chair Zoë stood on. I don't know why it's still here. Why we didn't burn it. I don't know what the hell Mary used. Don't know why Zoë brought these things down here. I don't know any of it."

"Jericho?" I follow him when he sits down and picks up the bottle.

"Why the hell would anyone want to be in here?"

I swallow, sit beside him, and take the bottle. I set it aside but keep hold of his hand.

"Come upstairs with me," I say.

He blinks like he's having a hard time keeping his eyes open. I wonder how full that bottle was earlier. "I'd better never find you down here, Isabelle."

My mouth opens. Does he think I'd hang myself? Is that what he's saying? "Come upstairs."

"Zeke knows," he says. "He knows why. I know he does."

I lay my head on his shoulder and squeeze his hand.

"It's why he killed dad."

That startles me and I pull back. "What?"

He puts his head in his hands. "Why?" he roars.

"You're drunk, Jericho. You're not thinking straight."

He gets to his feet, walks to where the box lies broken on the floor, the notes scattered. He stands in the middle of the mess and shakes his head.

I stand, go to him. I take one of his hands and press it to my belly.

"Take me upstairs. I'm tired and hungry and it's cold down here. The baby..."

He looks at me, mouth open, forehead furrowed.

He presses my stomach gently and sets his forehead on my shoulder.

"I don't understand why," he says, and I don't know if it's his words or the tone of them that breaks my heart in two.

"It's okay. Let's go upstairs."

He straightens to his full height, looks down at me, studies me for a long moment. "Your name means promise. Do you know that?"

I'm surprised he'd know that. "God's promise," I say. "My mom chose it."

"Fuck god. There is no fucking god and if there is, he doesn't deserve your affection." He shakes his head, closes his eyes then runs a hand into his hair and opens his eyes. "The baby. I hope it's not a girl. The St. James's girls...there's history you know? I don't want it to repeat."

"It won't."

"Angelique." He sighs.

"It won't repeat—"

"That's what history does," he interrupts. "It repeats. It's on an endless fucking loop."

I get in front of him, take his face in my hands. "Look at me."

"Endless."

"Look at me." He does. "Take me upstairs. I don't want to be down here. It's not good for the baby."

His eyes narrow thoughtfully, and he finally nods. He cups my face with one hand, thumb gentle on my cheekbone. He kisses my forehead, my cheek, my mouth.

"Promise," he says and takes my hand. He turns me and just as we're about to walk out of the room I feel a draft tickle my neck. Glancing back, I see something behind the picture that he knocked askew. A cubby hole. A place to hide something. And the edge of what looks like a beaded necklace dangling from behind the picture. It must have come loose when the box crashed into the frame.

"Your feet are bare," he says, dragging my attention away. He lifts me up just before switching the light off. He doesn't close the door but carries me to climb the stairs. "I don't want you coming down here again. Understand? It's not safe. It's cursed, that cellar. I don't want you in it."

I nod as he sets me on the floor in the main part of the house. I don't want to be down there.

He closes the door and I watch him. Watch this giant of a man who is back to being himself now, tall and powerful. The dragon tattoo moving on his back as he locks the door and slips the single, large key into the pocket of his pants. When he turns to me, the man I glimpsed downstairs, the broken one, he's gone. No, not gone. Hidden from view. He's in there. I've seen him now. I know.

"I mean it, Isabelle. I don't ever what you down there. Am I clear?"

I nod and my stomach growls loudly. I've only eaten a bowl of Catherine's brothy soup.

Jericho smiles. "I'll make you a sandwich." We walk into the kitchen, and I don't pull my hand free of his.

# 11

## JERICHO

Isabelle is five weeks pregnant. I wonder if the baby was conceived on our wedding night. I watch her when we return from the doctor's visit. She's distracted, sitting with Angelique going over her music lesson. But it's like she said when she first found out. She's nineteen years old. I'm sure being married to a man like me, a man who was a stranger to her, and having his baby wasn't on her to-do-by-the-time-I-turn-twenty list.

I meant what I said though. I will take care of her.

Even as I think it, I realize how strange it sounds. How different to when I first devised this plan.

Zeke has been on a business trip in Calgary since the night we last spoke. We have offices up there, but I know it's bullshit. He's avoiding me after our conversation. I don't blame him.

At nine o'clock on the dot the doorbell rings. Isabelle's excitement is palpable when we get to the door to find Catherine inviting her little group into the foyer. They're clearly impressed, if not intimidated, by the house. I see it in their faces as they set down their cases to take off jackets. They give them to Catherine who then hands them off to the girl whose name I always fail to remember. Isabelle would know. She knows the staff well. She spends time talking to them throughout her day and they seem to like her.

She charms everyone she comes in contact with. Her nature is sweet. Innocent. I understand it. But something about her relationships bother me, too. It's envy maybe. Not that I want to be friends with the staff. I just want Isabelle for myself.

"Holy shit, girl. If I knew you lived here, I'd insist we always have lessons at your place!" says Megs from the café as she and Isabelle hug. Megs is holding two bakery boxes so it's more Isabelle hugging her. I stand back and watch them.

There is one other girl. She's younger, maybe sixteen, seventeen. Maria. Then Maria's older brother, John. They, too, hug Isabelle.

I clear my throat and Isabelle turns to me. I smile at the group and put my hand on my wife's back. The smile feels forced.

"Um, this is Jericho," she says.

I wait. But when nothing else comes, I add, "Isabelle's husband."

There's clear confusion from Maria and John but after a quiet, awkward look exchanged between them they smile and shake my hand. Megs walks up to me. She's older, more confident. Less intimidated.

"Good to see you again, Jericho. How did your little girl like the cake shop?"

"Loved it. Can't get enough sugar."

"Well, that's good," she says and extends one of the boxes out to me. "Because this is for her. Is she still up?"

I take the box. "Sadly no. Bedtime was half an hour ago. I'll make sure she gets it in the morning."

"Great." She turns to Isabelle. "And these are for us."

Isabelle peeks into the box. "Oh, lemon scones. My favorite. Thanks, Megs."

"No problem. I'm glad to see you back with the group."

"Speaking of...where's Paul?" Isabelle asks.

Paul Hayes is their teacher. Twenty-eight years old, during the day he's a professor at a posh private music school in the city. He's a violinist who is supposed to be pretty good. Not that I know much about it, that's just based on his bio which he probably wrote himself. I ran background checks on all of them.

"He was right behind us but got caught at a

traffic light." Just as Megs says it, the doorbell rings again. "Speak of the devil."

John, who is closest to the door opens it, revealing Paul Hayes.

Except that this isn't the Paul Hayes I saw in photos.

"Paul!" Isabelle rushes to hug him and immediately my hackles rise. None of the others had this kind of reception from her. But it's not only that.

"Sorry I'm late," Paul says, keeping one arm around her as they draw apart. "Got caught at a light then had to stop to fill up the car."

He's about my height. Maybe an inch or two shorter. He's leaner than he used to be, too. A lot leaner. The photos of Paul Hayes I found had him about three-hundred pounds heavier.

"And, almost forgot," he says.

He didn't.

He reaches into his pocket to pull out a triangular shaped chocolate bar.

Isabelle's smile grows huge.

"Saw they had them at the station, so I grabbed one for you. I know how much you love these."

"They're my favorite! Thank you!" She takes the bar. Toblerone. I make a mental note. And then they hug again.

I step toward my wife and watch my own shadow fall over her. I clear my throat, close my hand around the back of her neck.

"I'm Isabelle's husband. Jericho St. James."

"Jericho," Isabelle starts but stops when I draw her away from Paul and closer to me.

Paul clears his throat, pastes a smile on his face. "I just heard you'd gotten married," he says, half to her, half to me. "Congratulations. You're a lucky man." He extends his hand and I look at it, at the long fingers, the soft skin of a violinist. The frayed edge of a cashmere sweater. I'm pretty sure he's never punched another man.

"You're her teacher," I say, squeezing his hand harder than I need to.

"The one and only." He turns to her. "As far as I know." He winks. And I want to break his face.

"Did you lose weight recently, Paul?" I ask.

He clears his throat again, that warm smile he seems to reserve for *my wife* faltering.

"Oh my god. I'm so sorry, Paul," Isabelle says, apologizing for me. Unbelievable.

"What? It's a fair question," I defend.

"No, it's fine. I did, actually," says Paul. "With surgery and the support of my family and some of the best doctors and nurses in the city, I lost over two-hundred pounds."

"He has a will of iron because he's even able to resist my treats," Megs says and comes between us to hug Paul. I notice the smile he gives her is different than the one he had for my wife. Their hug shorter.

"This way," Catherine says, and the group follows her to the library.

Isabelle turns to me, slipping from my grasp. "What the hell? That was so rude."

I drag my gaze from the back of Paul Hayes's head with its stylishly messy blond hair to Isabelle. "He wants to fuck you."

"What?"

"He," I say, pointing in the direction they went. "Wants to fuck you." I point to her.

"And you could gauge that all from the thirty seconds you spent with him?"

"I know men, Isabelle. You should have told me."

"Told you what exactly?"

My eye twitches. "That he isn't three-hundred-and-fifty pounds."

"What is wrong with you?" she asks and shakes her head. "I'm going." She steps away. Tries to. But I grab her arm and tug her back. She looks up at me. "What?" she snaps.

"Is there something between you two?"

"Me and Paul? He's my teacher. That's all. Seriously. What is wrong with you?"

"That's not all. Is there anything I should know? Because you're my wife now. That means something."

"You forced me to be your wife, remember?"

I tighten my grip when she tries to pull free. "You

are my wife. You are carrying my child but pregnant or not, I don't share."

"Not true when it came to Kimberly," she snaps, and she knows she's wrong to say it the moment the words are out of her mouth. I see it on her face. "Shit. Sorry. I didn't mean that."

I blink, draw in a tight breath. Truth is I haven't thought of Kimberly in days. Not like I used to anyway.

"I'm sorry," she says again, thinking it's her comment that upset me.

"It's fine. You're right." I walk her backward, trapping her between the wall and myself. I let my gaze roam her face. She's not wearing a stitch of makeup and she's so beautiful. More now that she's pregnant even with the shadows under her eyes after our long night. "You're mine. You know that don't you?"

She blinks, eyebrows coming together like she's confused. Something tender passes through her eyes but it's gone in the next instant, replaced by a hardness. "I'm yours because you want something."

"You're mine because I want you."

"And you're used to taking anything you want. Getting anything you want, aren't you?"

I slide my hands down her arms to her wrists and drag them over her head, pinning them to the wall. Her eyes darken as she licks her lips, her body preparing itself as if in anticipation.

"I am," I say darkly. "And pregnant or not, Bishop

or not, vengeance or not, you're what I want. Remember what I told you. Any man touches you, I will cut off their hands. That includes my brother. That includes Paul Hayes. Any. Man."

Her throat works to swallow and the pulse at her neck throbs.

"You're mine. Say it."

Her mouth opens, closes.

"Say it, Isabelle."

"I'm yours."

"Only mine."

"Only yours."

I kiss her hard, releasing one of her wrists to cup the back of her head and pull her to me. The fingers of my other hand intertwine with the fingers of hers. And I realize how much what I said is true. She's mine. Pregnant or not. Bishop or not. Vengeance or not.

Isabelle is mine.

Only mine.

She will only ever be mine.

## 12

## ISABELLE

I'm flushed when I walk into the lesson. I apologize to Paul again for Jericho but am distracted throughout the two hour lesson. I'm embarrassed by how Jericho behaved toward Paul but that's not what has me distracted. It's our conversation. What he said. What I said.

He wants me.

Pregnant or not. Bishop or not. Vengeance or not. I'm his.

When the lesson is over, and everyone gets ready to leave, I half expect Jericho to be standing in the hallway waiting for me his ear to the door. I'm not sure if I'm not a little disappointed when he's not.

Everyone leaves but Paul hangs back.

"I know I still owe you for a few lessons, but I should be able to send you a check in a week or so. I have a job now, but things have been...weird."

"You don't owe me. We're caught up."

"No, I think I'm three lessons behind. I know I am. I keep track. And I want to pay for those I missed too. I know you have other students who want my spot—"

"I'm not kicking you out, Isabelle. Besides, you letting us use your house is great. Saves on renting a room at the college."

"No. I'll pay you. As soon as I can."

"No worries."

"You're sweet. Hey, I'm sorry again about what happened."

"It's fine. My weight loss is no secret." He looks over my shoulder and steps closer. "It's just this whole marriage thing all came about out of nowhere. And he seems pretty possessive of you. You're okay?"

"Yeah. I'm fine."

"You're sure?"

"M-hm."

He studies me as if trying to gauge if I'm lying. I'm not. Not really.

"Okay," he finally says. "As long as you're fine. I was just surprised when Megs told me you were married. I mean, I didn't even know you were dating anyone."

"It was...sudden."

He nods, studies me. "I'll send you tickets to the show. We're still on, right? You'll be there?"

"Show?"

"You forgot?"

I think, then shake my head. "Shit. No, I didn't forget. Time has just been going so fast." Paul is playing in a quartet at a small theater. It's one of his first public appearances.

"Good. One ticket or two?"

"Um…" I know he has to buy the tickets and I don't want him to waste his money in case I can't get there. "I can buy the tickets."

"No, you're my guest. I'll just send two. So your husband doesn't get testy." He winks like he did earlier.

I giggle more out of nervousness than anything else and glance behind me.

He opens the door, and we look out at the rain. He turns back to me and pulls me to him for a hug. I hug him back. I've never thought of Paul as anything other than my teacher. I'm not attracted to him. Never have been. And the feeling is mutual. I think.

"I'll see you next week," I say, drawing back when the hug lasts longer than normal. Has he always held me like this? Or is it Jericho who has me paranoid?

"See you then."

I close the door when he's gone and turn back to the foyer. It's quiet, the rooms on the first floor, dark. I still expect Jericho to creep out of some corner and surprise me, but he doesn't. So, I head to the library.

I'll clean up before I go to bed. But I jump the instant I walk inside, because speak of the devil and there he is.

My husband.

He's sitting on the big leather chair where Paul was sitting and the other, smaller chairs are still set in a circle around it. He's got my violin in his hands.

"You scared me," I finally say, hoping I sound somewhat normal. "Why are you sitting here in the dark?" He's got his jacket off, the sleeves of his button-down rolled up to his forearms, the top two buttons undone.

"It's not dark. It's how you left it. Ambiance, I guess?"

"What?" the room is dimly lit by three soft lights. We'd turned off the brighter ones. "It's better for the mood when we're playing."

"*Paul* like it better that way?"

"You're being a child," I say and pick up a tray.

"Sit."

I look at him. "I'm going to clean up then go to bed."

"Sit, Isabelle."

I put the tray down and sit across from him, feeling the submissiveness of my position in the lower, smaller chair, him in the dominant position in the large leather chair. It didn't feel like this earlier when Paul had been sitting there.

He holds the violin out to me. "Play."

"I can't just play on demand." I start to get up. "I need to clean. I'm tired after last night's adventures." It's a low blow. I know it. He was upset last night, not just drunk but hurting. I don't apologize though, and I avert my gaze as I pick up the tray again.

A moment later, he's on his feet, hand around my arm, my violin and bow hanging limply from the other.

"You'll play for him but not for me?"

"Are you jealous?"

He snorts, setting my things down. He spins me so I'm looking away from him and bends me over the high arm of the leather sofa. My face is in the seat, my ass in the air.

"What are you doing?" I try to get up, but he keeps me pinned.

"What did I tell you?" he asks, flipping my skirt up, pushing my panties down. There's no ceremony in it. He's baring my flesh for his use. And it's strangely arousing when it should only be degrading.

I reach back to push my skirt over my butt. "Jericho—"

"Isabelle," he says, capturing my wrists and holding them in one hand. He flips the skirt back up and leans over so his warmth is at my back, his breath at my ear. "What did I tell you?"

I can feel him. He's hard.

And I'm aroused.

With his free hand he cups my ass, fingers digging into flesh. "What. Did. I. Tell. You?"

"I'm yours," I say, turning my head so I can see him.

He nods, satisfied, and straightens. Keeping me prone, he glances around. I don't know what he's looking for but a moment later, he leans toward the side table where someone's half-eaten scone sits on a plate. He scoops up the butter with two fingers.

"What are you doing?" I ask, trying to wriggle free when he smears it into the cleft of my ass.

"Lubricating you. You'll be thanking me in a minute," he says and then he's rubbing the butter into me.

Every muscle tenses. Instinct.

"Relax, Isabelle."

"Not there."

"There. And if I recall you came hard the last time I fucked your ass." He keeps his fingers on me and releases my wrists. "Put your hands on the sofa."

"No."

"No? Let me put it differently then. Keep your hands on the sofa and I'll let you come. Don't and I won't. Either way, I'm fucking this tight little hole. Which do you choose?"

"I don't—"

"Choices, Isabelle. Remember? What's yours? Come or don't. It doesn't matter much to me either way."

I crane my neck to look back at him and slowly slide my hands to the seat of the sofa.

"Smart. Now." He turns his attention back to my ass. "Relax." He slips the fingers of his now free hand between my legs to find my clit and the instant he does, I do what he wants. I relax.

He takes his time rubbing my clit while easing his fingers into my ass, stretching it, smearing lubricant inside it. As much as I want to hate it, hate him touching me like this, I'm going to come. I'm going to come hard when he's inside me. I remember the last time. How it hurt at first. How hard I came after.

I know he deems me ready when he pulls his fingers out and I hear him unzipping his slacks. I brace myself. He slips his cock into my pussy once, twice, and I'm open for him. Aroused enough that I stretch easily. I hope the other passage stretches as easily. He draws out and brings his cock to that entrance. I tense up and he rubs my lower back.

"Relax."

I nod. This is the hardest part. It's the thickest part I have to take. So I close my eyes and try not to fight the unnatural intrusion. It hurts at first, a moment of burn, but then he's in, the butter lubricating his way. He doesn't go slowly, doesn't take me inch by inch. He slides all the way in, and I hear myself moan as his fingers play with my clit.

"So tight." His voice is ragged, raw.

I arch my back as he pumps slowly then draws

his fingers from my clit to grip my hips, drawing my cheeks wide.

"So I don't get testy?" he asks when I look back. He meets my eyes and thrusts in hard.

I gasp, my body going rigid.

"Is that what he said?" he asks, drawing out and repeating.

"That hurts."

"And what did you say to him?"

I close my eyes, trying to prepare myself to take another punishing thrust, not ready when it comes.

"Please!"

"Look at me."

I shake my head.

He thrusts again.

I cry out, feel tears burn my eyes as I turn to look at him. He heard everything. And I know I was wrong.

"What did you say when he said that?" he asks, drawing out so only the tip is inside me. I know I'll take at least one more. And maybe I deserve it.

I swallow, can't answer.

"You giggled," he says and delivers his most punishing thrust yet.

"I'm sorry. I didn't know what to say. How to react."

"I can tell you how not to react. Don't fucking giggle when some asshole is hitting on you and trying to belittle your husband."

I nod. He's right.

"I'm sorry. I am. Please."

"You're going to take my cock in your ass but you're not going to come. That's your punishment. Spread your legs. I don't want you accidentally getting yourself off."

I do it. It's a small price to pay. And when he's satisfied, he takes me and I want to come. I want to come so bad. I almost do. All it would take would be the lightest touch of my fingers to my clit.

"Please," I say in a small voice as his thrusts grow harder, deeper, and I find myself meeting them. "Please let me come."

I slip one hand between my legs, and he grabs it, then the other and holds them at my lower back.

"No," he says, leaning over me as he fucks me.

"Please. I'm sorry. Please."

He grins, eyes dark. "Are you begging me, Isabelle?"

I nod. I don't even care.

"Fine. After."

After?

He straightens, keeps hold of my wrists and looks down at us, watches. When he thickens inside me, he lays his chest to my back. I feel the rumble of him, skin slick with sweat as he takes what he wants from me, uses me and fills me as his cock throbs his release.

"Fuck," he manages hoarsely as he slowly straightens, draws out. "Don't move."

I watch as he takes a used napkin and wipes his cock before tucking himself back into his pants. He turns back to me, looks at me spread out for him. His come leaking out of me. I want to cover myself. To get up and run out of the room.

But then he nods.

"Your turn," he says.

"What?"

"Do it. It's what you wanted, isn't it? What you asked for?"

"What?"

"Make yourself come."

I blink, feeling my face heat up.

"You heard me," he says. He resumes his seat in the armchair and picks up his whiskey glass. I hadn't even noticed it before. He sips. "Get yourself off while I watch. Now. And don't look away from me when you do it." He says that last part just as I am about to bury my face in the seat of the couch.

I keep my eyes on his as I slip my hand between my legs. He never shifts his gaze from mine as I begin to rub my clit, hearing myself pant as my breath comes in short bursts. I'm aroused. I'm so turned on. And feeling his seed slide over the cleft of my ass and down my thigh, I come. It's not as hard as when he fucks me, but I come. When it's over, he finishes the last of his whiskey, sets his glass down and claps his hands.

"That's a show worth watching," he says and stands. He moves behind me, bending to pick up my panties. He helps me step into them before pulling them up. "You'll sleep with my come inside you just so you remember this punishment." He flips my skirt down and helps me stand, then takes my face between his hands and kisses me hard on my mouth, leaving no doubt that I belong to him.

## 13

### ISABELLE

I don't see Jericho until the next evening. It's a strange week but this time of year is always hard. It's almost the anniversary of Christian's death and this may be the first year I don't go to his grave on the day. I could ask Jericho to take me. I don't know why I haven't.

Saturday is the concert and although I've been asking about mail, I've been told there wasn't anything for me. I wonder if Paul changed his mind about me coming because of Jericho. Not that I think Jericho will let me go or want to go himself.

Leontine, Angelique, and I are seated at the table when he walks in, taking off his suit jacket. He hands it and his tie to Catherine who comes around the corner at the same time.

"Evening," he says. His eyes on me, making me flush, remembering last night.

"Daddy, guess what we did today," Angelique starts as he rolls up his shirt sleeves—something I can't seem to look away from. Something that makes my mouth water in anticipation of those hands on me, those eyes on me. Him inside me.

I shake my head. It must be the pregnancy hormones. That or there is something seriously wrong with me.

"Tell me everything," he says, kissing her on top of her head and hugging her before kissing his mother on top of her head and then getting to me. "I'm famished," he says when he does. He tilts my head and kisses me on the mouth. It's not a deep kiss but it's hungry. Erotic rather than sensual. Dirty. "Sleep well last night?" he asks.

"Fine," I say, embarrassed. Feeling myself flush.

"Good," he says and brings his mouth to my ear. "I can still see it you know. See you bent over— "

I clear my throat, shake him off and busy myself with laying the napkin on my lap.

He grins, takes his seat at the head of the table. "Zeke still in Calgary?" he asks Leontine.

She nods. "He'll be back in a few days."

"Good."

Catherine enters followed by one of her helpers to serve dinner. A roast for them and plain home-made pasta for me. I've been less nauseous and haven't thrown up today. It's something. But I'm also eating a pretty bland diet.

"Is that enough?" Jericho asks when he sees my plate of pasta with olive oil, salt and pepper. I sprinkle a generous serving of spicy pepper flakes and pick up my fork and knife. "You need protein." He picks up the grated parmesan cheese and raises his eyebrows.

"A little," I say, not having tried it yet.

He sprinkles it on then we eat. Angelique and I drinking water out of fancy glasses while he and his mom drink red wine. Angelique proceeds to tell him all about our day. About what she learned in her lessons. About the flowers she collected outside with which she made a sort of bouquet for the table. She also asks about the next story time she will be allowed to go to.

Jericho smiles. "Maybe we can have story time here," he says. "But tonight, I was hoping Isabelle would play something for us after dinner. What do you think about that Angelique?" he asks her, not me.

"Oh! Yes! That's a great idea. Belle, maybe you can play the one you did this afternoon," she says to me then turns to her father. "It's from a story called Romeo and Juliet, daddy. Romeo and Juliet love each other but they can't be together because their families hate each other. It's so sad."

"Maybe we can stick to the happier fairy tales, Isabelle," Leontine says to me.

"Romeo and Juliet is closer to reality, don't you think?" I ask.

"She's right. Star-crossed lovers it'll be," Jericho says as he takes a bite of his food. "How are your lessons with Mrs. Strand?" he asks Angelique.

Her face darkens and she shrugs a shoulder. I walked by her room earlier today when Mrs. Strand was there. Through the door I could hear her raised voice. I almost went inside to see what was going on, but Leontine stopped me, saying Angelique hadn't done the work she was supposed to do. I didn't think it was reason enough to raise her voice at the little girl but walked away making a mental note to check on them at the following lesson.

"She's not nice," Angelique says.

"Well, not everyone is nice in life," Leontine tells her. "Why was she angry with you?"

Angelique sets her jaw. She looks just like her father when she does it, except that she's cute and I have to giggle.

"Those giggles get you in trouble," Jericho tells me but he's smiling at her too. I wonder if he sees the resemblance.

Once we're finished, he turns to me, takes an envelope out of his pocket and sets it on the table. He keeps his fingers on it but makes sure I can read that it's addressed to me.

"What's that?" I ask. He pushes it toward me. I

take it and open the flap which has already been opened.

"Two. So I won't get testy," Jericho says.

"You opened my mail? When did they come?"

"Yes and no idea. They were on my desk."

"It's a crime to open someone else's mail."

"Are you going to call the police?"

I glare.

He grins.

"Can we go?" I ask him.

"It's why I'm giving them to you." I open my mouth, but he puts up a finger. "One stipulation. You play for me tonight. For my family."

"That's blackmail."

"It's a choice. Choose."

I'm not sure why I don't want to play for him. Is it that I want to keep that piece of myself secret from him? Maybe keep control of one part of my life? Or maybe it's how vulnerable I feel when I play. How it opens me up. And him witnessing that scares me.

"Belle?" Angelique asks when I take too long to answer.

I look up at Jericho who leans toward me. "What are you afraid of?"

"I'm not."

"Then play for us and I'll take you to your concert."

"Okay."

He nods and we eat. When we're finished, he wipes his mouth with his napkin and stands. "Shall we?" he asks, holding out his hand to me, palm up. I slip mine into his.

## 14

### JERICHO

The library is alight with candles. There must be more than a hundred of them. I had Catherine set it up this way and place a chair for Isabelle beneath the arched, iron-clad windows where the moon casts an other-worldly light around her.

"Oh. Wow," Angelique says and I lay my hand on her head. My eyes are on Isabelle who slipped her hand free as soon as we got here, going in ahead of us. She's wearing a simple white dress and I think I should have put her in a gown. Something soft and flowing and beautiful. Like her.

She turns to me and bites the inside of her lip.

I tilt my head a little. It's almost imperceptible. I want her to like it. It's important that she likes it.

She smiles a small smile and her eyes glow. Tears. Not sad ones I think. She turns away and I notice her hand go to her face before she opens her violin case sitting on top of the coffee table.

We sit down and I can't take my eyes off her. Angelique holds one of my hands with both of hers and lays her head against my shoulder. My mother sits across from us. She's not looking at Isabelle. She's watching me.

Isabelle clears her throat. She doesn't quite look at any of us as she sits down in the chair set for her.

"I'm probably rusty," she says with a quick glance to me. "I'm not very good. I just—"

"She's very good," Angelique says over her.

"I'm sure she is," I say and nod to Isabelle.

And she begins.

And fuck.

Fuck me.

I know the piece Angelique mentioned earlier. I've heard it as background.

Romeo and Juliet.

A Thousand Times Goodnight.

Fuck.

I squeeze my daughter's hand. My gaze is riveted on my wife and breathing seems to get harder. Like the oxygen's being drawn out of the room and all that's left in its place is this emotion. This incredible feeling of sadness. No, not sadness. Of love. Of a love that will end in utter tragedy.

Romeo and Juliet were young. Idealistic and naïve. They still believed in love. They still hoped.

I'm not so young. So naïve.

My throat closes up and swallowing is hard. Looking at her is hard but looking away impossible.

Will she bear the tragedy of my actions?

Isabelle doesn't look at any of us directly. She keeps her gaze straight ahead, eyes unfocused. She's not looking at anything in particular. I wonder if she's following the music in her head. If she's seeing the notes as her bow moves over the strings of the violin.

Something shifts, something not palpable. Something inside her. I see it on her face. Do the others? It's soft and subtle but complete. And tragic. So very tragic.

She plays from memory. When she closes her eyes, she grows blurry in mine. Fuck. The music is so fucking beautiful.

My breath is a ragged sucking in of too-thin air.

My body is tense. And I'm squeezing Angelique's hand too hard.

Between the candlelight and the vision of Isabelle in the moonlight in white, I almost have to look away. Almost. But the vision of her face, her eyes, this thing that's come over her. This softness. This other-worldliness. I have to keep my eyes on her. Because she's not here right now. She's else-where. She's emotion and sound and feeling. Only feeling. And I feel her. God. I feel her inside my chest, my gut. I feel her like she's inside me.

When it ends, I blink and she blinks. Then she's wiping her face with the back of her hand. Her violin and bow still in her grip. I look at her. I just look at her. Can't look away.

A Thousand Times Goodnight.

And fuck me. I am fucked.

Because I know something now. Something I've been ignoring. Something I've tried to quash.

I'm hers. All those times I told her she was mine, I left out the other part of that equation. Denied it. But here it is. Clear as day.

Just as she's mine, so am I hers.

We belong to one another.

Until death do us part.

## 15

## ISABELLE

D ex drives us to the sold out concert. It's a small venue but still, it's something. Everyone is dressed in evening gowns, the men in tuxedos. Jericho too. Black on black for him. He is the devil, after all.

We take our seats in the front row.

"He went all out, didn't he?" Jericho says.

"Don't be mean."

He picks up a program, flips through it, snorts at Paul's picture and biography. "You'll start proper lessons in two weeks," he says, closing it and setting it on the still empty seat beside his.

"What?" I ask, tucking the program into my purse.

He turns to me and my breath catches. He's handsome, my husband. Ruggedly so with that five-o'clock shadow along his jaw, his strange eyes that always seem to convey power and possessiveness.

I think about what Paul said. How possessive Jericho is. It's no secret. And some part of me seems to lean into it. Feel safe within the boundary of his arms. It's ridiculous, I know.

"I've arranged for a retired teacher from the Oberlin Conservatory to teach you. He moved to New Orleans about a year ago so it's perfect timing."

"Wait, can you say all that again?"

"Professor Larder. Used to teach at Oberlin Conservatory. Heard it's a good school."

"Oberlin? It's one of the best."

"You'll have weekly lessons. More if you want."

"I have a teacher. A group."

"Now you have a better one."

"How expensive is he?"

"Don't worry about that, Isabelle."

"Tell me. I mean, Oberlin Conservatory?"

He leans toward me. "I have a lot of money in case you hadn't noticed," he says with a wink.

The lights blink twice signaling the concert will begin soon. People who've been milling around take their seats so we can't talk as openly.

"What about my group?"

He looks at me squarely. "Your group isn't my concern. You're talented, Isabelle. It's a waste of your gift not to pursue it."

I'm taken aback by this but then I remember

how he was with Paul. Wonder if he's only saying these things, arranging the lessons to get me away from Paul and my group. To isolate me even more than I already am.

"Jericho," I start, but before I can continue a woman comes toward us, looking hurried.

"Are you Isabelle St. James?"

We both look at her. She's young, dressed in black slacks and a black blouse, wearing a nametag. Amanda.

"Yes," I say.

"We have a problem. Kind of a big problem. One of the violinists who is to go on is caught in traffic. Her piece starts in twenty minutes, but she won't make it. Paul said you could maybe take her place?"

"What? I can't just—"

"Please. It's not a big part but it's important. Only ten minutes on stage then you can watch the rest of the show."

I look to Jericho whose eyes are narrowed like he doesn't trust this. He shifts his gaze to me, but the girl starts again.

"Please. We're desperate."

I nod, get to my feet. "I'll be back I guess," I say and before he can say anything, I'm walking backstage with the girl. "Where is Paul?" I ask.

"This way," she says, walking swiftly ahead of me and away from the stage. Three stagehands pass me. I hear the sound of the concert beginning, and a moment later, applause. I glance behind me to see if I can get a glimpse of Paul. I just catch sight of him in his seat on the stage and can't help my smile. I'm so proud of him. I see the other three seats on the stage are taken and wonder about the woman who is running late. I turn back to follow Amanda's rapidly moving footsteps and my mind doesn't process what happens next. It can't make sense of it. Amanda's gone and in her place stands a man I've never seen before.

I falter, stopping just before I walk straight into him. He's staring down at me and something about him makes me back up a step. Right into another man's chest.

I look from one to the other, two giants dressed in suits that are too tight, too wrong.

The one in front of me steps toward a closed door and opens it. "In," he says.

I turn to the one behind me, but he shoves me forward. I would scream but the music from the concert would drown out any sound. So when he places his hand at my back again, I move forward. I stop when I get to the door and see who's inside. I'm confused.

"Julia?"

The dressing room isn't brightly lit and there are costumes everywhere. The table she's sitting in front of is loaded with makeup and a scented candle burns on the corner. Cinnamon. I used to like the scent but now it makes my stomach turn. On her lap is a very sleepy Matty.

Julia gets to her feet, hugging her son to her body. He's in his pajamas, one thumb in his mouth, the other holding a little blue blanket with a rabbit on one corner. His head is on Julia's shoulder and he's so tired he can barely manage a smile.

"Thank you," Julia says to the man behind me. "Wait outside."

"Yes, ma'am."

I watch the two hulking men step outside and close the door. When I turn back, Julia smiles at me. She looks tired, too.

"What's going on?" I ask, hugging them both tight.

"Belle," Matty says around his thumb.

I kiss his little cheek and take him from Julia. "What are you doing here, buddy? It's late for you."

"He wanted to see you and this was the only way. He misses you. And I thought with the anniversary coming up..." Julia trails off.

The anniversary. The night Christian was killed.

We take a seat, she on the same chair she just vacated, me on a couch where there's just enough space for me to perch with all the costumes stacked on top of it.

I lay my hand on the back of Matty's head, feeling him grow heavier as he drifts off to sleep.

"I can't believe it's been three years," I say, speaking of the anniversary of Christian's death.

"No. It's gone fast," she acknowledges. "Anyway, we don't have much time. I'm sure your goon husband will have an army searching for you in a few minutes." I am surprised by this sharp turn in conversation but I'm not sure I want to talk about the night of the break in, or my brother's murder, with Julia. Or with anyone else.

"Those men... Who are those men?" I ask. "One of them shoved me."

"Shit. Sorry about that. I told them you were pregnant. Not to touch you."

"Who are they?"

"Protection," she says. "Carlton hired them for Matty and me after your husband threatened us."

"He did what?"

"He came to see Carlton the other day. Didn't he tell you?"

I don't mention that I'd caught the scent of her perfume clinging to my husband's suit. "Yes. Well, no. He said you were there, not Carlton."

"I don't think he likes dealing with strong women." I'm not quite sure how to take that, but she continues so I push it aside. "Anyway, he was expecting Carlton, but you know your brother. He was at the Cat House, as usual."

"Carlton? At the Cat House?" I feel my eyebrows knit together in confusion.

"Okay, maybe you don't know Carlton that way but, it doesn't matter. He's not why I'm here and I'm sure if he knew I came this close to Jericho St. James, he'd lose his shit."

"Okay, what happened exactly?"

She glances at Matty. "He came to gloat about the pregnancy. About how he was going to use the baby to take everything from us. The house. The land. The various properties. Any money that's left."

"What?"

She nods. "I don't know how he is with you. I guess he handles you with kid gloves, considering." She gestures toward my stomach and I swear there's a moment of something dark that passes through her eyes. "He's going to use that baby to steal it all, Isabelle. I told you that already. Now you've just given him what he wants."

"I didn't exactly give it to him."

"No? Did he force you? Not that it matters. I'm sure he has the cops and the courts in his pocket. Not to mention the Tribunal. I don't know where your head is in this. I can't imagine you've given a family any thought."

"A family, no—"

"Not that it would be a family," she continues quickly. I'm pretty sure she's not hearing me. She's caught up in her head. It's not like her. "Once he has the baby, he won't need you. You'll go the way of Nellie Bishop and any other Bishop who's had the misfortune of crossing their path. You should read their history. Your future is written in it."

"What does that mean?"

"He'll twist your mind. Have you believing exactly what he wants you to believe. You're malleable, Isabelle. It'll be easy for him."

"What?"'

"Never mind. We don't have time. Let me finish. He threatened Matty, Isabelle. Matty." Her eyes grow wet.

"What do you mean?" I ask, glancing at the tiny head on my shoulder with its blond curls. He looks like a little angel with his cherub-like face and that hair.

"He told me to stay away from you or he'd come after my family." She wipes a stray tear from her eye.

"He did what?" I feel myself shudder and hug the tiny boy in my arms closer.

"Look, I'm sure he's worried you'll miscarry, and he'll have to start all over again."

The way she says it makes me think about how Jericho is with Angelique. Makes me wonder about our child. How he'll be with him or her. If he'll love him or her like he does Angelique. The way Julia says it, the child isn't a human being. It's either a threat or a weapon depending on which side you're standing on.

"It's a baby," I say.

"I know, honey," she says. I wonder at the use of

the word honey. It's not like Julia to use endearments but this also isn't meant as an endearment. It's said like she'd say it to those she finds beneath her. I've seen this side of Julia with waiters and other staff. It's ugly. "To you and to me, it's a baby. But to him, it's a weapon. And once you hand that baby over, you'll never see it again. If you live to see anything at all."

I shudder and Matty stirs. I pat his head and whisper shh in his ear.

She checks her watch and stands up. "You should get back, but I wanted to tell you about what happened. I don't think he would have been honest about that. About threatening a four-year-old."

"Julia, he has a child himself. He wouldn't—"

"Don't be naïve," she snaps. She looks upset, really upset. She reaches into her purse and takes something out.

I look at what she has in her hand.

"You may not need them all but better safe than sorry."

"What are they?" I ask, chilled as I get to my feet.

"Mifepristone and misoprostol." She gestures for me to take the packages from her. There are six of them, each containing four small pills on one side and one larger pill on the other.

"Abortion pills?" Shit.

"They'll get rid of your problem."

*Your problem.*

I feel cold as I drag my gaze from the packages of pills to her. "It's a baby, Julia," I repeat.

She nods. "Don't think of it like that. This is the only way, Isabelle. You need to do it for yourself. For us. For Matty." She shoves the pills into the palm of my hand and takes her child from me. He mumbles but falls back asleep easily. "You need to go back. If he sees Matty and me here, I don't know what he'll do."

"He wouldn't hurt you or Matty. He's not like that."

"You think you know him? You don't, Isabelle. You don't know what he's capable of. And I won't risk my child's life. Go back to your husband before he comes looking for you. If there's one thing I'm sure of, it's that he will come looking. As long as you're carrying that thing inside you, he'll come."

Shocked at the vitriol in her words, I stand mute. She exhales like she's annoyed when she sees my expression.

"Just do it, Isabelle. Get rid of it."

"There has to be another way."

She shakes her head and walks out the door, leaving it open. I watch her hurry to an exit, the two hulking men flanking her. Matty's head bounces on her shoulder. I watch his little blankie drop from his too tired hand and I instinctively want to run to grab it. I hear Jericho then. Hear him threaten someone to get out of his way.

I watch Julia slip out the door and I wonder if she's right. If I'm being naïve. If he really is capable of hurting a woman or a child to get what he wants.

And I wonder if I'm capable of what Julia wants me to do. Because the little pills in my hand would do more than hurt the child I'm carrying. It would kill him or her.

# 16

## JERICHO

Something is wrong.

I get up to the annoyance of the idiots behind me. I could give a fuck. I move quickly in the direction Isabelle had gone. A man stops me at the door.

"Can I help you?" he asks in a low voice.

"My wife is back there. Amanda came to get her. I need to see her."

"I'm sorry, no guests backstage, sir. If you could take your seat, I'm sure—"

"Get the fuck out of my way."

"Sir?"

"Amanda. She's one of your colleagues." People start to shush me. "She took my wife—"

*She took my wife.*

Fuck.

"Sir, there's no one named Amanda who works

with us. I'm sorry, perhaps you're mistaken. If you'll—"

I shove him aside and dig my phone out of my pocket as I force my way through the door backstage. I text Dex. Tell him to look around the perimeter for Isabelle as I storm through the backstage area.

"Sir?" someone stops me. He's carrying a walkie talkie. "Are you supposed to be here?"

I look beyond him, but the corridor is empty.

"My wife," I tell him. "She's going to substitute for one of the violinists."

He looks confused and I must sound insane.

"Substitute? Sir, I think you're mistaken. The musicians are on stage now," he says, pointing to the stage.

"Fuck." I push my hands into my hair. "Amanda?"

"I'm sorry, sir, I'm going to have to ask you to return to your seat." He talks into his walkie talkie calling for security.

I walk away, scanning the large space with all its curtains and corridors and dark corners. I see something near one of the doors marked Exit at the far end. I walk toward it as two men hurry after me. I pick it up. It's a small, worn blanket with a rabbit at one end. Angelique had one similar to it once.

"Sir!" One of the men calls out as they reach me.

Just as he does, I see her. Isabelle. She steps out of one of the dressing rooms looking flushed. Guilty.

"Isabelle," I say, hearing the exhale of relief in my voice. I tuck the small blanket into my pocket.

She smiles but that smile falters as she walks to me. The man with the walkie talkie steps away as I go to my wife.

"She made it," Isabelle says.

I look her over. "What?"

"The woman. They didn't need me in the end."

I study her. Something is off. She takes my hand and turns back in the direction from where we came. "Let's go back."

My phone buzzes and I take it out of my pocket. It's Dex.

*Julia Bishop just got into a car with two goons and a kid. Tell me what to do.*

I stop, read it again. My brain rattles inside my skull. I turn to my lying wife.

She's working too hard to keep eye contact. She's a bad liar.

"You look flushed, Isabelle. Do you feel okay?"

"M-hm," she says too quickly.

"We can go."

"No. I'm fine. I want to be here. Please."

I smile tightly as my phone vibrates. I glance at it.

*Boss?*

"Sure," I tell her and type out my reply. *Follow them but stay out of sight.*

We resume our seats and I watch my wife as she pretends to watch the stage. I can see she's deep in thought. Her mind isn't here. It's on whatever poison Julia Bishop just spewed into her ear. And given my recent visit to the Bishop house, I can guess what it was.

## 17

---

## ISABELLE

He doesn't ask me any more questions that night. I find it strange, not like him. I expected twenty questions. But we took a taxi home after the concert. He said Dex hadn't felt well, so he'd dismissed him early. None of it really fits but when we get to the house, he gets a call and is quick to send me to bed as he disappears into his study.

I go upstairs relieved to have a little time alone. In my bedroom I beeline into the bathroom. The lock doesn't work anymore. He broke it the day I found out I was pregnant. I don't think it's an over-sight that he hasn't fixed it. I take the pills out of my purse. I study them, take in the strange six-sided shape of the four. Abortion pills.

Julia has given me the means to terminate this pregnancy. She called the baby an it. A weapon. And it doesn't sit right with me. This baby is a human being. A life. Does she already hate him or her?

No. That can't be. She's just scared. And I get it. My husband is a formidable man. A devil. It's what I'd thought him when I first laid eyes on him. A horned devil. And if he threatened Matty, well, I understand her desperation. And tonight, she was desperate.

But there's another side to Jericho St. James. I saw it the night I played for him. It was in his eyes when they shone wet as he listened. It's there every time he looks at his daughter. He's human, too. He feels, too. And there's something vulnerable inside him. I saw that in that room in the cellar.

I hear the bedroom door open.

"Isabelle?" It's Jericho. I hurry to drop the packets of pills into the back of a drawer—I'll hide them properly later—and busy myself brushing my teeth. He knocks on the bathroom door, opening it.

I wonder if he can see the guilt on my face so I bend my head to rinse. I take the towel he holds out to me and wipe my mouth.

"Are you going to fix the lock?" I ask.

"No."

"You don't trust me."

"Should I?" It's a rhetorical question. "Do you trust me, Isabelle?"

I don't answer.

"I didn't think so," he says after a moment. He

reaches into his pocket and pulls out Matty's little blanket. I look at it, my heart pounding. He can't know it's Matty's. How could he?

I slowly turn my gaze up to his. His eyes narrow but he doesn't speak.

"Come," he says, tucking the blanket back into his pocket.

I let him lead me out of my bathroom and through the door to his bedroom where he undresses me carefully looking me over as he does. I see the furrow between his eyebrows, the intensity in his gaze.

"I can do this," I say once I'm standing in my underwear.

His gaze shifts to my breasts which are already fuller, more tender. He sets his giant hand against my stomach. It spans the whole of it.

I think about what he's done with those hands. Who he's hurt. How he's threatened to cut off the hands of any man who touches me. Would he hurt Julia if he knew what she gave me? Would he hurt her if he knew one of the men Carlton hired to protect her shoved me like he did? Would he cut off their hands?

When I look back up at him, he's studying me intently.

What a pair we make.

Enemies. Lovers. Secret keepers.

He picks up Christian's T-shirt and tugs it over

my head. Spinning me around, my back is pulled into his front, and his hand moves possessively over my stomach once more.

He pushes my hair back from my ear, kisses my cheek, my neck. He brings his mouth to my ear. "You lied to me," he whispers.

I shudder. When I try to pull away, to turn to face him, he doesn't let me.

"You and I have many enemies, Isabelle. And they're ruthless. You give them an advantage when you lie to me."

I turn my head enough to look at his face. "Will you hurt me when the baby is born?"

He shakes his head.

"Will you take him or her from me?"

"Don't be her fool."

"She said you threatened Matty." His face is unreadable. "Is it true?"

"I won't hurt a child. You have to ask me that?" He releases me and I sit down. My legs feel wobbly. "What did she say to you?"

"Nothing. Just that," I lie again. Second time tonight. It's getting easier.

"Right. Maybe I'll ask her myself," he says.

"You scared her."

"Did I? If she was scared of me, how did she pull her trick tonight?"

I open my mouth, close it. He's right about that. Why would she come to the theater? Bring Matty?

How did she even know I'd be there? Maybe I mentioned it a long time ago? Maybe Paul told her. I don't know.

"She's fucking with you, Isabelle. With us," he says.

"Us?"

"And it's working." He takes Matty's blanket out of his pocket. "Maybe I'll return this. Remind her to stay the fuck away from my family."

He takes a step toward the door, and I jump to my feet. My brain barely registering his use of the word family. I grab his arm with both of my hands. "You can't hurt them. They're *my* family. Please!"

He looks down at where I'm holding onto him, my hands curled like claws around his bicep. He faces me, tugging both of my hands behind me, forcing my chest to jut up and into his.

"I don't hurt children."

"What about women?" I ask.

He stops at that. "Have I hurt you?"

I falter.

"I could have. Maybe I should have." He walks me back to the bed. "But have I hurt you, Isabelle?"

I shake my head.

He nods as if my answer means something. He pulls me to his side, draws the blankets back. "Get in bed."

His phone buzzes and he releases me to read the message. I sit again. Draw my knees up to my chest.

When he looks up from his phone his expression has changed, a crease of worry between his eyebrows.

"What is it?" I ask.

"It's been a long night," he says and tucks the blankets over me.

"What are you going to do?" I ask when he moves away.

He turns, studies me. "Not visit your cousin if that will help you sleep."

I exhale in relief.

He sees it and I can tell it irritates him. He comes back to me, touches my cheek with the knuckles of one hand, then cups the back of my head. His fingers intertwine with my hair and he rubs my skull. He could do it to hurt but he's not. He's taking care.

Kid gloves. It's what Julia had said.

"You just worry about one thing, Isabelle. Just one thing." I swallow and he brings his mouth to my cheek, kisses it, then whispers: "Whatever you do, do not betray me."

---

I CAN'T SLEEP. I'M NOT SURE IF IT'S MY conversations with both Jericho and Julia or the fact that with the anniversary coming, I'm anxious about the dream. I don't have it often, just a few times a year. The last time was in bed with Jericho and I don't want a repeat. But I know the pattern. My mind seems to ramp up the frequency in the weeks leading up to that night.

Jericho left over an hour ago. He took his little sports car. I wish I could get ahold of Julia, although I believe him when he says he's not going to see her. I don't know why but I do. Still, I should warn her that he knows she was there. I go into my bathroom, open the drawer where I'd dropped the pills. If he knew what she gave me, what would he do to her? He would hurt her. I'm sure of it.

I should flush them now. Get rid of them. Keep her safe. I have no intention of using them. But for some reason I don't. Instead, I tuck them into a zipped pocket in my violin case and head back to the bedroom. I dress in a pair of jeans, a warm wool sweater, and sneakers. I make my way down the stairs to the kitchen where I open the drawer I've seen a flashlight in. I take it out, check the batteries, then leave through the kitchen door.

If I wasn't pregnant, would Jericho feel as possessive when it comes to me? Would he be so careful?

I think of his non-answer when I asked him if he'd take the baby from me. Or maybe that silence is the answer.

Once I've cleared the patio and the pool area and am almost in the woods, I switch on the flashlight. A cool wind blows tonight, and the sky is clear for a change. I draw the sleeves of my sweater down to my hands and hurry toward the chapel. I'm grateful for the sneakers on my feet. I know what to expect in these woods.

It's not Jericho's actions that have me out here on this midnight stroll. It's Julia's words. *You should read their history. Your future is written in it.*

I will read them tonight. I don't know why I haven't yet. I'd forgotten about the book on the altar of the small chapel.

The air is still and cold when I reach the grave-yard. I glance around. Part of me wants to go back to the house. Get back into his bed. Feel safe even if that safety is false at worst, temporary at best.

I open the creaky gate and walk through, my gaze moving toward the grave of Nellie Bishop. I see the discarded whiskey bottle still in the ground, dug into the muddy earth from the rains over the last few weeks. I think it's the one Jericho had left here the night I accused him of being a terrible father to Angelique. The night he lost his mind when he saw how I'd cleared and decorated Nellie's grave.

I walk toward the grave. It's overgrown again. I should tend to it. I will tomorrow. Tonight, I have other work to do.

I take a few steps before noticing the cigarette butts on the ground. Three of them. I squat down to get a closer look. They haven't been here long or they'd have deteriorated further with the rain. I wonder who smokes. A groundskeeper maybe.

Wiping off my hands, I stand and go to the chapel. I climb the stairs, pulling the heavy door open, remembering the last time I was here. Well, not here but in the room behind the chapel. Where the pillory is.

Butterflies flutter their wings at the memory, and I shake my head. The sensation, the desire at odds with what I should be feeling. I wonder if it's the pregnancy hormones skewing things. Making me think I feel things for my husband that I don't. That I shouldn't.

Jericho St. James is a walking contradiction. And he confuses me. His possessiveness. His protectiveness. The way the predator lurks just beneath the protector.

My mind wanders to what Julia said again. How Jericho didn't answer my question. But maybe I didn't ask the right one.

I walk into the chapel where only the tabernacle lamp is lit. Like last time, I pick up the faint scent of incense. It's a comfort and a concern. I wonder who they are and when they are coming here to burn it.

Using the flashlight, I walk along the center aisle making a point of looking down at the grave markers. I read Draca's name. The dates of his birth. His death. I don't linger on Mary's. Nineteen is too young to die. To kill yourself.

My mind wanders to Nellie Bishop. Did she truly

kill herself? Throw herself into that well? Or did
Draca murder her?

*You should read their history. Your future is written
in it.*

I shudder at the thought although consciously I
can't make sense of why. What does Julia know? I
have no doubt she has some knowledge of the ugly
history between the families. How much can she
know? What does IVI know? That's got to be where
she'd get her information from. Or from Carlton or
the Bishop library. I don't see how there could be
much on the St. James's there. Unless they stole
something at some point in the last centuries. Which
isn't that outrageous an idea. They have hated each
other for hundreds of years.

When I step up to the altar, I set the flashlight
down and light all the candles. There are about half
a dozen. Draca's book sits unmoved from the last
time. Set on the altar like some sort of bible. Like the
word of Draca St. James is what is worshipped here.

Draca. It means dragon. It's where the dragons
come from, I guess. The tattoo on my back tingles
and I shudder. The idea of Jericho's mark on me
gives me some comfort, some protection against this
horrible man who hates me even from beyond the
grave. For no other reason than the blood that runs
in my veins.

I lift the heavy tome off the stand and set it down
in front of me. I can't help but glance back at the

door like some sort of thief as I open the front cover. Guilt.

My first thought is, it's beautiful. It belongs in a museum. I probably shouldn't handle it without gloves but it's here, others seem to be handling it, and I need information. I need to know if Julia is right.

No. I need to prove her wrong.

Wrong about my future.

Wrong about Jericho.

Because I know one thing about myself. I'm very clear on it, in fact. I don't want him to be my devil. I want him to be my angel.

So I begin to read Draca's history. I read about how the St. James family is connected to IVI. How lowly their beginnings were. I read about the work Draca did within The Society. See how he built a fortune for himself. For his eventual family. I see how hard his life was.

The script is difficult to decipher in some places. It's faded in spots and the handwriting old-fashioned. But when I see the first reference to a Bishop within a few pages, I go back several paragraphs to make sure I haven't missed anything.

Draca St. James and Reginald Bishop hated each other from the beginning. From when Draca worked for the Bishop family. As he grew wealthier and became more valuable to The Society, Reginald resented him. At least that's how Draca wrote it.

I read how he purchased Bishop land. This part Jericho left out of his story. He'd tricked Reginald Bishop. Well, not quite tricked. It had all been done legally. He just made sure Bishop was backed into a corner when he presented the offer. Because Reginald had run into trouble with The Society. According to Draca, he was a gambler, a drunk and worse.

He goes on at length and I skip several pages of Draca spewing hate. It's strangely visceral to read the words and I shudder, glancing back at the stone covering his grave more than once as if expecting him to rise up from beneath it, hate bringing him back to life.

I pick up the book and carry it to one of the pews. I sit down, setting it on my lap and turn the next few pages until I see Mary's name. Her story is as Jericho told it. Draca fell in love with her at first sight and married her within weeks. The wall hadn't been erected to divide the properties yet, but I wonder if what happened to her is what caused it to be built.

Mary's story is a sad one. I read every word of it. Even the moment he found his beloved wife hanging from the wooden support in the cellar of the house he'd been building for her. It was their bedroom according to this account. I find myself feeling for Draca St. James. I feel his pain. His loss. I feel his heartbreak. And in some way, I understand the root of his hate, though I still can't reconcile it with hate for all Bishops.

I glance to his grave again and shudder. I turn the page. This one is worn so badly I can't make out many words, so I keep turning until I see Nellie's name written in an angry oversized scrawl at the top of a sheet. This is different than the story-telling of the earlier pages. Here, Draca didn't bother to weave any romantic tale. Nellie wasn't a person. She was a thing. A pawn.

*Like me.*

I know this thought...these words are true. I am Jericho's pawn. The devil's pawn. The devil's bride. The question is will I survive his game? His vengeance? Can I become his redemption?

Draca used bullet points in the pages devoted to Nellie Bishop. And I feel a little sick to read them.

The first entry is the night he took her. His initiating of the Rite. The Councilor, a man names David Bonaventure, signed off to give Nellie Bishop to Draca St. James.

The second bullet point describes Nellie. Describes how he stripped her bare and examined her. How he had her work as the lowest of the low of staff, keeping her naked as she scrubbed floors and cleaned bedpans. How he would wake her to send her to fetch water in the middle of the night. How he abused her until he exhausted her to the point she was skin and bones.

I think about the night Jericho took me. How he stripped me. There is a similarity, but where Draca was ruthless, Jericho gave me the shirt off his back, his warmth still clinging to it.

He talks about how he used her sexually. How he made sure never to deposit his seed where it might take root.

The next page describes the first game he played with her. *The chase*, he called it. He would blindfold her, and in the middle of the night, take her to a random place on the property, forcing her to return to the well, in what he himself writes, is an unachievable space of time. He'd punished her when she arrived too late. How cruel he was in his punishments.

We played that game, too. A similar one at least. If I hadn't fallen and hit my head, if I hadn't passed out, would Jericho have punished me like Draca did Nellie? I still remember his words that night. How he meant to draw the first drops of blood from me.

I consider closing the book, wanting to go back to the house. Back into his bed. To the warmth and comfort of it. I want to forget what I've read. But Julia's words haunt me.

*You should read their history. Your future is written in it.*

I'm on borrowed time. I touch my stomach. I have nine months. Less.

I make myself read another passage. Another

bullet point. A detailed account of how he brought her into this chapel. How he chained her to the altar. Whipped her until she bled so her blood would seep into the stone floor. I look up at the altar. Are the chains still there? Back in the shadows?

I turn the page. Jericho has said he won't hurt me but, as I skip the next page and a half dozen bullet points, I wonder again if I didn't ask the right question. If I should have asked if he would kill me once I gave him a child.

Draca St. James had Nellie dig her own grave the night before her execution. Her death was meant to be an execution. But the next morning, they'd found her body in the well. I'm sick to my stomach when I read Draca St. James's words. His utter disappointment that he could not murder the innocent girl himself. How he could not hang her from a tree where her father would watch her corpse rot before he finally buried it when the stink got too bad and the flies became unbearable.

I feel physically ill at his words.

I close the book wanting to be away from it. Wanting to scrub any part of myself that touched it. Wanting to be away from this place. I stand, forgetting the flashlight that drops with a loud noise to the stone floor. It reverberates off the walls. I bend and have to stretch my arm under the pew to reach it.

That's when I hear the chapel door open. I swear my heart stops then. I swear it just drops right to my stomach as footsteps draw closer. I'm crouched down hidden by the pew, the light of my flashlight giving me away.

When I look up, I remember something Jericho asked. If I'd be able to tell him and his brother apart if they were masked. They're built the same, the way they walk and stand is the same. But before seeing his face, I only know it's Ezekiel from his cologne. A subtle but distinct difference from Jericho's signature scent. As I drag my gaze up to face the man standing before me, I think I should feel relief it's not Jericho. I should. But I don't.

# 18

## JERICHO

I meet Dex down the street from the run-down house in the Seventh Ward. Our cars stand out among the dilapidated vehicles.

He called me to meet him here soon after I got Isabelle back to the house. When he explained why I knew I had to come see for myself.

Dex climbs out of the Rolls Royce as I park. I see him tuck a pistol into the back of his pants.

"Which one is it?" I ask.

"End of the street. The garage door sticks."

"You're sure about this?"

"Positive. They pulled into the driveway. She must have left the kid in the car because they didn't make any stops. She and two men walked right in the front door. And you'll find this interesting," he says as we make our way down the street toward the house. "Did a little research while I waited for you to get here. Guess who owns the house."

I turn to him, curious. "Don't tell me the Bishops."

"No, even better. The deed is in the name Marjorie Gibson."

"Gibson?" I remember it but it's a common enough name.

"Mother of Danny and Gerald Gibson, the former is currently serving a life sentence for the murder of Christian York."

I stop. Try to make sense of what Dex is telling me.

"Marjorie's dead if you wanted to know. Had a heart attack about six years ago. Her deadbeat sons lived in the house separately and together off and on. That's mostly public record by the way."

"Are you fucking kidding me? Julia Bishop hired Danny Gibson's brother to run Isabelle down?"

He shrugs a shoulder as we get to the house. A TV is on. I can see the flashes of color through the curtains and hear the jingle of a commercial through the closed window.

"He hasn't moved since they left," Dex says.

I look to the garage with its partially open door. It looks jammed at an angle. I lean down, and can see the white van with its dirty license plate. I walk up the driveway as a group of three men noisily cross the street. They pause to look at us. Dex takes two steps toward them and they scurry off. They're young and Dex is intimidating. It's one of the reasons I hired him.

I can hear the TV in the house when I reach the garage. Dex stands outside when I duck my head to enter. I take out my phone to use the flashlight and I'm sure this was the van. I recognize the first few digits of the license plate.

The driver's side window is down. When I peer inside, I have to hold my breath against the stink. I can see empty containers from fast food joints. A half-full pack of cigarettes. Lighters. More Trash. And hanging from a small noose on the rear-view mirror is a teddy bear.

Sick fuck.

I switch off the flashlight and walk back outside. We stand on the dark driveway.

"Do we go in?" Dex asks.

I want to. Fuck do I want to. But I shake my head. "Get a couple guys out here to watch him."

Dex nods. "Involve IVI?"

"No. Get our own guys. I don't want anyone to catch on that we know anything just yet."

"Got it." He already has his phone out of his pocket texting a message.

I glance back to the house as I open my car door. If there was any doubt as to Julia Bishop's involvement in Carlton's scheme, it's gone. This revelation complicates things because Isabelle trusts Julia. She has a relationship with her that's very different than the one with her brother. There's also the matter of Julia's kid to consider.

I get in the car and start the engine.

If there was a moment I hoped things would be different where Julia was concerned, for Isabelle's sake, it's gone. Things just went sideways in a very bad way.

# 19

## ISABELLE

"What are you doing here, Isabelle?" Ezekiel asks me. He extends a hand to help me up.

I grab the flashlight and take his hand. He helps me stand and I dust off my jeans to buy some time.

"I was... I couldn't sleep."

He releases me and bends to pick up the book. "What happened to making a cup of warm milk if you can't sleep?" he asks casually, his focus on straightening the bent page. Reading it. It's the one about Nellie. "There's a library in the house if you want something to read." He closes it, placing it back on the altar.

"I didn't know you were home."

"No, I guess you didn't. I just got back." He looks me over, eyes falling on the dust still clinging to the knees of my jeans. "What were you doing? And don't tell me praying."

"I had a fight with your brother. Well, not a fight... just, things are weird." I take a deep breath. He's not stupid. I'm not going to try to make up some story of why I'm here. What would be the point? "I wanted to know what Draca did to Nellie," I say, gesturing to Draca's grave.

"To ready yourself for what Jericho might do?"

I don't answer.

"Hm." His forehead is creased, eyes dark and intent. Just like how Jericho looks at me, as if he sees right through me. "And does knowing help you?"

I rub my arms at a sudden chill and look around. I shake my head.

"He was a piece of work, wasn't he?" he asks, tracing the carved wood cover of the book.

"He hated Nellie even though she had nothing to do with what happened to Mary. It was her father who was guilty."

"Sins of the father. You know how that goes."

"Or the half-brother in my case." I sit down on the pew again and he joins me.

"You're not afraid to be in here alone in the middle of the night?"

I shrug a shoulder. "A little. But sometimes I'm more scared to be inside the house."

The corner of his mouth curves upward and he

exhales. "My brother can be an intimidating prick, but he won't hurt you, Isabelle."

I smile. "I agree whole-heartedly with that first part."

He grins.

"But why do you think he won't hurt me? Is it because of the baby?" I realize when I say it that I'm not sure if Ezekiel knows about the pregnancy. But given his expression, it's not news.

"No, it has nothing to do with the baby. He just won't." He looks up at the altar. "He may have planned to, but he won't. He can't."

"Can't?"

He turns back to me and I see shadows under his eyes. A little bit of graying hair at his temple. "Come on, I'll walk you back to the house," he says, standing.

"What are you doing out here in the middle of the night, anyway? Just taking a walk in the woods?" I ask, standing.

"Visiting the dead," he says. "Let's go." He closes his hand over my arm.

"Just a minute," I say, remembering the candles I lit on the altar.

"Not sure you have a minute. My brother got home a little while ago."

My heart drops to my stomach for the second time that night. "What?"

"He was on a call in his study. If you're lucky, you can get upstairs before he realizes you're gone."

"I'm never lucky," I say just as the chapel door opens as if to confirm the truth of my statement.

I gasp. A gust of wind blows out two of the candles and my husband stands on the threshold of the chapel. The little bit of light shining around him casts him in a shadow so dark, so menacing, I find myself shrinking from his gaze.

But it's not me he's glaring it.

It's his brother.

I feel Ezekiel's hand on me, wrapped around my arm. Then I remember what Jericho said about any man touching me.

"Brother," Jericho says.

Jericho remains where he is, unblinking. His eyes move from Ezekiel's hand on my arm, to me. He steps into the chapel letting the door slam shut behind him. I swear it rattles even the stone walls of this ancient building.

"Brother," Ezekiel replies.

I swallow, my heart racing as Jericho eats up the space between them, moving as swift as a shadow. He grips Ezekiel's wrist. I wonder if Ezekiel had forgotten he was holding me or if he keeps his hand on my arm to taunt his brother.

"We discussed this," Jericho says, face inches from his brother. Two giants readying for battle. "You don't touch what's mine."

I glance from Jericho's hard face to Ezekiel's and see one corner of his mouth curl upward. "See what I mean, Isabelle?" he asks. I assume he's referring to the intimidating prick comment but for as casual as he sounds, he hasn't shifted his eyes from his brother.

"He didn't touch me," I hurry to say.

Ezekiel releases me. Smiles. "I'm not afraid of my brother, sweetheart."

"Sweetheart?" Jericho gets in Ezekiel's face, his big body nudging me aside. "Maybe you should be," Jericho tells him.

"Relax," Ezekiel says, his expression and body language confirming he's not afraid. But he is ready to do battle. I wonder if this is about Kimberly. If this is a years' old battle that will happen whether it's tonight or another night. Or if it's truly about me. If he feels that possessive about me. But why would he? I'm a means to an end. It's Kimberly he loved.

*Kimberly he loved.*

I feel my forehead crease as I look to the stone floor, my gaze landing on the carving of Draca's name on his grave. To Mary's. I think about how much he loved her. What he did to avenge her.

I shake my head at the direction my thoughts take. Jericho St. James does not love me. This isn't even about love. Not for either of us. So why do I feel that tightening in my chest?

"It's just an expression," Ezekiel says, drawing my attention back to the moment. He removes Jericho's hand from his wrist. "You and I need to talk."

"Yeah. We do. But first I need to deal with my wife."

I find myself taking a step away at his sideways glance.

Ezekiel glances at me too, but only briefly, then turns to his brother. "Don't punish her. We weren't here together. I surprised her."

"Whether or not I punish my wife is not your concern."

I put my hand against my stomach to stop the flutter of anticipation of what's to come.

"Take it out on me. Not her," Ezekiel says.

"Get out."

Ezekiel opens his mouth, but I reach my hand to his arm to stop him. "Go. It's okay," I say.

A rattle like that of a snake warning of impending attack comes from Jericho's chest. It takes all I have to steel myself. To stand up tall even if I still come to the middle of their chests.

"I'm not scared of him either," I say to Ezekiel even though my eyes are locked with Jericho's.

"That was a mistake," Jericho says and takes my arm. "Get out, Zeke," he hisses the words, never looking away from me.

Ezekiel doesn't move and he doesn't reply right

away. But then he glances at Draca's book on the altar and it's as if he understands something because his posture changes. He shakes his head, grips Jericho by the collar and forces him off me. "Don't be a fucking idiot," he tells him.

"Get the fuck out," Jericho tells him.

"If you're planning to do what I think you're planning to do then no. I won't allow it."

"You won't allow it?"

"No. I won't."

"She's not yours."

"No, she's not. But if you're going to play that idiotic game our ancestor played—"

"It won't go that far," Jericho cuts him off.

There's a long moment of silence, the tension so thick it's almost hard to breathe around it.

"If it does, I'll fucking kill you," Ezekiel says.

"A Bishop coming between us," Jericho says, his words wounding me in a way they shouldn't.

"Don't be stupid, Jericho. Don't fuck this up," Ezekiel says.

"I said it won't go that far," Jericho repeats tightly.

Ezekiel studies him, then glances at me, hesitation clear in his eyes. I want to tell him to stay. Not to leave me here with my husband. My own husband. But he does. And he should. Because Jericho is right. Whatever Ezekiel is warning him about isn't his to deal with. It's ours. Mine and Jericho's. And I know in that moment that what happens next, what he does or doesn't do will change things for us. It will change everything.

---

## 20

## ISABELLE

"Strip."

He releases me, walking around the altar. It's pitch black so I'm not sure what he's doing. But then I hear the rattle of chains and remember the passage in Draca's diary.

"Nothing happened. He didn't do anything. I didn't," I hurry to say as Jericho walks back into the candlelight.

He steps before me. "Strip," he repeats then walks around the other side. I know what he's doing when I hear that same sound. Another game.

No, not a game. A punishment.

He means to punish me like Draca St. James punished Nellie Bishop.

I break out in a sweat, unable to move, or breathe when he comes around the corner. I suck in a breath when I see the braided handle of the whip in his hand, the long, thin tails that my ancestor endured. He places it on the altar as if that cruel thing was an offering to Draca.

I need to run. I need to run right now. But I just stand there and watch him as he takes off his jacket, folds it over the back of a pew then rolls up the sleeves of his shirt.

"I'm beginning to wonder if I need to have your hearing checked."

I swallow, blink hard as I glance to the door, then to him.

"Don't bother, Isabelle. I'm faster than you. Stronger than you."

"Nothing happened."

"I believe you."

"Then why are you going to punish me?"

He steps toward me, forcing me back a step. My back touches the altar. "To teach you once and for all that you're mine." He grips my sweater and tears it down the middle.

"No!" I try to run past him, but his arm is around my middle. He tugs me to him, my back to his chest, as he undoes the button and zipper on my jeans.

"It'll go easier if you submit."

"I don't want this!" I try to push at his arm but he's like a fucking brick wall.

"I don't suppose Nellie did either. Submit or don't. Choose."

I push the heels of my hands into my eyes. "Please!"

"Submit or don't. Choose," he repeats.

I nod. Try to get my breathing under control. He won't hurt me. Ezekiel said it. Jericho has shown he would hurt himself before he hurts me. I have to believe this. But maybe what he saw tonight, me with his brother, me disobeying his law after I lied to him about Julia, maybe he changed his mind. Maybe it was too much, too many betrayals.

"No it is then," he says and begins to push down my jeans.

"I'll do it!" I scream, shoving at his arm, at him. I hook my hands into the waistband of my jeans and push them off, half inside-out, my shoes discarded at the same time, my feet bare on the cold stone.

He unhooks my bra and it slips off my arms. Before I straighten, he walks me back the few steps to the altar. We'd moved away from it in our struggle.

I resist. I can't not. But he's so much stronger than me and keeps hold of my wrists, stretching one arm out to the side of the altar where he locks it into an icy iron cuff. I cry out when he does it, trying to pull free as he takes my other arm and stretches it as wide as the altar, locking me in place with the second restraint. He moves behind the altar and tugs at the restraints, forcing me to bend over almost flat with the shortened chains.

When he steps away from me, I glance up at Jesus on the cross.

"Don't tell me you're praying," Jericho says as he wraps his hand around the braided handle of the whip and makes a point of dragging it out from under me. "There is no god, Isabelle. Or if there is, he forgot about us centuries ago. Think about it," he says, sliding the taut handle of the whip between my legs. "If he were real, if he gave a fuck about any of us, would you be here right now? Would you be chained to the same spot your ancestor was centuries ago? Where my ancestor bled her to pay for her father's sins?"

"Please, Jericho. You're not thinking. God. Please."

"How many times do I have to tell you there is no god!"

"I—"

"If there was, would Mary have been raped by that monster? Would she have hanged herself? Would Zoë? Would my daughter be motherless?"

He stops then and I turn my head. My shoulders hurt, my arms too wide.

"Jericho?"

I feel him at my back fingers in the waistband of my panties. He pushes them down without ceremony.

"Would your brother be dead?" he asks more quietly.

I drop my forehead to the altar. He's right. I've doubted the existence of god for years but never consciously. Never daring to go that far.

"But that's not what this is about, is it? That's not why we're here, you and I." He cups my ass roughly, fingers digging into flesh, forcing me up on tip toe. I'm looking straight ahead, body taut. He's at my back again, breath at my ear. I feel the whip in the hand that snakes around to my stomach.

I turn my face a little so I can see him and he can see me.

"Who do you belong to?" he asks and before I can answer, he slaps my ass making me jump. "Who?"

"You!"

He slaps again. "Say it. All of it."

"You!" Another slap. "I belong to you!"

"What did I tell you before I left tonight?"

I think. He spanks. But he's still got the whip in his other hand. And he's not hurting me. Not really.

"Isabelle."

"Not to betray you."

"And why were you in the chapel with my brother?"

"I wasn't. I swear. I came in here to read that book. I wanted to read it. I needed to know what he did to her."

"Because you're afraid I'm going to do it to you. Even though I told you I won't hurt you."

"You're hurting me now."

"Am I? A little spanking is not what she endured."

"No. He bled her. He whipped her until she bled."

"Right. I'm sure he ripped her back open."

"And you're holding that same whip."

"Am I using it?" he rubs the space he just spanked, his touch almost tender.

I shake my head, drop it to the altar because I can't do this anymore. I can't.

"I don't know up from down with you," I say, my voice a whisper. "I don't understand what's happening. What to believe. Who to trust."

"I'll tell you, Isabelle. You choose me. You trust me."

"You have me chained, Jericho. Literally chained. How can I trust you?"

He grips my hair, lifts my head, and turns it, forcing me to look at him. "My chains will keep you safe. My chains will keep our baby safe."

*Our baby.*

My God. What a mess we've made.

I exhale, tears pouring from my eyes, my lips salty with them. He kisses me and I think he must taste them too, those tears. It's what he wanted when he took me. To watch me cry. To bleed me.

I hear the whip drop to the floor and he's behind me, pushing the hair off my neck, kissing along my shoulder, my jaw. He nudges my legs wider and a moment later, he's inside me.

"Trust me, Isabelle. You need to trust me. To choose me."

*Choose him.*

He thrusts into me, wrapping one arm around my middle to lay the flat of his hand over my belly, over our baby. The other he slips between my legs, expert fingers finding my clit, knowing just how to manipulate it.

"I want to," I tell him. It's true. I do want to.

"Then do. I won't hurt you. Haven't I already told you that? I choose you."

*I choose you.*

He draws his arms to either side of my own and a moment later, I'm free of the chains. He's turning me, holding me. I cling to him, my back to the altar, my legs wrapped around him, our mouths locked, eyes open.

"I won't hurt you," he says again.

"You promise?"

"I promise. You just have to choose me. Be mine. Only mine."

I want to believe him. I need to. Because this is too hard. And so I nod, closing my eyes, and holding tight to him as the first wave of orgasm comes. I drop my head into the crook of his neck, his skin salty against my tongue. I moan, coming and feel him come, feel him shudder. I think about this act in this chapel, this holy place. I think about Draca and Nellie. What he did to her in this same place. And I think maybe one cancels out the other. Love canceling out hate.

Love.

Love overwriting hate.

*Choose me... I choose you.*

I feel fresh tears slip from my eyes. Warm and wet and sad. Because I think I love him. I know I do. And I also know that when he says he won't hurt me, it has nothing to do with my heart. I am chained to him. I am his prisoner. His. But there's too much history between us for anything close to love. Centuries worth. And even if he wants to choose me, I don't think Jericho St. James can put his vengeance aside to love me.

## 21

---

## JERICHO

I don't bother to knock before I walk into Zeke's office after taking Isabelle to bed. I can't think about what happened between us tonight. Can't process it. I meant what I said. I won't hurt her. I won't let anyone else hurt her either. I choose her. But that choice is wrought with too much history. Too much tragedy.

The night I took her it was my intention to use her for my vengeance. But everything is different. Every single thing. And I don't look at her like I should. Like I meant to. I care about her, and it has nothing to do with her carrying my baby. It's her.

Zeke pushes back from his desk and looks at me like he was expecting this.

"What were you doing out there with my wife?"

"What do you think I would be doing?"

"I don't know, Zeke. You tell me. Because you keep a lot of secrets."

He snorts, gets to his feet. "Isn't that the trademark of our family?" he says, moving around the desk to stand inches from me. He has never been cowed by me. I sometimes wonder if he wouldn't like a fight. Get some of that old anger out. My brother has always been my equal in size and strength. At least since we were adults. He was skinnier than me when he was a kid. Like he and Zoë seemed to split the weight between them until they were about fourteen. That's when he started to grow into himself. Zoë remained petite, developing slowly. She was still a girl when she died.

Zoë. Shit. I miss my scrawny, goofy little sister. Not that she was that way toward the end. In the half year leading up to her suicide she'd grown so quiet and secretive. Dark. The few times I tried to reach her I couldn't. I wonder if I hadn't given up she'd be here today.

I shake my head. To think of that is like drowning. I can't dwell in that place. On the waste of it. The loss of her. I couldn't save her. I couldn't save Kimberly. Now there's Isabelle who needs saving. Will I fail her too? My track record would suggest so.

I push my hand into my hair and step away from Zeke. "Why were you out there?"

"It's where I always go when I come home."

"The chapel?"

He shakes his head. "The graveyard."

He's a better man than me. I've never made visiting Zoë or Kimberly my priority. I realize how shitty that makes me. "Leaving flowers at their graves."

He nods.

"Dad's too?" I ask, needing to deflect my own lack.

He slaps his hand to my chest and shoves me. "Fuck you, brother."

I grab his wrist. "What were you doing with my wife?"

He tugs free. "Your wife was already there. In the chapel. I saw the candles were lit and went inside to investigate only to find Isabelle there."

He's not lying. I can see that. He's never lied to me. That goes both ways. But we do keep secrets and secrets are as bad as lies.

"She went to the chapel on her own?"

He nods. "Catching up on her reading."

I feel my breathing tighten.

"She's all right?" he asks.

I study him understanding his meaning. He knew what I would do tonight. He's read Draca's diary. We all have. "I said I wouldn't go that far. I didn't lie."

"But you wanted to scare her."

I don't answer because what kind of devil would admitting that make me? I already know the monster I am. No need to admit it to my brother.

"You know, Draca St. James wasn't one to idolize either, brother," he says. "But you have a bad track record when it comes to choosing your gods, don't you?"

Dad. He means dad. And I remember our last conversation in my study. I remember how that conversation moved from dad to Zoë. To her death. To him finding her hanging in the cellar. And again, that nagging feeling returns. It should have been me. I was the older brother. I should have found her and spared him that.

"What did he do to her?" I ask and I swear he knows exactly what I'm talking about. I see it on the lines that etch his face, in the darkness that casts shadows from inside him. It's when I see the similarities between him and Zoë. The only time. For a moment, I just watch as my brother breaks. Just for a split second I see it. I see the fissure that's been there for years. Deep. Deepening. The one he's so good at hiding beneath a casual, cool exterior.

"Leave it," he says in an almost unrecognizable voice. He clears his throat. Stands up straighter. "We have a more urgent problem." He reaches into his pocket for something. He opens his palm and I see a cigarette butt.

Confused, I look up at him.

"I don't think your wife smokes. I haven't picked

up the habit and I know how you feel about it," Zeke says.

I hate the smell of cigarette smoke. Always have. Dad smoked. It was one of the things I couldn't stand about him. He stank when he smoked. And he chain smoked when he was in one of his moods. It was usually a sign of bad things to come.

The staff sign a contract agreeing not to smoke on or around the property. If they do, it's immediate termination.

"Where did you find that?"

"Graveyard. There's more of them."

"Do we have a new gardener or something?"

He shakes his head. "Unless you hired someone. Where were you tonight by the way?"

"Let's have a drink," I say. He nods and I move to the couch while he pours a tumbler of whiskey for each of us. "Bring the bottle," I tell him. He does and joins me.

"I'm not your enemy. You know that, right?" Zeke asks me.

I study him, nod. "You should tell me, though. The thing with dad. It's history. Long past."

"You don't want to know this, Jericho. I'll carry this one."

"Share the weight."

"No." He sips. "Tell me about tonight."

I take a deep breath in, then out. "Did you know Danny Gibson has a brother."

"Why would I care?" he asks. He recognizes the name.

"I took Isabelle to a concert that teacher of hers invited her to and she disappeared for a while. When I found her, she lied about who she was with."

"Who was she with?"

"Julia Bishop."

His eyebrows knit together.

"Dex saw Julia get into a car with two men and her kid. He followed them to a house in the Seventh Ward where it turns out Gerald Gibson lives. That van that almost killed Isabelle the other day was parked in the garage."

"Wait a minute. *Julia* Bishop? Not Carlton?"

I finish my drink, pick up the bottle and pour another. "This was Julia. I'm not sure if she's working with Carlton or on her own. I didn't want to question Gibson yet. Figured I'd tail him for a while. But either way, one of them hired Gerald Gibson to finish the job his brother started."

He's quiet for a very long minute. "Where does Carlton fall in this?"

"That's a great question. I just got off the phone with Santiago. He's looking into the charity from which Danny was paid. Julia's been managing it for years."

"Does Isabelle have any idea?"

I shake my head. "And she won't believe me if I tell her. I need proof. But even if I have it, the pregnancy is too new. She's been so sick. I don't want to risk upsetting her."

"That wasn't your concern tonight."

"Low blow, brother."

"But deserved." He finishes his drink and pours another. "How can I help you?"

"I should keep Isabelle under lock and key, but that's easier said than done. And I don't like the cigarette butts on the property anyway. If someone managed to get inside—"

"I'll do a perimeter check tomorrow. Make sure the wall hasn't been compromised."

"Thank you. Dex is watching the Bishop house tonight, but I want him here with Angelique and Isabelle. We need more men. And not from IVI."

"Not an issue." He takes out his phone and scrolls through his contacts. He puts the phone to his ear. "We need to meet," he says, then after a pause: "I'll be there in twenty." He tucks the phone back into his pocket and stands, finishes his whiskey. "I'll meet with my contact now. We'll have men here by morning."

"I'll come with you," I say, standing.

"Your wife and daughter need you more."

I get up and go to him. Pat his arm. "Thank you for taking care of her tonight."

He nods and we walk out, going our separate ways. I'm at the bottom of the stairs and he's at the front door when I stop.

"Zeke?"

He looks back at me.

"You're going to tell me about dad. You have to."

He shakes his head.

"One way or another, I'm going to find out the truth."

He walks out the front door and I climb the stairs, stopping to look in on my daughter. She smiles in her sleep when I kiss her forehead. I continue to my bedroom where I find my wife exactly where I left her for a change. Asleep in my bed, curled around my pillow. I smile, brush hair from her face. She smiles in her sleep but settles again. And I wonder when she did this thing to me.

When she made me care.

## 22

### ISABELLE

The next two weeks pass quietly although I notice more men are stationed around the house. When I ask Jericho about them, he casually distracts me, telling me it's nothing, just additional security for the family. When he says family, he takes care that I know I'm a part of that equation. He's different with me since that night in the chapel. More tender. Our lovemaking has shifted too. Morphed into something erotic and sensual, deeply satisfying on a level that is so much more than sexual. Jericho St. James knows how to manipulate a woman's body and bend it to his will. I knew that from day one. But what's happening between us now is so much more.

And I find myself feeling strangely happy.

Jericho has even opened a bank account for me —well, a joint account—where he deposits way too much money for the weekly lessons I'm giving Angelique. I'm aware that he set it up as a joint account so he can control the funds or at least know what I do with them. He's even given me both an ATM card and a credit card which are both great, except that I never leave the house, so also useless. I guess it's a gesture, though. And I've been able to send Paul a check for the missed lessons, which I feel good about.

He and Zeke are spending more time together huddled in their studies. I do notice the shift when they meet. See the looks exchanged between them.

I spend my days with Angelique mostly and I've started my lessons with Professor Larder. He's a nice man, I guess, but he is a strict teacher. While I know I will learn a lot from him, I miss my little group. I miss Paul and Megs and the others. Jericho isn't convinced Paul wasn't involved in the incident the night of the concert though. He's told me in no uncertain terms that if Paul is to be allowed back into the house, he will first need to submit to a thorough questioning. That's his condition. And it's my choice to make. As usual, Jericho is giving me impossible choices. But right now, it's just easier to say I'll deal with it another day.

At least he allows Megs to visit even if we aren't allowed to go out.

I'm just dozing off when the echo of the steel

door opening and closing jars me awake. Someone was in the cellar?

"The meeting is arranged," Zeke says to Jericho as they come around the corner into the living room. I'm sitting in a comfortable, high-back leather chair, the book I was reading face-down on my lap. I'm curled into a ball so I'm pretty sure they don't see me. "All the hands that need to be greased have been greased."

"Corrupt assholes," Jericho says, and I hold my breath.

"You sure you don't want me to go?"

"No, I want to see him with my own eyes. Hear him tell the story with my own ears."

"Flights will get you there and back the same day, so you won't be missed."

Jericho walks to the mantle where he picks up one of Angelique's discarded toys. I make the slightest movement and the book on my lap drops to the floor, catching his attention.

Our eyes meet.

Heat flushes through me instantly. I'm caught. He stands still taking me in. A moment later Zeke comes into view. The two of them together like this, on the same side, watching me like they are, it's unnerving.

I yawn and uncurl my legs to pick the book up off the floor.

"Were you reading?" Jericho asks, getting to the

book before I do. He holds it out to me and I look up at him.

"I was," I say, taking it from him. "But I must have dozed off."

"You should go upstairs and nap properly when you're tired."

"I'm fine," I say. "Catherine made a big lunch." I've been eating more, my appetite furious some days. And the nausea has subsided. "And I guess this wasn't the most exciting book." I hold up the book for him to see, talking too fast. I'm sure he can hear it. I'm sure he knows I was eavesdropping even if it wasn't intentional, so I get to my feet.

He smiles. "I'm glad to hear that."

"I'll see you later," Zeke says. "I need to head to the office for a few hours."

Jericho turns to him and nods.

"Goodbye, Isabelle," he says.

"Bye." I wait until he leaves before turning to my husband. "Are you going somewhere?"

"I thought you were dozing."

I shrug a shoulder.

"Thought so." He smiles. "Come with me. I have more of the vitamins from Dr. Barnes. They were delivered this morning."

"Are you?" I ask as we head to his study.

"A day trip," he says as he opens the door and gestures for me to enter ahead of him. I do and watch as he closes the door, walking around the desk. He takes the cellar key out of his pocket and drops it into a drawer, then holds two bottles out to me. "Here. Same as what you have upstairs. Two a day."

I take them. "Thanks. Where are you going?"

He checks his cell phone, types out a response to a message then tucks it into his pocket and turns to me. "Atlanta. Business." He tucks my hair behind my ear and cups my cheek. "I'm glad you're feeling better." He kisses me, just a peck. "You look beautiful, Isabelle. Dare I say happy?"

I smile and shrug a shoulder trying to be casual. I drop my gaze as emotion raises goosebumps up and down my arms. I remember that night in the chapel. What he said. What he asked of me. What I chose.

Someone knocks on the door then and he clears his throat to answer. "Yes?" He doesn't move away or take his hand from my face.

"I'm sorry to interrupt," Catherine says, peering her head inside. "But you have a visitor," she says to me.

"Me?" I ask.

"What visitor?" Jericho asks.

She turns to Jericho. "Mrs. De La Rosa and her children. They're waiting in the library."

"Ivy?" I smile.

"I thought that would be all right, sir?" Catherine asks, unsure suddenly.

"Of course. I'll say hello too."

Catherine's smile is one of relief as she holds the door open for me and Jericho to pass. His hand is on the small of my back as he leads me toward the study. I can already hear the sound of a little girl's voice and it instantly makes me smile.

Jericho opens the door, where we find Ivy and her children standing at a bookshelf. The little girl on tip-toe is trying to reach for a book, while Ivy is trying to hold her wriggling baby and get the book at the same time.

"Let me," Jericho says and hurries to them.

They all turn to us, Ivy smiling, a little flushed. The little girl has a look on her face that belongs to an older, more cynical person. And the sweetest little baby with the biggest green eyes I've ever seen, has his mouth open in a tiny O showing one small tooth.

"Oh my gosh!" I say, hurrying to them myself. I hug Ivy and the baby at once and she smiles when I pull back. "You came!"

"I thought it may be easier than getting you to my house and I really needed to get this one out," she says, gesturing to the little girl.

"Your family is beautiful," I say, taking them all in.

"Thank you. Elena, say hello," she says, putting a hand to the little girl's head.

Elena glances up at me, flashes a smile showing a perfect row of tiny, straight teeth. She turns back to Jericho who is crouched down beside her balancing about five books for her to choose from.

It's so funny seeing him like this. He's so different with kids. Like the pressure is off because they're not so scared of him. Even though I'd think they would be given his size and gruff manner.

"That one used to be my little girl's favorite," he says when Elena chooses her book.

"I like the horses," Elena says then holds the book back out to him when he straightens to put the others back. "Read it to me."

"Elena," Ivy says, putting a hand on the little girl's shoulder. "I'm sure Mr. St. James is busy."

"No, it's fine," Jericho says, clearly taken aback. "I have a few minutes."

Elena smiles at her mom then turns to Jericho. She slips her hand into his and leads the way to the seat beneath the large window.

"Well, she's always been a very confident little girl," Ivy says with a proud smile.

"I think it's great," I say as I watch Jericho settle into the seat with the little girl tucking herself almost under his arm as he opens the book. "It's so weird to see this side of him," I tell Ivy just loud enough for her ears.

"Santiago is the same. It's kind of amazing to see men like that with kids. They become big teddy bears."

I chuckle and turn back to her. "And who are you?" I ask the little one in her arms.

He makes a gurgling sound and nudges his face against his mom's neck.

"This is Santi, short of Santiago."

"It's wonderful to meet you, Santi," I say as Ivy hands him over to me. I take the warm bundle into my arms and sniff the baby smell of his head when I cuddle him to me. "He's so sweet."

"Santi is a flirt," Ivy says as the little boy reaches up to take a handful of my hair, that smile irresistible.

"He is."

The study door opens then, and Catherine walks in with a tray of refreshments.

"Cookies!" Elena jumps up from her seat and rushes toward Catherine who smiles lovingly.

"I just baked these this morning. They're Angelique's favorite."

"Who's Angelique?" Elena asks as she chomps on a cookie.

"Please wait until you're offered, Elena," Ivy tells her.

Jericho comes over to us and hands Ivy the book. "She can have this if she likes. Angelique has outgrown it."

"Thank you, that's very kind. And I'm sorry about that," Ivy tells him. "Thanks for reading to her but cookies always take priority."

"I understand and it was a pleasure. She's a sweet girl."

"I'll go get Angelique," I say, checking my watch. "I'm sure Mrs. Strand won't mind wrapping up her lessons a few minutes early."

"I'm sure she won't. Ivy, nice to see you. Say hello to your husband for me."

"I will. It was nice to see you, too," she pauses.

"Jericho," he fills in.

"Jericho. Nice to see you again."

Jericho leaves and Elena helps herself to a second cookie as Catherine pours her a glass of milk.

"Want to come with me to get Angelique?" I ask Ivy. "She'll be so surprised to see the baby but I'm afraid if you're out of sight, he'll get upset."

"Sure. I'd love that."

"Catherine, we'll just be a few minutes. Do you mind staying with Elena?"

"Not at all," Catherine says and settles into the sofa.

Ivy and I walk out into the hallway and up the stairs with little Santi still in my arms.

"You seem more at ease," Ivy says.

"I am. Things are better I guess."

"Good. I'm glad to hear it."

I stop at the top of the stairs and turn to her. "I'm seven weeks pregnant," I tell her, my heart racing as I do. A pregnancy is happy news, but I haven't told anyone. Not Megs, not anyone. And Julia, well, how

Julia's been about the pregnancy, I guess I didn't realize how heavy the burden of it all has been. Not until this moment, this normal moment when I tell a friend what should be and is happy news. In a way, it feels like this joy I should be feeling has been stifled, stolen.

"Oh, Isabelle!" tears spring to her eyes. "That's such wonderful news."

I realize I'm teary too when she hugs me. I have to wipe my eyes. "We haven't told anyone, and it was...unexpected."

"One day I'll tell you my story with Santiago," she says, wiping some of my tears. "It wasn't pretty when we got married. I didn't want to be there. He and I...well, let's just say he didn't marry me because he loved me. Not then. But it's all changed so much, and I can't imagine life without him anymore. You and Jericho, you remind me a lot of us and I'm just happy to see you settling in and happy. Are you happy?"

I suck in a deep breath and force myself to stop the tears. "I don't know. Things are weird but Jericho and I are in a better place. I just didn't expect to be married and pregnant at nineteen."

"I understand." She opens her mouth to say more but then we both hear the sound of someone crying from Angelique's room.

I hand the baby back to Ivy and hurry down the hall. Ivy follows and I slow my steps as I near the door. I hear quiet sniffles from the other side of the door, making my heart hurt. But what I hear next makes me furious.

"Stop that. No one's going to give you any attention when you're sniveling. You're a spoiled little girl."

"I'm not."

I put my hand on the doorknob, rage making it shake.

"You're lucky your father won't let you go to a normal school for normal children. What with your strange eyes you'd probably sc—"

She doesn't get to say more though because I push the door open so hard it slams against the wall. The older woman is clearly caught. She straightens and I see how she's squeezing Angelique's ear hard, the little girl's head tilted at an angle. She's standing on tiptoe to ease the pain.

Ivy gasps behind me.

"Get your hands off her!" I say, my voice trembling with rage. I've never felt this angry before, this protective. It's like I'm on autopilot, my legs moving swiftly across the room. I'm pretty sure I'll attack the woman, but she must sense it and scrambles away. I pull Angelique physically farther from the witch, red-hot blood pumping hard through my veins. I drop to my knees and hug Angelique to me, holding her tight.

"It wasn't what you think," Mrs. Strand starts, her face drained of any color.

"Get out. Get out of this room. Get out of this house. And don't you ever come back," I hiss, my voice foreign to me, my chest tight.

Angelique buries her face in my neck and clings to me, her body racked by sobs.

"I'm so sorry, sweetheart," I tell her, hugging her, rubbing her back. "I'm so sorry." I look up at the older woman from over Angelique's head. She's still standing there. "Get. Out."

Ivy hurries across the room to where the woman's briefcase is sitting on top of the desk. Santi fusses in her arms and she bounces him as she snaps it closed and hands it to Mrs. Strand.

"I'll walk you out," Ivy says.

"I know the way," Mrs. Strand says and turns toward the door.

I turn my attention to Angelique who is holding on so tight that when I straighten to stand, I lift her with me.

Ivy walks out of the room after the woman, and I sit on the bed with Angelique in my arms.

"Don't tell daddy what she said," she whispers in my ear, her voice choked on the words as her body is racked by the after effect of violent sobs.

"Oh, sweetheart. It wasn't true. You're not spoiled. You're the sweetest little girl."

She sucks in shaky upset breaths and shakes her

head. "I mean about my...my eyes. Daddy will think his are weird too." She starts to sob all over again.

"Oh, honey." I'm crying with her now. I close my hand over the back of her head. "There's nothing weird about them. They're beautiful. You're beautiful inside and out. That woman is just mean."

"She's a witch. It's why she always wears black," she manages against my ear, my neck and face wet from her tears.

Ivy walks back inside and goes into the bathroom to return a moment later with a box of tissues. She carries it over to us.

"Is she gone?" I ask her, taking the box.

"Jericho heard the commotion. He's um...dealing with her."

"Oh."

Angelique draws back and I wipe her eyes and nose. She glances up at Ivy and the baby, then quickly back down. Something occurs to me. I wonder if at least a part of her shyness is about her eyes. The difference in color between them. I wonder if all this time she's been trying to hide them.

"Hello, sweetheart," Ivy says, crouching down. She touches Angelique's head. "I'm Ivy and this is my baby, Santi. Would you like to meet Santi?"

Santi coos as if on cue. Flirt for sure.

Angelique looks up from beneath long, thick lashes at the baby. I watch her smile because he's smiling at her, reaching out to her. He captures two handfuls of her curls and she giggles. A moment later, her body heaves with a breath.

"I bet that awful woman would think my eyes were weird too," Ivy says to her.

Angelique looks at her more closely and so do I.

Ivy opens her eyes wide, and I see the strange bleeding of the pupil into the pretty green of one eye. It makes it look like a cat's eye.

"It's not weird," Angelique tells her. "It's pretty. You're pretty."

"So are your eyes and so are you, sweetheart. Different doesn't mean weird."

Angelique smiles just as Jericho steps into the doorway. He looks rushed, enraged, upset, and helpless, all of those things at once. When his eyes fall on his little girl, I watch as something inside him breaks. I swear I see it. Angelique slips from my arms and runs to her father. He crouches down to catch her. He hugs her so tight that it squeezes my heart and makes it swell at the same time.

I may see a devil when I see Jericho St. James. But even the devil was an angel once. I know this devil now. He's dark, without a doubt. And he is fierce. He's haunted by the past and broken in ways he may never be whole again. But he's my devil. Mine and Angelique's and our baby's. A devil to watch over us.

---

## 23

## JERICHO

When Angelique was born on the day she should have died, I changed. It happened in that same moment that two paramedics held me back while another sliced Kimberly's stomach open. The same moment I heard my daughter's first cry. I remember it as I stand watching her sleep now.

Angelique was born violently. Cut into the world moments after Kimberly's death. She'd kicked. That's what one of the paramedics had told me later. That he'd seen the kick like she was trying to call for help. Like she knew her mother was dying or dead. If they'd waited any longer, she'd have died too.

That moment I heard her strangled cry, any innocence, any stupid, youthful, blind ideals, aspirations, hopes, they vanished. And in their place a darkness settled. A vast, empty darkness. The only reason I lived was because she lived. Our child survived the attack that killed her mother.

At first, she was the last piece of Kimberly. I clung to that idea, to anything that could tether me, no matter how elusive that tether, to the mother of my child. And then she became Angelique, her personality forming, her sweet nature so much like her mother's. I was glad for that.

I didn't think I'd ever love anyone again after holding my fiancée as she died in my arms, but I loved our baby. I loved her fiercely, desperately. Violently. Exactly the way she came into the world.

And when I heard what happened here today under my own roof, what that woman said, well, I would have killed her if Ivy hadn't come down the stairs after her. If Dex hadn't come to take my hands from around her neck and lead the woman out of the house. I would have committed murder with my child in the house.

I have killed. Over the last five years I've dealt with many evil men. I don't regret a single death. I don't lose sleep over any of them. The first were the two who were responsible for pulling the trigger. The assassins themselves. They each suffered very slow, very painful deaths, each watching the other die.

After them, I went up the ladder. Until I got to Felix Pérez and his recording of the meeting that confirmed where the order came from. I wanted to be the one to end Pérez too, but his death belonged to another. And she killed him with the pearl handled dagger I provided so that's something at least.

At the heart of it all is Carlton Bishop. He was the man who began it. Who put the hit out on me. Although now I'm wondering if it's Julia Bishop who was holding the reins all along. For centuries our families have been at odds. Battling. Bishops fighting to take back what they consider theirs. St. James's holding on fiercely. Growing slowly wealthier and more and more powerful as the Bishops slowly declined.

Carlton went a step too far. He's as bad as Reginald. The man who started it all. As rotten.

But I digress.

I take a sip of whiskey and watch my little girl sleep. What I feel guilt over isn't the blood on my hands but the knowledge that this woman, a woman I hired and paid and invited into my home spewed lies and hate into my daughter's ear and made her feel lesser.

Isabelle told me what Angelique said to her. That she didn't want to tell me the comment about the eyes because we share those strange eyes, and I might have my feelings hurt.

That's the part that breaks my heart in two.

I swallow the last of the whiskey, a fresh rage burning from the inside. I walk out of the bedroom and into the dark hallway. I need to hit something. But almost at exactly the same moment my bedroom door opens at the end of the hall and Isabelle comes rushing out. She goes immediately to the banister like she's running from something. I rush to her.

"Isabelle?" I say, hearing her heavy breaths. I'm not sure she hears me. "Isabelle," I repeat when I get to her, taking hold of her arms. "What is it? What happened?"

She blinks. Looks up at me, then around herself. She looks like a ghost in this shadowy corridor in the long white night dress she's wearing. I see her little toes with their pink polish peeking out from beneath the hem. I assume her brother's t-shirt is in the wash or she'd be wearing that.

She takes a deep breath in, calming a little.

"Are you all right?" I ask.

She nods. When I let go of her, she wipes at her forehead, and I see the beads of sweat at her hairline.

"The dream?"

"Yeah." She takes another deep breath in then out. I wonder if she's learned to do that to calm herself down. To get herself under control. She looks up at me.

"Do you want to tell me about it?" I ask carefully.

She shakes her head. "What are you doing out here?" she asks, changing the subject.

I glance down the hall to Angelique's room. "I changed my mind," I tell Isabelle.

"What do you mean you changed your mind?" she asks, following my gaze. She touches my face, brushes my hair back from my forehead.

"I'm going to kill that woman."

"No, you're not. You're tired. I'm tired. Come to bed."

"I don't know what damage she's done. Right under my nose."

"Jericho, stop."

I look down at her, her soft face, long hair loose down her back. She looks like an angel. An angel for a devil.

"I'm glad Angelique has you," I tell her, brushing her hair over her shoulder. "You're good for her."

"So are you."

"I let it happen, Isabelle."

"I was here too, remember. I let it happen too. But it's over now and we just have to show her what a wonderful little girl she is. How loved she is. How kind and good. That's all we can do."

I nod although I'm still thinking about how I'm going to murder the old bag. "I'll take you to bed," I tell her, taking her hand to walk her back into the bedroom. I draw the blankets back for her. She sits on the edge of the bed and smooths out the pillow.

"Stay with me," she says, taking my hand and intertwining our fingers.

"I won't sleep tonight," I tell her.

"Please." There's a strange expression on her face. She looks at our hands together on her lap, then at me. "The dreams get worse now."

I study her. "The anniversary is coming up." The night of the break-in. The anniversary of her brother's murder.

When I look at her what I see is a girl who needs someone to take care of her. A girl who needs a guardian angel. I'm no angel but I'll have to do.

"It's a pattern that doesn't seem to change."

"Lie down," I tell her and stand to strip off my clothes. She does as I say and a moment later, I slip into the bed to hold her. She lays her head against my chest.

"Thank you," she says.

"Do you want to talk about it?"

"No. Not really. I mean, the man who did it is behind bars. He was caught. Justice is being served. But Christian's still dead, you know?"

I hug her closer when I hear her sniffle. "I know, sweetheart. I wish I could bring him back for you. We'll go to the cemetery on the day if you like."

She lifts her head to look at me. "Yes. I'd like that. I usually go and spend a little time there with him. I didn't think you'd let me."

"I'm not an ogre, Isabelle."

"I know that." She rests her head again. "Thank you."

"You don't have to thank me for that."

"I am anyway." It's quiet for a long minute before she speaks. "Do you have dreams? Near the anniversary of Kimberly's death?"

"The day Kimberly was killed was the day Angelique was born. I've always tried to keep those two things separate. Try to give Angelique that day. Make it happy for her."

"You're a good father, Jericho St. James."

"That's debatable."

"You know what Ivy called you when you let Elena lead you to that window seat to read?"

I look down at her. She's got her head tilted up to see me. "What?"

"A big teddy bear."

I smile at that. "A bear, yes."

She smiles too and climbs up on her knees to straddle me.

I look up at her, watch her draw the nightdress off over her head, her hair cascading down her bare shoulders like a waterfall. She's completely naked underneath. I reach out to run my hand over the soft strands and let my gaze wander over her breasts, cradling one, brushing my thumb over her nipple before I cup the back of her head and bring her face to mine to kiss her.

"Are you trying to distract me or yourself?" I ask as she snakes her way down, taking off my briefs and looking at me from beneath dark lashes as she licks the length of my cock.

"Both of us." She rises up on her elbows to take me into her mouth and I think this is the sexiest she has ever looked. Naked, long hair wild all around her, her eyes heavy lidded, lips wrapped around my cock.

"Fuck, Isabelle." I weave my fingers into her long hair and guide her over my length. "Fuck."

## 24

## JERICHO

The jet leaves early to the high-security prison in Colorado where Danny Gibson is currently housed. The sun is just cresting the horizon as we take off.

Isabelle was asleep when I slipped out of bed. She clung to me the whole night long. Having her in my bed has become so natural I think I'd miss her if she wasn't there which is something I'm having a hard time wrapping my brain around. This isn't how it was supposed to be. And her holding onto me like she did, clinging to me to keep her nightmares at bay, it does something to me.

She needs me.

She is choosing me.

And it makes me that much more protective of her.

I rub the back of my neck with both hands. This is so fucked up.

"Sir, can I bring you some coffee or tea?," the flight attendant asks.

I turn from the window to look at her. Fuck I'm tired. I didn't sleep. "Yes, please. Coffee. Black."

She smiles, walks away and a few moments later she's back with a mug of coffee and a choice of croissants. I drink the coffee but leave the food and reach to the folder on the seat beside mine to open the file Santiago gave me on Danny Gibson.

I know what he did. I've memorized the file. But I want to hear it from him. And what I need out of this meeting is to know concretely if Julia Bishop was involved before I even knew Isabelle. Back when she was Isabelle York and had no idea of her relation to the Bishop family.

I spend the flight reading that file, checking for anything I missed, making myself focus on the task at hand. When we land two and a half hours later in Pueblo, Colorado the skies are cloudy and dark. I get into the waiting SUV, the air chillier here than in New Orleans. The driver greets me then begins the almost hour-long journey to Florence.

Once we arrive, I'm met by Mr. Holzman, the director of the facility. He shakes my hand and leads me inside while I try to remember what we paid him.

"How was your flight, Mr. St. James?"

"It was fine. Uneventful."

"Looks like we'll be getting a storm later. Hope that won't impact your return."

"I'll be out long before then. Thanks for making this meeting happen so quickly," I say as he leads me through several secure areas where no one asks any questions. At this rate, I could be carrying an assault rifle into the place and I'm pretty sure these guards would turn a blind eye. It's amazing what money can buy.

"I put Mr. Gibson in our most private and secure room. You won't be disturbed. I have stationed a guard right outside the door if you need assistance," he pauses. "Or if Mr. Gibson needs encouragement to talk."

No question on his meaning. "I'm sure I can manage. Has he had any other visitors since coming to this facility?" He was transferred here a year ago.

"A couple of men a few months back."

"Names?"

"I don't recall."

Right.

"This way, Mr. St. James." We're buzzed through a narrow corridor, and I follow him down another maze before we finally reach the guarded door.

Holzman stops. "You don't have any weapons on you? Anything sharp?" he asks me.

I shake my head. "I'm not here to break him out."

"No, of course. I ask for your safety."

"I can take care of myself, Mr. Holzman."

"Well, as a precaution he is cuffed to the table which is nailed down."

"Actually, I prefer him unbound."

Holzman pauses, then nods.

I gesture to the door, but he tells the guard to give us a moment. Once the guard is gone, he leans against the wall and cracks a smile that makes me want to break his teeth. This man is slime.

"I did have to make extreme accommodations for your visit," he starts. "It was a lot of work, to be honest with you."

"And I believe you were compensated for your efforts."

"Yes, your brother was generous. I just wanted to be sure you knew—"

I step toward him. Standing at my full height I have about six inches on him. "Let's get to the point. You want more money, Mr. Holzman? Is that what this is?"

He clears his throat, straightens up. "No, like I said. Your brother was generous. Just if you plan to rough him up... The health and safety of our inmates is of course a priority for us."

"Hm. Of course it is." He'll let me beat the shit out of Danny Gibson for the right price. I'm undecided if I will or not. I take out my wallet, having expected this, and make a point of counting out ten hundred-dollar bills. I shove them into his jacket pocket. "I'm on a tight schedule."

"Of course. Guard!"

The guard returns and unlocks the door.

"Uncuff Mr. Gibson," he tells the man who hesitates but does as he's told.

Holzman steps aside and I enter the room where Danny Gibson is sitting on the other side of the table. An ugly smirk on his face as he takes my measure.

He looks different than he had in the photos I saw. Bulkier with muscle. And meaner. His head is shaved showing off a tattoo of the year 1999. I guess it was a significant one for him. His face is pockmarked and he's a big guy. The thought of him touching Isabelle makes my blood boil. Turns my hands into fists.

The door closes behind me and I pull the chair out. Gibson is still sizing me up. He doesn't know who I am.

"That bitch send you? I already told her I'd shut my mouth. I have, haven't I?"

"What bitch would that be?"

He goes quiet, probably worried he's already said too much.

"No one sent me, Danny. I'm here to hear your side of the story," I say, pulling out the chair and taking a seat. At least he doesn't stink. I guess I expected him to stink.

"What, are you from the state? No. No way. Not dressed like you are."

"Just a private citizen."

"And what's in it for me?"

"Tell me what happened the night you murdered Christian York."

"Like I asked, what's in it for me?"

"That'll depend on how honest I think you're being."

He snorts but leans back and studies me some more. "I'd been casing the house. Just planning to grab a few things and get out before anyone was the wiser. That's it."

"So, if you were casing the place then you'd have known the girl would be home."

He swallows and I watch his throat, think what a delicate thing life is. How easily it can be snuffed out. One slit and it's over.

"What did you want to steal exactly? It's not like they had anything of value."

"Everyone's got something."

"Yeah, but you weren't there to take anything from them," I say, leaning closer. "That gash have something to do with your updated story?"

He looks momentarily uncomfortable and looks away.

"Because from what I've read, you swore up and down you were hired to do a bigger job than steal some trinkets."

He draws in a deep breath and exhales. "Who are you?"

"I'm the husband of the woman you tried to rape that night. She was sixteen years old at the time. Did you know that?"

His face loses all color and sweat breaks out across his forehead.

"I guess that didn't matter much," I add, knowing it's true. Scum. "What was the amount you were paid?"

He grits his teeth, fingers intertwined so tightly the veins on the backs of his hands are popping.

"What's rape worth these days anyway?" I ask.

"What the fuck is this?" he asks me. "Guard!" he shouts to the closed door.

"Or weren't you hired to rape her first? I'm really curious about that part."

"I'm done in here. Guard!"

"He won't come."

"Guard!"

Nothing.

"Who paid you?"

He shakes his head.

I lean across the narrow table, half getting up, and wrap my hand around his throat. "Tell me who the fuck paid you and what exactly they hired you to do."

I squeeze.

His eyes bulge.

I need to put the thought of Isabelle trying to fight him off out of my mind before I kill the fucker. I ease my hold, sit back down.

"Fuck it," Gibson says with a shake of his head. "He wasn't supposed to show up."

I wait.

"I was fucked up then. In a bad fucking place."

If he wants my pity, he'll be waiting a long time. Until hell freezes over.

He swallows hard. "The girl was the target. That what you want to hear?"

"What I want to hear is the truth."

"Well, then you just heard it." His eyes narrow and I wonder if he's less stupid than I thought. "The guy said he didn't care what I did or what I took as long as the girl was dead at the end. I had to make it look like a break-in gone wrong."

"Guy?"

He nods.

"Name?"

"I don't fucking know. We didn't exactly exchange business cards."

"How did he find you?"

"My reputation precedes me," he says with something akin to pride. Asshole.

"I bet. Go on."

"Gave me some cash to think about it. Show me he was serious. A down payment, he said. Judging by the amount he was dead serious," he pauses. "Told me I could walk away with it. I should have. But he promised me two more payments just like it. One when I agreed, the other when the job was done. I should have known something was up when that second payment showed up in some fucking bank account I couldn't touch." He shakes his head.

The funds were wired from a charity. My guess is the money was tied up. The Bishop's are cash poor, I know that, but it surprises me they'd take a chance on the money trail being discovered.

"Assholes," he says then leans toward me. "He did have one specific request about your wife, though."

*My wife.*

He must see how him saying the words gets under my skin because one corner of his mouth curves upward.

"And what was that?" I ask stonily.

"Make it bloody."

I study him. My hands clench and unclench at my sides. I'm almost done here.

"One more question."

"Shoot," he says casually, balancing on the back legs of the chair. You'd think he'd know how dangerous that is.

"Did you put your dick inside her?"

That grin spreads across his face. "Just the tip."

It's in that moment I decide I'll get my thousand dollars' worth.

## 25

---

### ISABELLE

The house is practically empty. Jericho was gone when I woke up. I guess it's his business trip to Atlanta. Zeke took Leontine and Angelique to a movie after lunch. They invited me but I declined. There's something I want to do while I have the opportunity and the new guards stationed around the house are not as observant as Dex, who mentioned needing to run an errand and that he'd be back within the hour. Whatever errand he was running seemed urgent.

Once they're all gone, I tell Catherine I'm going to take a nap before Professor Larder arrives for my lesson and head out of the kitchen but before turning to go up the stairs, I make my way to Jericho's study like it's perfectly normal for me to be going there. The less suspicious I look the better.

When I get to the door, I realize it may be locked

but am relieved to find it's not. I wonder if he simply forgot to lock it or doesn't bother to.

I walk into Jericho's space, close the door, and lean back, my hands still on the doorknob behind me. It smells like him in here.

I feel a momentary twinge of guilt when, after taking a deep breath of his lingering aftershave, I make my way to his desk. The surface is clear of most things, a laptop sits closed on one corner, there are a few sheets of paper and several photos of Angelique. I am relieved there isn't one of Kimberly. I know I shouldn't feel jealous of her. She was Angelique's mother. But I'm glad he doesn't keep a photo of her on his desk.

Taking a seat in his chair, I open the top right-hand drawer. It's where I saw him drop the key to the cellar door. It's still there. I recognize it. My heart races as I reach in and take it out. I'll be quick. Get it back here before he's home. I just want to see what he was looking for. See what it was behind that picture he knocked askew.

I close the drawer and get to my feet, hurrying out of the office toward the cellar before I can chicken out.

It's good there's no one around because in my guilty haste I fumble with the key, dropping it once before I finally get it into the slot and unlock it. Once open, I take a deep breath, slip into the staircase, closing the door behind me, and switching on the light.

It's instantly several degrees cooler and even the smell of it, the closed up underground space, is eerie. I hold onto the railing and move quickly. I don't want to give myself time to think. At the bottom of the stairs, I glance right but turn left toward the room I found Jericho in the other night. I move more slowly here, having to feel my way as the light from the stairs fades. When I manage to flip on the light switch, nothing happens. I remember how the bulb had flickered on and off that first night too.

I don't allow myself to look at the closed doors on either side of me. Instead, I hurry to the last door, which is still standing open. The one where I'd found Jericho that night. When I reach the door, it's almost too dark to see so I reach my arm around the corner to feel for the light switch. I am relieved when it doesn't take me long. A moment later, the bulb blinks on and I'm standing in this room that almost looks like a little girl's room, complete with a doll house, except it's not. No parent would put a child in here. It's too eerie.

Something cool brushes the back of my neck and I shudder. I take two quick steps into the room, turning to look behind me, half expecting someone to be there. My heart races as I'm met by empty space, so I hug my arms to myself. It's almost like the air in here is unsettled. Restless.

I just have one thing to do and then I can get out. The ghost that lives here, she doesn't want to hurt me. She doesn't have anything against me.

She.

Mary or Zoë.

The chair Zoë stood on to hang herself is still in the corner. I look up at the ancient wooden beam. History. History he's afraid will repeat with his own daughter. With me.

I take a deep breath in of the musty air and hurry to the wall where the picture still hangs askew, the box broken at my feet, letters strewn about. I see the edge of the beaded chain and lift the picture off its nail. It's only an 8x10 but it's dusty. The glass is broken and a shard drops to the ground, breaking into two pieces with a light tinkling sound. I set the picture aside and look behind it where someone has carved a small cubby hole into the stone. In that hiding place is what I'd thought was a beaded necklace, but I see now it's a rosary. And it's wrapped around several sheets of paper.

Is this why Jericho was here? Have I found what he was looking for?

My hand trembles as I reach for it and I realize the air around me has settled. I lift the papers. They're torn out of a spiral notebook, the edges uneven.

I unwind the rosary and unfold the sheet. It's dated March 20 ten years ago. I think at first it might be some sort of love letter but realize quickly it's not. And I wish it were. Because what I read is chilling.

It's not addressed to anyone in particular. It just starts.

*It's not right. Not normal.*

*He comes when everyone is sleeping. He smells like that whiskey he drinks and he's rough with anger and I'm too scared to move. To make a sound.*

*He tells me it's the rule. That girls become women and women are dirty and need to pray for forgiveness to save their souls. I don't believe him, though. I don't believe girls or women are dirty. At least I didn't before. But I still pray. Now I pray for strength to do what I decided I would do because although I'm relieved to have decided I'm still scared. I almost changed my mind, too, when he was away for a few weeks and when he came home, he didn't come to my room. I thought it was over, and I wouldn't have to do it again, but I was wrong. It will never be over, and I have to stick with my decision.*

*When I tried to tell Zeke, he told me to stop being weird. He didn't understand and it's too strange to say the words out loud. To say what happens those nights. I feel dirty to think about it. I feel disgusting.*

*I can't tell mom. He'll just hurt her if I do. He told me he would, and he likes hurting her because she's a filthy woman too. He hates us for being women.*

*But it will be fine now. It will be over. I decided.*

*I brought the rope down a few days ago. Brought*

*down my favorite stuffed animal. I know I'm too old for a stuffed bear, but I don't care.*

*It started almost one year ago. I was late to develop and when Zeke started to grow taller and stronger and more like a man than a boy, I looked like I was his little sister. Not his twin. I would never be as tall as either of my brothers but that was fine. My mom said she'd developed late too. I remember how much I wanted to hurry things along. Jealous of the girls in my class who already had breasts and shaved their legs and other things. I changed in the bathroom for gym because I was embarrassed of my flat chest and straight body and having no hair there.*

*Now I wish I'd stayed that way because when I did start to develop, he noticed. I think it's the first time he noticed me since I was born. He was never affectionate with any of us but at least my brothers served some purpose, especially Jericho. He's the oldest. His successor. He's the most like our father and sometimes that side of him scares me, but I have to remember Jericho isn't our father. He's kind and sweet and even when he tries to act like dad, as soon as he sees that I'm scared, he's himself again.*

*He's bigger than Zeke but Zeke's getting there. And they both said they'll always protect me because being so small I probably need a lot of protecting. I do. They don't know how much. How right they are. But thing is, neither of them can protect me against him. He's too wicked. Too clever. Too hateful.*

*He hates me. It's why he does it.*

I take a breath in and turn the page over, sitting on the bed to read it. The frame creaks but I'm too wrapped up to care.

*It started the night I got my first period. He knew somehow and when everyone was asleep, he came to my room. I was asleep too when I felt him pull the blanket away. He said I was dirty now. Like my mother. He said I needed to pray. To beg forgiveness for my sins. He never said what those sins were. He gave me a special rosary then made me kneel to say my prayers. That happened for a full week. I had to kneel and pray while he watched until he was satisfied.*

*I was so tired everyone noticed but I never said a word and I hid the rosary between my mattress and the box spring.*

*Then when my period was over, he stopped coming and I thought that was it. But then my cycle repeated, and the punishment changed. He made me take off my clothes before I knelt. It was cold I remember that, and he opened the window and let in more cold air and told me to pray. For the full week while I bled, he would make me strip and kneel and pray and beg for forgiveness.*

*The next time I had my period again he said it wasn't working. Said I was too dirty to pray and instead he would need to punish me as long as I bled. It was the rule he said. And every night that week he punished me. His punishment was wicked and hurt inside me. He hurt me so badly I had a hard time getting out of my bed those days.*

I stop reading.

Oh my God.

Jesus.

No.

I turn to the last page and realize I'm crying when a tear falls on the sheet blotting the ink. I smear it away and make myself read.

*It went on for a full year like this. A full year where for one week every month I was made to strip and kneel and pray and be punished. He changed the punishments sometimes, but they were all bad. They all hurt and made me feel bad especially when something happened while he was inside me. When for a few moments it felt good.*

*I feel sicker at the thought of that. Sicker than when he touched me. And I prayed on my own then after those nights. I knelt and prayed, my fingers running over bead after bead of that rosary. I prayed for it to stop. I prayed for forgiveness. Because he was right. I was a filthy girl and he always knew it.*

*The rope is ready. I'm ready. And before I have one more period, I have to finish this. Before he can come into my room one more time, I will end it.*

*I'll miss Zeke the most. I wish I could tell him. I wish he could protect me like he promised he would. I'll miss Jericho too. And mom. I will leave the letter where Zeke will find it in our hiding place. I hope he'll under-*

*stand. Hope they all will understand that I had no choice.*

*And that I'm sorry. I'm sorry I wasn't strong like them.*

Tears stream down my face by the time I'm finished reading. I turn the page over but it's empty. And I look at the rosary in my hand. It's broken. I wonder if she did that.

The letter is unsigned, but I have no doubt it's Zoë who wrote it. It's her suicide note. That's what he was searching for. He was trying to understand. Does Zeke know? Does Leontine? And what will I do with it now that I know?

I get to my feet feeling that strange calming of the air again. Like the ghost here was Zoë's. Maybe she was waiting for someone to find her letter. For her mother and brothers to understand.

I wrap the rosary back around the pages and slip them into my pocket, then make my way back down the corridor to the stairs. I'm not afraid and I don't hurry. And when I'm back upstairs I lock the steel door behind me, return the key to Jericho's study and close the desk drawer.

The pages are burning a hole in my pocket and I'm about to stand when something on his desk catches my eye. I feel cold at the sight of it. It's Jericho's handwriting on a sheet of paper. I recognize it from the time he'd left me the note the morning after he tattooed me. That feels like ages ago. But this isn't random scribbling. It's the name of a prison. The prison Danny Gibson was transferred to part way into serving his sentence.

I pull the sheet close to see if there's anything else but there isn't.

The prison is near Pueblo, Colorado. Getting to Pueblo, though, can't be easy from here. It has to be a connecting flight which would take hours, not to mention security and all the additional time. I'm wrong. That's not where he is. It can't be.

But I stop. My gaze lands on one of the photos of him and Angelique. Behind them is a private jet.

Jericho St. James wouldn't fly commercially. He would have taken a private jet which would get him there in about two-and-a-half, three hours, I guess. No waiting for security checks. No connecting flights.

I remember his comment about money when he told me he'd hired a professor from a prestigious conservatory to be my private violin teacher. Of course, he'd charter a jet if he doesn't own one outright.

What is he doing going to see Danny Gibson? Is he even allowed visitors? What does he want to know from that man?

I feel clammy and my hands are shaking when I finally get to my feet.

What does he want to know? And what will Danny Gibson tell him about what he did? I remember last night. The nightmare that plays on repeat this time of year. He asked if I wanted to talk about it. Talk about Christian's death, I guess. If he knew what I dreamed, though, would he think less of me? Because no matter what happened to me, what that man did to me, I'm alive. Christian is dead. He's the one I should dream about. His death the thing that wakes me in the middle of the night. Not what *almost* happened to me.

## 26

## JERICHO

The house is quiet when I walk in well after one in the morning. Turned out I was wrong about getting out long before the storm. By the time I got through with Gibson and headed back to the airport, that storm had begun, and we were grounded into the night.

Dex heads off to bed and I strip off my jacket on my way to the study. I'm tired after not sleeping last night, but I need a drink before I go to bed. I flex my right hand. It's stiff, the knuckles raw and bruised. Gibson's face was harder than I expected.

*Just the tip.*

Mother. Fucker.

I'm surprised when I open my study door to find the lamp on beside the couch and the room occupied. Isabelle is looking like she's been waiting for me all night. I can't quite gauge where her head is from the look on her face.

"Why aren't you in bed?" I ask, closing the door and walking to the liquor cabinet. I pour myself a glass of whiskey.

"I was waiting up for you. How was *Atlanta*?"

I put the lid on the bottle and turn to her, leaning against the cabinet as I sip and study her. She knows I wasn't in Atlanta.

"Would you like something?"

She shakes her head. "Why are you so late? Your brother thought you'd be home by dinner."

"Storm. We got delayed."

"Really? Because it was a clear, sunny day in Atlanta."

I smile, drink again and move to sit behind my desk. "What's this about, Isabelle?" I ask, realizing I already know. I'm pretty meticulous with how I leave things on my desk and I remember everything. Although I'm not sure she was trying to hide this.

"Snooping while I was gone?" I ask, crumbling the piece of paper with the name of the prison on it. "Let me be very clear, Isabelle. You're not to come in here without my invitation."

She stands and walks toward me, gripping the edge of the desk, her face hard. "Why?"

I lean back against the seat and study her. She's livid and anxious at once.

"Why would you go to see him?"

I see the crease between her eyebrows, the delicate skin pink around her eyes. Her gaze falls to my hand then, the one holding the tumbler of whiskey. The one that beat Danny Gibson to within an inch of his life.

"What did you do?" she asks, lowering herself to one of the chairs in front of my desk.

I consider what to tell her. If she's ready to hear the truth about her half-brother and cousin. But Danny Gibson's words taunt me. I know Christian got there in time to save her from being raped. I know because I am the one who claimed her virginity the night I took her to my bed. But how close did she come to being raped? And those nightmares, are they about her dead brother or about almost being raped? Being attacked by that piece of shit?

"Tell me about that night," I say, feeling a tenderness toward her. I want to hold her. Remind her that she's safe.

"There's nothing to tell that you don't know, I'm guessing."

"Tell me anyway."

"Why? What did he say?"

"It doesn't matter what he said. I want to hear it from you."

Her eyes grow misty and she's quiet for a long moment as she studies the wall just beyond my shoulder. When she finally looks back at me, her expression is guarded, closed. "A man broke into our house to rob us. He found me at home and thought he'd have some fun. But before he could finish what he started, my brother surprised him and got himself killed saving my life. Is that good enough for you?"

I watch her hug her arms around herself. She's trembling. "And the nightmares, tell me about them."

"It's not them plural. It's just one. One nightmare." She juts her jaw stubbornly. "You want to know what it is? Want to know how selfish I am?"

I don't answer. Just watch.

"It's not what you'd think. What normal people would dream about. It's not my brother." She stands up, walks halfway around the chair then turns back to me. "I mean, he lost his life that night. I lost him but I'm still alive and if it weren't for me, he'd be here now. If it weren't for him trying to get that man off me." She swallows, wipes the tears from her eyes with the heels of her hands. "After what he did to save me, it's not even him I see in my dreams. It's that horrible man. His face. The way he felt. The way he smelled. His hot breath on my neck." She looks like she might throw up, but she draws in a deep, shuddering breath and focuses on me. "I can't stop seeing that man's face, but I'm forgetting what Christian looked like. Do you know that?"

"That's normal, Isabelle. You don't have to feel guilt over that."

"Yes, I do. That nightmare is all about me. All about what happened to me. Not him." She shakes her head. "I get to the part where... where he's pushing off my jeans. I can feel his hands like they're on me—"

"I broke his hands. His fingers."

She looks at me and I imagine she's processing as she speaks. "That's when I wake up. When Christian came into the room."

"Isabelle—"

"I dream about when I felt that man between my legs." She's looking straight at me, eyes huge and wild. "I dream about him almost raping me. Even though I got to walk away."

"You didn't exactly walk away." I get to my feet, walking around the desk toward her. She shakes her head, backs away.

"It doesn't matter, Jericho. I'm here, aren't I? I'm alive. Christian is in the ground when he should never have been there to begin with. If I hadn't called him, he'd have been safe. It's why he came, you know that?" She wipes more tears. "I'd called to ask him to bring me my favorite soup from the deli nearby. I was sick and he'd gone to work. I asked him to get me soup like he wasn't busy enough already. If I hadn't been so selfish—"

"You're not selfish."

"He brought the soup during his shift break and got himself killed."

She's backed herself into a corner. I take her arms, squeeze them, and don't let her go when she tries to scoot past me.

"If he hadn't come home, a lot worse would have happened to you," I tell her, deciding it's time. Because she's been carrying the guilt of her brother's death on her shoulders for years when it wasn't her fault at all. When it was the fault of those who pretended to care about her.

She struggles against me and I pull her into my chest, cup my hand around the back of her head.

"I would have survived," she says, talking against my chest. "Even if he'd succeeded and done what he'd wanted to do, I would have lived." A sob wracks her body and she wraps her arms around my middle.

"No, you wouldn't, sweetheart." I keep her cheek against my chest and hold her tight.

"He didn't need to die," she says like she hasn't heard me.

"It would have been you who died if Christian hadn't come home."

She shakes her head. "You don't know that," she says, drawing back to look up at me.

I waver again. Is she ready to hear this? Even with the proof I have? She's fragile still. So is the pregnancy. But I can't keep it from her any longer. It's not right.

"I do, Isabelle. I do know."

Her eyebrows furrow as she tries to understand.

"Danny Gibson was hired to kill you that night. He was told to make it look like a break in."

She shakes her head. "What? No. That makes no sense. Why? You're wrong."

"Carlton Bishop learned about your existence years before publicly claiming you as his half-sister. He only did because he was bound to the way the inheritance is written."

"Inheritance? What does my brother's murder have to do with a stupid inheritance?" she shoves at me, walks away. "I don't care about any inheritance!"

"I know you don't," I tell her, closing the space between us to rub her arms, to hold onto her as I tell her the truth.

"Let go."

"No. You need to know."

"He lied to you. That man lied to you," she says.

"I have proof. I've had proof since almost the very beginning."

She just shakes her head.

"Carlton wanted you out of the way. You needed to be dead. The line needed to end for him to keep hold of the inheritance. He has no heirs."

"He didn't know who I was."

"He did. And he hired Danny Gibson to make it look like a robbery gone wrong."

She sets one hand against her stomach as if protecting the small life inside. The other is wrapped around my bicep.

"Gibson was paid out of one of the Bishop charities. It was diverted via several accounts and then withdrawn. It's an intricate scheme but is doable if you know what you're doing."

"The trial...they never found any trail. There was no money trail, Jericho."

"The bastard deserves to rot in prison, but so does Carlton Bishop."

She moves to sit down, and I follow to sit beside her. "You're wrong. You have to be."

"I wish I were."

She presses her hands to her face, rubs, shakes her head. "He came to the hospital. He took me in. Took care of me."

"Because he had to. IVI knew about your existence and so did the executors of the Bishop estate. He could no longer hide you, so he took you in to control you. Maybe to wait for his next opportunity."

At that she shoves my hands away and jumps to her feet. "No! No. I don't believe that."

I'm up too as she walks toward the door. "He gave just one instruction to Danny Gibson. Do you want to know what it was?"

She shakes her head, opens the office door.

"Make it bloody. That's it."

She stops. Drops her head.

"That was his one requirement." I get to her, wrap my arm around her from behind. "I'm sorry, Isabelle. I don't want to hurt you but it's the truth. I'll show you the proof. I'll show you."

She turns in my arms to face me, studies me for a long, long time as if trying to gauge if I'm telling the truth.

"So, Carlton is trying to kill me and he tried to kill you?"

My gaze narrows.

"Makes a lot of sense. Why would he try to kill you or me? What's the point? Why? And why go to such lengths?"

"Our families hate each other. If you look back throughout our history—"

"I have looked back and you're right," she says, pushing my hands off. "We hate each other."

I wait. Watch.

She stands up taller and takes a step away putting space between us. "You and I are enemies. I'll always be a Bishop. You'll always be a St. James. The baby I'm carrying, the one that has Bishop blood, will give you everything you want to have your revenge. Carlton and Julia and Matty will be out on the street. Me with them, probably."

"No, Isabelle." I take a step toward her, but when she takes one back, I stop. I don't know how I expected this to go. I knew this conversation was coming but still I'm unprepared. "Not you. I told you—"

"I know what you told me, and I understand why. But I think caring about my well-being has an expiration date. It's about nine months."

"Fuck, Isabelle." I stop because I thought we were past this part. "You think that still? After everything?"

She pushes her hands into her hair. "To believe you I have to believe Carlton wants to hurt me. To not believe you I have to believe you want to hurt me."

"I don't."

She looks up at me. "Either way I lose."

"You chose me the other night. Don't you remember?"

She shakes her head, walks toward the stairs, stops when she reaches them and turns a half circle to face me. "It's too much. I can't do this."

"Sweetheart." I go to her but she puts her hands up to stop me.

"I want to see Julia. I want to talk to her."

"No. That won't be possible."

"She told me you'd do this. Twist my mind. My thoughts."

I feel anger growing. "Do you remember the van that almost ran you down?"

She shakes her head. "I don't want to hear any

more." She hurries up the stairs, tripping in her haste to get away from me.

I catch up with her on the landing, grab hold of her arm and walk her to my bedroom. I close the door behind us. "Do you know where your cousin went the night after she came to see you at the theater?"

"Let me go!"

"She went to see the man who owns that van."

She stops, shakes her head. "No. I don't believe you. She wouldn't."

I take both her arms and give her a shake. I need her to hear me. To see reason. To believe me. "He's Danny Gibson's brother. She went to meet with Danny Gibson's brother."

"No. No." She slips out of my grasp and walks to the other side of the room. "Why are you doing this? You've already taken everything from me! I'm your prisoner. And you have what you want. Julia knew. She knew all along. I told her she was wrong, that it couldn't be. But you'd been swapping out my pills. So how can I believe you about this? How can I believe you about anything? You want me isolated. You have me under lock and key. Why are you doing this now? Why would you try to make me think...make me believe the one person who's been my friend—"

"She's not your friend. She was never your friend!" I walk to the dresser and open a drawer to take out one of the syringes Dr. Barnes left. She sees it before I can tuck it into my pocket.

"What is that for?" She asks as I eat up the space between us and take her by the arms. She's not going to see reason tonight. "Let me go!"

"We'll talk tomorrow. I'll show you the proof. Right now, you need to calm down before you hurt yourself or the baby."

"You don't care about me. You care about the baby. At least be honest about that! You want to hurt me some more by telling me about this man...this man who is Christian's murderer's brother? You want me to believe he's trying to kill me. That Julia would..."

"Isabelle. Last warning."

"That she would do something like that? Something only monsters and devils are capable of, Jericho St. James. And you are a devil. It's what I thought that first day. Did you know that? And when you're done with me—"

"I'm not going to be done with you." I spin her to face away from me, uncap the syringe with my teeth and spit the cap out. "Don't you get it?"

"Let me go!" She fights but she's not strong enough. Not even close. I nudge her leggings down a little and push the needle into her hip.

"No!"

But it's too late. It's already working. When I pull

out the empty barrel, her knees give out and I lift her in my arms to carry her to the bed.

"I'm sorry," I tell her. "I didn't want to do this. Didn't want to tell you this way."

"When you're done with me, are you going to bury me beside Nellie? Let weeds grow over my grave so no one remembers me?" she asks, words slurring.

"That again?" I pull her to a seat, hug her to me. "No. Never. Never."

I sit on the bed holding her on my lap. "Why do you hate me so much?" she asks, her voice almost too low to be heard.

"I don't hate you. The opposite. God knows I never intended to, but it's true."

I feel the weight of her head drop to my shoulder. I close my eyes, holding on to her tight. So tight.

It's true. What I feel for her is the opposite of hate. It's love. And hurting her tonight hurts me as if someone's got hold of the muscle inside my chest and is squeezing hard.

"I'm sorry," I whisper as I lay her down, lift her legs onto the bed. I look at her so small and vulnerable and innocent in a world of devils. "I'm so sorry, sweetheart."

I brush her hair back from her face and stand up, slip off her shoes, her leggings. When I do, something falls out of her pocket and lands on the floor. I tuck her in, bending to pick it up and my heart stops.

Because I've seen the rosary before. I recognize the handwriting on the sheet of paper it's wrapped around. And I swear I smell the stench of the cellar on the sheets.

I lower myself to sit on the edge of the bed and look at the papers in my hand. Look at the sleeping Isabelle. And I unwrap the rosary to open the letter.

## 27

### JERICHO

I read that letter a dozen times and I still don't understand. I still can't make sense of it.

Zoë's suicide note. She did leave one. She'd left it for Zeke and he must have read it then hidden it only to have Isabelle find it.

Fuck.

I swallow a deep mouthful of whiskey and look at the mausoleum wall. Look at her name. The date of her birth and of her death. At least the whiskey isn't my father's brand. I hate the stuff he used to drink. Always have.

I read the letter through again, the rosary wrapped around my fist, biting into the back of my hand as it clenches into a fist.

Zoë killed herself because our father was hurting her. Touching her.

A wave of nausea has me thinking I'll throw up,

but I don't. How could we not know? How could that go on for a full year and we didn't fucking know?

I get to the part about us. About myself.

*He's the most like our father and sometimes that side of him scares me.*

Carlton Bishop's taunt comes back to me. Something about history repeating itself. Did he mean the suicides? Or did he mean something else? I think about my own daughter.

Jesus.

I feel sick.

How can a father do that to his own child? How twisted must you be to do that to your own flesh and blood?

With a roar I smash the bottle against his marker on the mausoleum wall. I'm standing too close though and feel a cut on my forehead from a splintering of glass that ricochets off. I don't care. I welcome the pain. But it's not enough. So I draw my fist back and smash it against the stone protecting the space where his bones rest. Where the pieces recovered after the accident Zeke arranged lie too close to my little sister even in death. I beat my fist against it again and again and think about how I'll remove his corpse. Burn what's left of it. Let the ashes scatter where they may. I will get him away from her. Away for my baby sister. Even if it's too late to change anything.

"Brother."

I turn to find Zeke standing a few feet from me. My hand throbs at my side. I look back to the blood and whiskey-stained stone and crash my fist against it again. I hear my own scream. It's loud enough to wake the dead.

"Jericho!" Zeke's hand closes over my fist when I draw it back. We stand staring at each other for a long minute.

"You knew?"

He studies me, eyes narrowing once his gaze shifts to my other hand clutching Zoë's crumpled letter.

"Did you fucking know?" I ask, drawing his attention back to my face. His has lost some of its color.

He nods a single, solemn nod. "I found the letter exactly as she meant for me to." He drops his arm. I draw mine back and punch him.

"You fucking asshole! You knew all along. You fucking knew what he did. Why she did it. Why she fucking died."

He touches his jaw. He'll have a bruise, but he barely stumbled.

"Did you know before she died?"

"Fuck no."

"She tried to tell you." I wave the letter in front of his face. "Where the fuck were you when she tried to fucking tell you?"

"Where the fuck were you?" he yells back, the

step he takes toward me angry. "Huh? Where the fuck were you, brother? Oh yeah. Gone most of the fucking time leaving us here with that monster."

I stumble back at his accusation. Although he's right. Every single word fits. I was gone. When things got bad, I left.

"What? No answer for that, big brother?"

I look down at my bleeding fist. It's raw and fucking throbbing. But I need more. I deserve more. And so, I turn back to that bastard's name and beat the stone wall until I can't anymore. Until Zeke finally manages to pull me from it. To take me down to the ground. Into the dirt and mud, my baby sister's letter, her final, terrible words ruined in the dirt.

"How could I not know?" I ask, my voice breaking. "How could I not fucking know? Not see." I lean against the nearest gravestone.

"I was her twin. If anyone should have known, it was me. Hell. She tried to tell me. I remember when she tried. She'd gotten so skinny, remember? Didn't sleep anymore. Didn't eat. Didn't do much but go through the motions."

I push my hand into my hair and look up at Zoë's name, notice the flowers that are dying. Time for new ones. I turn to my brother.

"Mom?"

He nods once.

"How long?"

"I told her before I left for Austria. Told her why I was going. What I was going to do."

I don't want to know how she took it. "Why didn't you tell me?"

"It doesn't matter, Jericho. Not anymore." He sounds tired suddenly. Exhausted. And that darkness I've glimpsed a handful of times, that shadow, it settles over his features. Aging him before my eyes.

"I'm sorry," I tell him. "I'm sorry I wasn't there for her. For you. I'm sorry I wasn't there to kill that bastard myself. Not leave it to you."

"I would soak my hands in his blood over and over again if I could. You have nothing to apologize for."

We sit in silence for a long time. I study my hand.

"When did you find the letter?" Zeke asks.

I turn to him. "I didn't. Isabelle did."

"Isabelle?"

I nod once, thinking of her in my bed. God. Could this night get any worse? Could it go farther off the rails?

"Let's go back to the house. Get some sleep."

"I'll be there soon. Go ahead."

"Jericho, there's nothing you can do out here. Breaking your hand isn't going to change anything."

"I just need a little time." I open the letter again, clean off the mud and read. After a while, Zeke leaves me alone. I'm not done punishing myself. Not yet.

## 28

### ISABELLE

When I wake up it's mid-morning and someone is pulling the curtains back. I half-expect Leontine or Catherine but it's a man. For a moment I think it's Jericho. He's dressed in a dark sweater and black jeans which is unusual for him. Then he turns, and I realize it's not him. It's Ezekiel.

I sit up, my mouth feeling dry. I'm still wearing the sweater I'd worn yesterday but I can see my leggings on the floor where Jericho must have dropped them after undressing me.

"Good morning," Zeke says. "I'm sorry to come in here and wake you."

I look up at him trying to work through the memory of last night, of what Jericho told me. What he did to me.

I push the blanket off and cross the room to the

dresser, not caring that I'm only wearing underwear and the sweater. It's oversized so it hopefully covers enough of me, but I just don't care. I pull the drawer open where he got that damn syringe and rifle through it, finding two more. I grab them, stalk into the bathroom and empty the barrels into the toilet before throwing them away. When I turn, I see my reflection in the mirror. See how haggard I look. I wash my face, rinse my mouth, and step into the doorway to ask Ezekiel what he wants. What message Jericho sent him to deliver. I fold my arms across my chest.

"What do you want?"

"You shouldn't have given it to him," he says. His arms are crossed over his chest too.

I'm confused. "What are you talking about?"

"The letter, Isabelle. It's not how he should have found out."

I look on the floor to my leggings. Zoë's letter. It must have fallen out of my pocket when he took them off to tuck me into the bed. As if my comfort matters to him.

But my forehead furrows when I think about what was in that letter. I look up at Zeke.

"It was Zoë's suicide note."

He nods although it's not a question. "How did you find it?"

"Jericho was in that room down in the cellar a few nights ago. He was looking for something and when he didn't find it, he threw a box at the wall. He knocked the picture askew. I saw the beads of the rosary and went down to investigate later when I was alone."

"It wasn't your place. That letter wasn't for you."

I bite my lip. "I didn't know what I'd find and you're right that it wasn't for me, but it was for Jericho." I am surprised to hear myself say it. Hear myself defending my husband.

He presses his lips together in a thin line. "I was protecting my brother."

I nod, walk back into the room. "I know. I'm sorry for what happened to her." I feel my eyes fill with tears.

"Thank you. But that's not why I'm here."

"Why are you here?"

"Jericho's in bad shape Isabelle. Really bad."

I feel my forehead wrinkle but before I can ask anything he continues.

"I found him at the cemetery last night. Heard what I thought was an animal out there, but it was my brother beating his fist to a pulp against the stone of the mausoleum."

"Shit. He went out there after reading it?"

Ezekiel nods. "He feels guilty."

"I'm so sorry," I say, wondering if I should have just left it in its hiding place.

"He's downstairs now. Locked up in his study.

Probably drinking another bottle of whiskey. Will you go to him?"

"Me?"

"I've tried. Leontine tried. I think you may be the only one who can reach him."

"Me?" I ask again, surprised.

"You. Leontine took Angelique out. Dex is with them. I don't want her coming home and seeing her father this way."

"Okay," I say, nodding. "Just let me get dressed."

"There's no time." He reaches into his pocket and pulls out a key. He holds it up to me. "Key to his office," he says, and I see the bruise on his jaw. I wonder if that was Jericho.

"Okay."

Ezekiel opens the door and I take the key as I pass him. Before I've even reached the bottom stair, I hear music coming from the study. He has the volume way up. I recognize the piece. Mozart's requiem.

Catherine is standing nearby looking worried. She meets my gaze and I try to give her a reassuring look then walk to the door. I don't bother to knock, just slip the key into the lock, and push the door open. The music is so loud in here I can't hear myself think. The curtains are drawn, the only light is the one I'd left on last night. There, sitting in my vacated seat is my husband. My husband looking like a broken man. A near empty bottle of whiskey on the table beside him. He's learning forward, elbows on knees, hands clasped between them, head hanging, hair messy. His clothes are dirty. His shoes off. And the smell of whiskey and pain permeates the room.

I don't think he hears me enter because he doesn't look up. I quietly lock the door behind me and look at him again. At my husband sitting in this dark room smelling of alcohol and regret. Looking beaten. Hopeless. Not the devil I know.

He lifts his head. When his gaze meets mine my heart twists at the sight of him. My eyes mist and last night is somehow forgotten. Forgiven.

I go to him, and he sits back against the couch. I see his face more clearly as I approach, see the blood on it, the dirt. The scruff of five-o'clock shadow. His shirt was once white, but it's ruined. Ripped in places. Smeared with mud and blood. For a moment I wonder whose but then I see his hands. The right one is worse than the left. It's swollen, bloody, possibly a finger or two broken.

I drop to my knees between his legs and touch his hands, hear his hiss of pain. They weren't this bad last night. This isn't from what he did to Danny Gibson. No. It's from what he did to himself after he found that letter in my pocket. I look in his eyes and touch his face, the cut at his forehead. He looks hopelessly at me. He's far away. Too far. I need to bring him back.

"What did you do to yourself?" I ask him.

He doesn't speak but he brushes the knuckles of his better hand across my cheek. Reaching beyond me, he takes hold of the neck of the whiskey bottle.

"No," I say, closing my hand around the bottle.

He blinks, eyes focusing on me. He tries again.

"No, Jericho. It's enough."

I don't know what to expect but I'm glad when he doesn't fight me. I set it back on the table and stand. I know one way to draw Jericho St. James out.

I reach underneath my sweater and slip off my panties. He watches as I straddle him, not bothering to undress completely.

"You stupid man," I tell him as I undo his belt and pants, sliding my hand inside his briefs to grip his still soft cock. "Are you trying to kill yourself?" I ask, kissing his mouth. He doesn't kiss me back at first. He's unresponsive. But I move my hand over the length of him. As he hardens in my grip, his pupils begin to focus on mine and he closes one hand around the back of my head.

I raise myself up and adjust my position to mount him, taking him inside me, kissing him as I do. Our eyes are open, mouths touching, tongues wet. He's hard inside me as I ride him slow and deep.

He moans. "Isabelle."

"Shh." I kiss him again as I grip the hem of my sweater. I pull it off, then rip his shirt open, the fabric tearing easily so we're skin to skin. I need to get closer. As close as we can be.

He reaches around me, holding onto me with one arm as he grabs the whiskey with the other and brings it to his mouth.

"No," I tell him. This time he resists but I shake my head. He allows me to take it from him. I let the bottle drop to the carpet. "I need you, Jericho," I tell him, moving my hips and squeezing my muscles in that way I know he likes. I can feel him grow harder inside me as his hands come to my hips. "I need you here with me, do you understand?"

He doesn't speak but begins to move me, grinding me against him.

"Our baby needs you. Your daughter needs you. Do you hear me?"

"It's all so much worse than I ever imagined," he says more to himself than me. "All fucking gone to hell." His grip hardens around my hips.

"Stay here with me," I say, cupping his face and making him look at me. "Be here with me now. I need you. Do you hear me? I need you, Jericho."

He looks at me, eyes tired and full of so much pain.

"Please," I say.

"I am like him. Zoë knew too. I idolized that man."

"No. You're not like him. I know."

"I'm a devil. You said it yourself."

"You could have hurt me. Really hurt me. So many times. But you didn't. Not once."

He shakes his head. "Isabelle—"

"And you're my devil. I need my devil now, do you understand?"

"I knew you wouldn't want a pregnancy. I changed your pills out. It's worse than lying. You know that. I know that."

"Shut up."

"And eventually, I'll hurt you. Don't you see?"

"Shut up. Just shut up. Shut up and make me come. I need you to make me come."

He swallows hard, eyes darkening. He grips my hips and pulls me down hard, grinding against himself. Then he lifts me and places me on the couch, spreading my legs and kneeling on the floor between them. He pulls me to the edge of the seat and buries his face. All I can do is grip a handful of hair and bite down on the back of my hand to keep from crying out. The scruff on his jaw is rough against my thighs, his mouth soft as he dips his tongue inside me before closing his mouth over my clit.

I come, my body shuddering with the orgasm. When it's over he's up again, knees on the edge of the sofa, face to face as he takes me. Something is different between us, our eyes wide open, never wavering from the other's face. When we come, we cling to each other, my arms around his neck, him gripping a handful of hair. He forces my head back and kisses me the moment I feel him empty inside me. I swallow his moan, knowing we belong to each other. Me to him and him to me. This is right. The way it was always meant to be. Me and him. Bishop and St. James.

And the baby inside my stomach has her destiny laid out for her. Her purpose. She will heal old wounds. She will close the history book and write a new future. Because even if the words aren't spoken, I love Jericho St. James. And I need him. I know it's the same for him. However this started, however he meant it to be, it's something other now. Something whole and perfect and right. Strong enough to face all the ugliness of our world.

# 29

## JERICHO

She cleans my hands. My face. The antiseptic stings but I try not to move as I watch her. She's beautiful. So beautiful. Even when she tells me how stupid I am to battle stone. She's right. She prattles on about what Angelique will think when she sees me like this. How we'd better get me bandaged up and not stinking of a distillery before she gets home. It's good. Distracting.

That's twice now that Dex has taken my mother and Angelique out. I need to talk to him about that. It's like my household is revolting silently behind my back.

Isabelle tucks a strand of wet hair behind her ear and looks at me. After our shower she dressed in a lightweight sweater dress. Her legs and feet are bare, the dress hugging her round ass. When she turns to throw away the bloody cloth she used to clean my wounds, I'm tempted to bend her over the foot of the bed, push her dress up to her waist and take her again.

"What?" she asks when she turns back to me.

I realize I have a grin on my face. To be honest I feel like I'm in a dream state. Probably at least partly due to the amount of alcohol I consumed and the fact that I haven't slept in forty-eight hours.

"Your ass looks good in that dress."

She rolls her eyes but smiles and draws the sheets back on the bed. "You need to eat this and sleep." She points to the sandwich on the nightstand. "You need something to soak up all that whiskey."

"Sit," I tell her.

"Eat," she replies, folding her arms across her chest.

"I'll eat if you sit." She doesn't move. "We need to talk, Isabelle." As soon as the words are out, it's like that high begins to evaporate for both of us.

She sits beside me, tucking her legs up under herself. "Eat first."

I nod and eat the sandwich in about three bites. I am hungry.

"Maybe chew?"

I smile, wipe my mouth, and turn to her. "What I told you last night. Do you remember?"

Her face darkens and she nods. "I threw away the other syringes. If you ever do that to me again—"

"I won't."

"If you ever do, I'll kill you Jericho St. James."

I smile at that. "Okay. I'll hold you to it." She pushes my hair back, her face softening. "What I said though," I continue. "What I told you about the night your brother was killed. You remember?"

She shifts her gaze to her dress, brushing off imaginary lint. "I need to think."

"I wish I were wrong, Isabelle. But I have proof."

"I just need to think. Need to get through the next few weeks first. Okay?"

The anniversary of his death.

"Okay."

I wrap an arm around her as she smiles weakly at me. "I won't hurt you, Isabelle. I promise. Not now. Not when you have the baby. Not ever. Do you believe me?"

She wipes her eyes.

"You never have to worry about that. I care about you. I will take care of you. Do you remember what I said once? Pregnant or not, Bishop or not, vengeance or not, you're what I want. That hasn't changed. It's not going to change." I touch her cheek, pull her to my chest as more tears come.

She sniffles, her body wracked by a sudden sob, so I hold her to me. I wish I could see her smile more. I wish I could hear her laugh. Have I ever heard her laugh? Giggles now and again with Angelique when she doesn't know I'm listening. But I don't think I've ever heard her laugh.

"And I won't betray you. You just have to trust me and keep choosing me."

## 30

### ISABELLE

Jericho sleeps long and hard. That afternoon I walk out to the chapel on the grounds. It's a cool, overcast day as I make my way along the path, feeling like the weeks leading up to Christian's murder are always cool and overcast. At least they have been for the last three years.

I pick wildflowers on my way, finding bunches in blues and yellows. By the time I get to the cemetery I have enough for four small bouquets. I lay one at Kimberly's grave, one at Nellie's and take a third to Zoë's. After arranging the flowers in the little pot before her name, I spend a few minutes thinking about her. Her short, sad life. Her terrible death. I think about her two brothers and how they couldn't save her. I see Jericho's hopeless face. The pain in his eyes.

"I'm sorry for what happened to you," I tell her,

remembering the sensation of someone being there with me in the cellar when I found the letter. The cool presence of something no longer of this world. As I think it, goosebumps rise along my body and a shiver has me hugging my arms to myself. It's not frightening though. It's her. Maybe she's left the cellar now that the secret is out. Maybe she can rest.

A lump forms in my throat and tears warm my eyes. I brush away dirt from the Z of her name and shift my gaze to the name on the stone beside hers. The one with the residue of what I know is Jericho's blood. Her father.

How can she rest with him so nearby?

But Jericho will take care of that. As early as tomorrow morning. Someone is coming to erase his name from the stone once his remains are removed from the crypt so that Zoë can finally rest.

I take a deep breath and head toward the chapel. I have my own dead to remember now. And over the last three years I have created my own memorial ceremony. Carlton never cared about it even though when prodded by Julia he pretended to. I can't blame him. He didn't know Christian. Julia though, I think she cared. She even joined me at the cemetery a few times, telling me she understood when I told her about my ceremony. How I remembered him.

Like I had the other night, I spot a few old cigarette butts on the ground in front of the chapel. I don't know why they stand out to me. It's not that out of the ordinary for someone to smoke if they are working out here.

Ignoring it I go into the chapel and walk to the altar. The tabernacle lamp is lit but the others aren't, so I set my last bouquet of flowers down, pick up the box of matches and start lighting them. I open the shoulder bag I brought with me and take out my small, framed photo of Christian and me. I study his face, see how the smile lights up his eyes. It was taken a few years before my parents' accident. I was only twelve.

We had taken a road trip to Miami. It was one of our few family vacations and I know how long my parents had to save for it. We stayed at roadside motels as we went, and I still remember the little bottles of shampoo I'd only use a little bit of so I could bring them home. We'd had so much fun, though. All of us laughing and happy. So happy.

My eyes fill up at the memory. They're all gone now. Every one of them. How life turns on a dime.

I set the photo down on the altar and arrange the bouquet of flowers before it. I take a small tea light out of my bag and light that too, placing it right in front of the picture before taking a seat on the front pew. I ignore Draca's book, ignore his name engraved on the large stone at the center aisle, and instead focus on Christian. Saying the prayers I know for him. Asking God to give him peace. To give them all peace.

I never felt their presence after they died. Not my mother or father. Not Christian. I thought I would. I think you should be able to feel your loved ones after they depart this world. It would be a kindness to those of us left behind.

But I don't linger on the thought. Instead, I take out my own sort of diary. A notebook I kept after Christian died. I had already started forgetting so many things after mom and dad's passing, only realizing that fact when I'd look through old family albums, trying to remember where or when a photo was taken. After Christian was killed, I wrote down everything I could remember about him. From the way he'd mess up my hair and call me a chicken when it came to scary movies, to the way he'd hog the bathroom on the rare nights he had a date. How I'd make fun of him for spending so much time on his hair.

I smile at that one. He always overdid the cologne too. At Christmas I'd go to department stores, ask for samples of various men's colognes and make him a gift out of them. I'd do the same for my mom with perfume. My dad would get a framed photo of us every year. We didn't have money growing up, but I never really noticed or felt a lack of anything. We loved each other and we didn't need more. Although I guess my parents may have seen that differently, working multiple jobs to keep us fed, clothed and housed.

I take a minute to thank God for those days. Even though my family was taken too early, we were happy. We loved each other. We never hurt each other. We were richer than Jericho's family, if I think about the tragedies they've endured.

I check my watch. It's almost time for my afternoon lesson with Angelique. Ever since Mrs. Strand was fired, Leontine and I have been splitting time with her, reading to her, doing simple lessons. And Leontine has been talking to Jericho about enrolling her in school more and more. Once the anniversary of Christian's death passes, I'll talk to him too. I just need to get through the next few weeks first.

And then the next part. The part where I try to understand why Julia would do what Jericho says she did. Where I try to come to terms with something I can't make sense of.

According to Jericho, Carlton hired Danny Gibson to murder me. All because he knew I was his half-sister and a threat to his inheritance.

Do I believe Jericho? I believe he believes it. And he has some sort of proof to back up his belief. I need to see that for myself. If it's true, he's known all along that Carlton was responsible for Christian's death. Is that what he is holding over Carlton? Is that how he got Carlton to agree to our marriage, knowing the threat of my having a baby would be exponentially higher? It makes sense that was Jericho's plan. It is the only thing that makes sense.

But is Carlton capable of murder? Because even if he didn't commit the act, he commissioned it.

And then there's Julia.

Is it true that the night she came to the theater to tell me Jericho had threatened Matty and to give me those pills, that she went to that man's house? The man who drove the van that almost ran me over? Wasn't that an accident? Bad timing? Or am I naïve?

Carlton is one thing, although I'm not sure I believe he's capable of the things Jericho is accusing him of. But Julia? She's been a friend to me. She's Matty's mother. I see how she is with him. She loves him. She'd do anything for him.

That night at the theater, she said Jericho would try to twist my mind. Make me believe whatever he wanted me to believe. That he'd treat me with kid gloves because I was carrying his baby, the tool for his vengeance. She said I'm malleable.

It's not true. He has sworn up and down he wants me. That he'll take care of me and not just for the baby. I believe him. More than that. I have feelings for him.

And that could all be exactly what Julia said. It could be him playing me like a puppet.

I get up because I don't want to think about this anymore. Besides, it's time to return to the house. I leave the tea light burning but blow out the other candles on the altar, pick up my bag and walk out of the chapel. The sky is darker, clouds denser. We'll have a storm tonight but it's not raining yet, so I hurry down the chapel stairs and cross the grave-yard. Something catches my eye making me look toward Nellie's grave. I gasp and stop with one hand on the cemetery gate.

There, standing against the marker is a shovel that I swear hadn't been there just half an hour ago when I laid the flowers on top of her grave.

A cold chill runs through me, and I glance around. Am I imagining the smell of cigarette smoke?

"Is someone there?" I call out. Maybe it's a groundskeeper come to do some work. It's the only thing that makes sense.

No one answers but a small flash of red lights up a dense cropping of trees in the distance.

"Hello?" I ask again. Is someone out there smok-ing? Is that what the red is?

But it goes dark again and there's still no answer. I glance once more at the shovel set at the grave and push the gate open to hurry back to the house. Feeling eyes on me the whole way, feeling watched. Feeling suddenly afraid.

## 31

## JERICHO

Erasing the name and date from the stone that marks my father's life is easier than exhuming the remains behind it. After the accident only a few bones were interred to begin with, but I want any trace of him out. Gone. I want my sister free to rest.

I remember the first night Isabelle was in the house. How she mentioned a presence in the cellar. I wonder if that presence was Zoë. I've gone down there since Isabelle found the letter. It's gone. The air is empty like the rest of the house. Maybe she'd been waiting for us to discover the letter. I wonder what she expected Zeke to do with the information. How she thought he could share it with us, something so terrible and impossible.

When I told my mother what I intended to do with my father's remains she only nodded once. We didn't speak of why. Didn't mention Zoë's suicide note. Didn't mention the abuse she'd endured. Honestly, I'm not sure my mother could take hearing it again. I'm sure she's gone through her own hell many times over at her daughter's death. And then learning the reasons behind it.

I watch from a distance as two men work to remove the stones behind which are his bones. I don't feel anything as I look on. Nothing but disgust for the man. The death Zeke dealt him was too good.

"Jericho."

I turn to find my brother approaching. I hadn't heard him over the noise of the workers. He glances to the mausoleum then back to me, a tell-tale line of worry between his eyebrows.

"What's happened?" I ask, on alert.

"I don't know. We've been summoned to IVI headquarters."

"Summoned?"

"I just got off the phone with Hildebrand's secretary. They're calling in Sovereign Sons. Meeting starts in half an hour."

"That's unusual. Any idea what it is?"

He shakes his head. "The compound is on lockdown. That's all I know."

"Lockdown?" The last time that happened was during an execution over two years ago.

"We should go."

I nod. "I'll get Dex out here to manage this." I tell

the men I'm leaving and get my phone out to text Dex on my way. I want to tell Isabelle where I'm going but hear her from just beyond the library door. She's having her lesson and I take a moment to appreciate the music, but decide not to interrupt. I'll see her when I'm back.

Zeke drives us to the compound. We arrive with a string of other vehicles and hand the car off to the waiting valets. Men exchange greetings with one another and it's obvious no one knows what this is about. Judge and Santiago approach as we're ushered to the main building.

"Any idea what's going on?" I ask after we shake hands.

"Not sure," Judge says. "All I know is something happened at the Cat House last night."

The Cat House is essentially a high-end whore house. The most beautiful of courtesans are kept by The Society for use by Sovereign Sons. I realize how fucked up it sounds, but they're supposedly paid well and work of their own free will. I guess it's some of what our fees buy. Another perk.

"I don't think it's a simple reprimand if they've called us all in," Santiago says because there have been one or two instances where things got out of hand, and someone needed to be reprimanded.

"No," Judge agrees, expression serious. I wonder if he knows more than he's letting on, but our conversation comes to an end when we enter one of the more somber rooms within the compound where large meetings are conducted. It's one of the few, outside of the ballrooms, that can hold us all.

Zeke and I take our seats alongside each other at the ancient oak table. Santiago and Judge are across from us. There's a buzz of noise as people speculate what is going on. Why the urgency. They only quiet once the last of the men enters, the door is closed and the gong sounds.

I look around the table. Every seat is taken and a few men stand along the walls. No refreshments apart from water is offered, which is rare for any meeting at the compound.

This is serious. And I know when I glance to my brother that he and I are just realizing the same thing. Carlton Bishop is absent.

The door opens then and the silence becomes absolute as Councilor Hildebrand enters wearing his official robe. One of the guards guides him to his seat at the head of the table and sets the folder in front of the councilor. We all watch and wait as, once he's settled, he glances to the other guard and nods.

The door he just came through is opened once more and to my shock, in comes Julia Bishop holding her son's hand. The little boy is about four years old with a mop of curly blond hair and big, frightened blue eyes. He's wearing a dark suit and has his thumb in his mouth. She walks swiftly but his steps are slow as he takes in this room full of strangers. I see her tug at his hand to hurry him along.

This is no place for a child. The boy is clearly frightened. Why would she bring him here? And what the hell is she doing here?

I realize then she's dressed more somberly than usual. Almost more modestly. Almost. She's wearing a long-sleeved black dress with a high neck that hangs just beneath her knees, paired with five-inch black patent leather heels. Her hair is contained in a simple but elegant bun at the nape of her neck, and she's pinned a black lace bobble into it. Her eyes are lined with dark liner and her lips are painted clown-red.

She comes to stand at Hildebrand's right hand and must realize her son is sucking his thumb because she pulls his hand away from his mouth. He looks up at her and sets his little hand at his side, but I see the effort it takes him to keep it there. It's when she lifts her downcast gaze to the men gathered around the table and they land on me, that I get a sinking feeling I know what is coming.

"Gentlemen," Hildebrand begins.

"It's Bishop," Zeke whispers.

I nod but don't reply as Hildebrand continues. "As you know the compound is on lockdown. This is something the other Councilors and I take very seriously. Given the circumstances and the delicacy of the situation, we deemed it appropriate."

"What's going on, Hildebrand?" Someone calls out. "Let's not stand on ceremony."

Hildebrand seems irritated by the interruption but gathers himself. "I invited you here today with both sad and happy news. First, the sad. I would like to advise you about an incident that took place in The Cat House early this morning. At approximately four o'clock, a few of our guests were indulging in..." he pauses and I'm sure it's a practiced pause, "a group activity," he says. He glances at the little boy with a look that makes it clear he has no idea how to behave around a small child. "It was during this event that our own Carlton Bishop met with tragedy. He succumbed to a heart attack and passed away on the premises."

There's an immediate and collective noise as the men gathered start to murmur their surprise and shock. The questions begin, but the Councilor raises his hand to quiet the table. It takes me a full minute to process this news.

My gaze shifts from Hildebrand to Julia Bishop. Because what the fuck is she doing here? Women are never or very rarely allowed to attend such a gathering even if Carlton Bishop is her cousin.

"And while we investigate the details of this unfortunate event, I have learned of happy news," he says, again glancing at the boy.

He forces his mouth into a smile and extends a hand to the boy who recoils. I get it. His mother, though, takes his hand, the one that wasn't in his mouth, and sets it in Hildebrand's ancient one. Hildebrand tugs the boy forward and the child begins to suck vigorously on his free thumb again.

My heartbeat is somehow controlled. My face a mask. I am calm as I watch what's going on. I feel the eyes of the men around the table slowly fall on me as we all begin to understand the only thing this can be about. Why a woman and her four-year-old boy are in this room at all.

"It turns out that our dear Carlton Bishop, whose wives failed to produce a single heir, was a father after all."

Hildebrand's eyes land on me. I meet them, then shift them to Julia standing behind him. Her gaze locks on mine the moment I meet hers. She's barely able to keep one corner of her mouth from curving upward.

"Mathew Bishop is the product of a love affair between Carlton and his cousin, Julia Bishop."

Someone makes a gagging noise. They are first cousins. Is that even legal? At least it wipes that satisfied smirk off Julia's face. As she shifts her gaze to the man who made the sound, I can see her mind working. Cataloging the name.

"As times are modern, of course, such a pairing would not be approved by The Society and thus the two had kept their love a secret." What love is he talking about? The man died at a whore house.

Probably balls deep in one of the courtesans. "But now that Mr. Bishop has passed, well, the important thing is we welcome his descendent into the fold with all the respect due him." Hildebrand stands and turns to the child looking up at the old man towering over him. Matty immediately begins to sob.

Hildebrand isn't bothered.

"Welcome, boy. Welcome to the class of Sovereign Sons."

As the men clap and stand, I hear sounds of "at least he died happy." And "fucking your cousin? What the fuck?" And "Well, cousin or not, I'd fuck her too. Look at her."

But it takes all I have to drag myself up to standing. I feel Zeke's hand on my shoulder as I try to process what I've just heard. As I try to understand how that woman managed this. All the while she stares only at me, a victor's smile wide on her face. Because if this is true, then she certainly is the victor.

But I'll be damned if I take it at face value.

I'll be looking into the boy's paternity myself. And into the circumstances surrounding Carlton Bishop's death. This is all just too perfectly put together. Too perfectly timed. And I don't buy it. Not one word of it.

## 32

## JERICHO

"Where is the DNA report?" I ask Hildebrand. Zeke, the councilor, Julia and I are in his private office not twenty minutes after the announcement.

"Everything is in order, Mr. St. James," Hildebrand says. I bet he's secretly pleased by this development. The St. James's are not natural born Sovereign Sons. This development secures the Bishop's inheritance and effectively nullifies any right mine and Isabelle's child may have to it.

If it's true.

And that's a big fucking if.

"With all due respect, Councilor, I'd like to study it myself." I glance to Julia who is watching me from a few feet away. She has her arms folded across her chest and looks like the cat who swallowed the fucking canary.

Hildebrand settles himself into his seat. "I understand your concern, but I can assure you—"

I slam my fist onto his desk. "I don't give a fuck what you assure. I don't buy it. Carlton Bishop has been unable to produce an heir with four wives. Four! You're telling me he fucked his cousin and magically impregnated her?"

"Brother," Zeke lays a hand on my shoulder. I shrug it off.

Hildebrand leans back in his seat but it's not out of fear of me. "Stand down, Mr. St. James or I'll have you taken to a cell to cool off."

"Jericho," Zeke says close to my ear. "Calm down."

I suck in a tight breath and glance to Julia who is watching in that calculated way, her features completely under her control, face giving nothing away.

"I'd like to see the report," I tell Hildebrand. "And run my own tests to corroborate this happy news." There is nothing happy in my tone.

"Do you think we haven't done that?" he asks. "Investigated Ms. Bishop's claim?"

"Doesn't hurt to have a second opinion, does it? If only to confirm there was no contamination." That last part I say with a glance to Julia.

Hildebrand studies me, glances to Julia, then turns back to me. "Ms. Bishop came to me in strictest confidence with what sounded to me at first an impossible tale," he starts. I wonder if she sucked his wrinkled old dick to get him to even hear her out. "This was several weeks ago and without Carlton Bishop's knowledge. Their affair, as you can imagine, would be...frowned upon. Cousin or not, he was a married man after all."

"In the midst of divorcing his wife," Julia adds.

"Married none the less and we'll still be discussing that sin, Ms. Bishop. I advise you to keep quiet." He turns back to me. "Of course, for the sake of transparency, I'll have the reports and samples sent to a lab you name, Mr. St. James. I don't anticipate you'll find anything other than what we did. When you don't, I'll of course expect you to apologize to Ms. Bishop for your behavior at this unfortunate time for her family."

Julia snorts.

"By the way, I hear your wife is pregnant. Congratulations."

It takes all I have and my brother's hand on my shoulder to not tell him to fuck off.

"Of course, I hope you will show grace as you accept that the Bishop boy displaces your as of yet unborn child in the line to inherit the Bishop estate in whole."

"If it's true," I add, my mind working on how I'll get fresh samples to the lab.

"I need to get back to my son," Julia says, stepping forward. "I'm sure he has questions about his father's sudden absence from his life."

"Understandable. I'll be in touch once arrangements have been made for the service," Hildebrand tells her.

"Thank you for your help, Councilor, and your discretion. It has been a tumultuous few years, but I am glad, with Carlton gone, that I came to you when I did."

"Convenient timing," I mutter.

"St. James," Hildebrand warns.

"No, it's all right," Julia Bishop says and turns to me. "I understand how disappointing such an announcement must be to one who bought his place into the upper echelon of The Society. I'm sure he hoped to climb the ladder using my family as rungs to be stepped upon." Her lips turn down into a sneer at the end.

"Perhaps you can learn from Ms. Bishop and muster some grace," Hildebrand says, standing. "Julia, my driver will take you and the boy home."

"Thank you, Councilor," she says and now I'm sure there was some dick sucking involved here.

She shifts her gaze to me. "Mr. St. James. I do hope you'll allow my cousin to attend her half-brother's funeral."

"Don't you dare," I start but she cuts me off.

"Surely you wouldn't deny her that in her own time of need."

I take a step toward her. "This is not over."

"Isn't it?"

## 33

## ISABELLE

I don't see Jericho until late that night. He and Zeke walk into the house after ten o'clock and they both look like shit. Like they've been through an ordeal.

"Where have you been?" I ask. I've been waiting for them.

Zeke pours them each a whiskey and they stand at the mantle by the large fireplace.

"What's happened?"

Zeke looks at me, then turns to his brother. "I'll see you in the morning."

Jericho nods to him, swallows half his tumbler of whiskey and shifts his gaze to me. He leans one arm on the mantle.

"What is it?" I ask, going to him, all but forgetting about what I thought I saw in the woods.

He takes a deep breath in, exhales and drains his

glass. After setting it down on the mantle he steps toward me. "Carlton Bishop is dead."

It takes me a minute. I hear the words almost slowly, give a shake of my head and shift my gaze to the fire, then back up to him.

"What did you say?"

"Bishop's dead. Had a heart attack while fucking one of the courtesans at the Cat House. Allegedly."

"I'm sorry. Can you back up a minute?"

"Fuck." He pushes his hand into his hair, looking away for a long moment before returning his attention to me. "IVI went into lockdown this afternoon. It will remain that way until morning. I assume the Cat House will remain closed for now."

"The Cat House, that's the…"

"Whore house."

"He had a heart attack while he was there?"

"Allegedly."

"What do you mean?"

"I'll be conducting my own investigation."

I drop into one of the armchairs and try to process. "Carlton's dead?"

"Hildebrand called us in this afternoon to tell us. You were in your lesson and I didn't want to interrupt. We were all there, all the Sovereign Sons. As well as Julia Bishop and her son."

My gaze snaps to his. "Julia? Why?"

"Your resourceful cousin had been meeting with Hildebrand for some time."

"What are you talking about?"

"She claims Mathew is Carlton Bishop's son."

My mouth falls open.

"They'd allegedly been having an affair for years. Being first cousins, a marriage would not be sanctioned, and so they kept it all hush-hush. This is all according to Julia Bishop of course. No one to corroborate her story."

"Matty is Carlton's son?"

"Unverified as far as I'm concerned."

"But there's some proof? Surely Councilor Hildebrand would want some proof."

Jericho quiets at this.

"Jericho?"

"DNA tests. I'll be conducting my own. That bitch is a liar and possibly a murderer."

"No, Jericho, she's—"

"Stop being naïve, Isabelle!"

I'm taken aback by his tone, but I see he regrets it too.

"Carlton's dead," I say. "He's dead. And if they were together all these years, she's probably beside herself with grief. Especially given the circumstances of his death. I mean, he was with another woman?"

"Multiple. And a man. Some sort of orgy, I assume, and these others witnessed him literally drop dead."

"Oh my God. How's Matty?"

"She brought him in there like he is a fucking puppet. Kid was scared."

"She brought him where?"

"Into the meeting where Hildebrand announced Bishop's death and welcomed the boy into the fold of Sovereign Sons. Fuck. I need another drink." He pours himself another whiskey.

"Carlton's dead." I rub my face. It's not that I feel sad. Not yet. I'm in shock. I stand up. "Julia needs me, Jericho. I need to go to her. She's alone apart from Matty."

His eyebrows rise high on his forehead and he looks at me like I'm insane. "I don't think so, sweetheart. Go upstairs. I need to think."

"What?" I walk toward him. "No. I won't be sent to my room like a child. My half-brother is dead."

He steps to me, standing up to his full height. I have to crane my neck to look up at him unless I back away which I don't.

"Your half-brother who is responsible for your brother's death. For the attack on you. Not to mention others. And that bitch is in it up to her eyeballs. I promise you that."

"You're being unreasonable. He's dead. And if Matty's his son, it doesn't matter anymore. The inheritance doesn't matter."

"This isn't just about an inheritance, Isabelle."

I take that step back. "I know that. It's about vengeance. *He's dead.* Will you let it go?"

"Let it go? He's the reason Angelique doesn't have a mother."

I have nothing to say to that and I hate the little nudge of selfishness at the mention of Kimberly. But I shake my head. We can't have this discussion. Not tonight. Possibly not ever. "When is the funeral?"

"Doesn't matter. You won't be attending."

"Yes, I will!"

"No, Isabelle you won't."

"Jericho, please! My half-brother is dead. My cousin is alone. Not to mention her four-year-old son who loves me. Whom I love. He sees me as an aunt, Jericho. I need to be there for them."

"She tried to kill you."

"I don't believe that. I can't. Don't you see?"

"For fuck's sake, Isabelle. Open your fucking eyes."

"I'm going to the funeral. And I'm going to see Julia. This can be over, Jericho. Don't you want it to be over? Isn't it time for us all to put it behind us? We're having a baby. You and I are bringing a child into this world. If we can choose whether to raise the child in love or hate, why would we ever choose hate?"

He doesn't answer right away, just drinks and looks at me. I think of what Julia said. Treating me with kid gloves. Turning my head, making me believe anything he wants. The kid gloves are half off, I think. This turn of events will force Jericho's hand.

"If Matty is the heir, it will change things," I say.

"That's a big if."

"It will change everything, Jericho." Everything between us. It will lay the truth bare. I'm not sure I'm ready.

"It changes nothing." His phone rings and he digs it out of his pocket, looks at the screen. "Go to bed, Isabelle. I need to take this."

I put my hand to my stomach. I know it's early and it's probably in my mind, but I swear I feel the beginnings of a swelling belly. I look at him as he answers his call, eyes on me as he listens to what the person has to say. He signals for me to go upstairs and turns his back to me, walking toward his office, out of earshot, leaving me standing there alone.

## 34

### ISABELLE

Jericho doesn't come to bed that night and the following morning when I go downstairs, I'm told he's in his office and is not to be disturbed.

I sit with Leontine while Angelique plays with her dolls in one corner of the library.

"You know what happened?" I ask her.

She nods. "Zeke filled me in earlier this morning."

"He says he won't let me go to the funeral."

"Why would you want to? He wasn't a good man and you know that. My son has your best interests at heart, Isabelle," she says, eyes on Angelique. "Jericho will protect his family. He learned the hard way what that protection has to look like." She turns back to me. "And you *are* his family. You're carrying his child."

"Does he even want this baby now that he knows Matty is the heir?"

"What kind of question is that? A child is a child." I feel guilty as soon as she says it. "You'll have that child. A little brother or sister to Angelique. There's no question about that, Isabelle. The child will be born."

"That's not what I meant," I hurry to correct.

"Really? What did you mean then?" she asks squarely, tone harsher.

"I just... I didn't mean I didn't want to have it."

Jericho enters the room just then and my heartbeat ramps up when his gaze falls on me. He's still wearing the same suit he had on yesterday and he looks like he hasn't slept. "Mother, please take Angelique to her room," he says, eyes locked on me.

Leontine looks from her son to me, then gets to her feet and goes to Angelique. "Come, Angelique, let's play in your room." She leads her out by the hand and I stand up as Jericho closes and locks the door behind them.

"You didn't come to bed—"

"What were you saying to my mother?" he asks, cutting me off.

"Were you listening at the door?"

"What did you say about the baby."

"Nothing. She misunderstood."

He steps toward me, eyes narrowing. "What did she misunderstand?"

"Nothing. Why are you being like this with me?" I sit back down and pull my knees up to my chest. "Will I never be accepted in this house? Will I always be under suspicion?"

"Isabelle," he says my name like a sigh. He sits down beside me and takes my face in his hands. I'm sure I look like death. "Did you sleep last night?"

"I was waiting for you. I needed to talk to you."

"There are a lot of things I need to take care of. You shouldn't have waited for me. You need to take care of yourself and the baby now."

I study him, searching his eyes. They're full of secrets. I touch his face. "You told me to trust you. To choose you. I am. But this has to be a two-way street. You're not choosing me, Jericho."

His eyes soften at that and he pulls me onto his lap. "I do choose you. I want you. That hasn't changed. But what's happened, the timing of it, it's too convenient. And it's not you I don't trust. It's her."

"What do you think she did? Cause his heart attack?"

He doesn't answer.

"Oh my God, you do. Are you being serious?" I push off his lap and stand.

"There are ways. You're too innocent to comprehend those ways, Isabelle."

"Do you mean too stupid?"

"I mean what I said. Innocent. You're good. She's

not." He stops, shakes his head. "I always say the wrong thing, don't I?"

I don't say anything.

He stands up. "I don't want you hurt. That's what this comes down to."

"I won't be hurt. You'll protect me. Just don't do it by locking me up and throwing away the key."

"I'm trying." He draws in a deep breath and exhales. "I had a call from Hildebrand's secretary a few minutes ago."

"The Councilor?"

He nods. "Seems your cousin has some information she came across while clearing out Carlton's desk. She's just a fountain of insights these days, isn't she?"

"What information?" I ask, ignoring the dig.

"We'll need to go to the compound to hear it."

"We?"

"You and me. He wants us both there."

"Or you wouldn't tell me."

"Your safety is my priority."

"How exactly do you think I'd be unsafe?"

"Like I said, Isabelle, I don't trust her. She wants something."

"What could she want?"

"In this case I can take a guess."

"Care to enlighten me?"

"I requested a second autopsy."

I'm confused.

"She'll want to block it. That's the reason for this coincidental timing of the revelation she's about to spring on us."

"Why do you want a second autopsy? What did the first one prove?"

"Heart attack."

I throw my hands into the air. "What do you think a second one will reveal exactly? He had a heart attack. There were witnesses. A coroner said so."

He stands, checks his watch. "We're expected within the hour."

"I guess the conversation's over then. Because you get to decide when our conversations are over. This isn't a partnership. This is a dictatorship."

He cocks his head. "Who told you it was a part-nership?"

"You're fucking unbelievable, you know that?" I turn to walk away but he grabs my arm.

"I'm trying, Isabelle."

"Try harder!"

His hand squeezes and I see the effort it takes him to ease up. But he does. And forces a tight breath. "She'll ask that my autopsy request be denied. Mark my words."

"And then you'll win?"

"No, Isabelle. I lost a long time ago. There is no winning when you're playing this sort of game.

There's remembering the dead. There's avenging them."

"What about the living? What happens to the living?" My eyes fill up with tears.

He lets me go, turns away and wraps his hand around the back of his neck. He's under pressure. And he's losing control.

"Jericho," I say, touching a hand to his shoulder. But before I can continue, he turns to me.

"Did you eat breakfast?"

Again, the conversation is over. "Not yet."

"You'll eat while I shower and change." He walks to the door, opens it, and waits for me.

I follow, stop in front of him. "What are you thinking happened to Carlton, Jericho? Why a second autopsy really? Tell me. Trust me enough to tell me."

"Heart attacks can be induced. Unless you know to look for the signs, you'll miss them. The Society has a dark history with poisons and your cousin is full of surprises these days."

## 35

## JERICHO

Isabelle is quiet but anxious on the drive to the compound. I'd prefer not to take her. Honestly, I'd like nothing better than to do what she said. Lock her up in the house until this threat passes. Because Julia Bishop is a threat. Perhaps a bigger one than I at first imagined. But Isabelle won't believe me and with Carlton Bishop's death, she has that much more sympathy for her cousin.

We arrive at the compound and are escorted to Hildebrand's office where Julia Bishop is already sitting, dressed in black from head to toe. A pantsuit this time that must have been tailor-made to her body. When she sees Isabelle, she rushes to her. The way the two embrace I wonder if Isabelle has heard a word I've said.

Hildebrand stands behind his desk and one of his men closes the office door.

"Are you doing okay?" Isabelle asks Julia who looks the part of grieving lover when I see her face. Less makeup. Eyes puffy. "How is Matty?"

"We'll be fine. It was a shock and I wish it didn't happen the way it did but..." she trails off, shrugging her shoulders.

"You two were together?"

"He didn't want to tell anyone. Not even you. I'm sorry I kept it from you. It was just, well, you know how people would be."

"I know, but I wouldn't."

"Because you're good," Julia says, pulling back, glancing at me beyond Isabelle's shoulder. "How are *you*?" she tilts her head, touches a subtle hand to Isabelle's stomach.

"I'm fine," Isabelle says, uncomfortable as she glances at me. My eyes are narrowed on Julia's hand. "The baby's fine," she adds. The comment seems out of place. An odd thing to say.

Julia studies her a beat too long. "You're sure it's what you want?" she asks, the way she asks, it's strange. Vague.

"I'm sure." Isabelle takes her hand and squeezes it.

Hildebrand clears his throat and the two move apart. Isabelle comes to stand beside me. I wrap a hand around the back of her neck.

"Coffee? Tea?" Hildebrand asks when his secretary enters carrying a large silver tray.

"Let's just get to it, shall we?" I gesture for Isabelle to sit in one of the empty chairs and take the seat beside her. I cross one ankle over the opposite knee and lean back. "I'm dying to hear of this next earth-shattering revelation."

Julia moves to the side of the desk and looks at Hildebrand with unsure eyes. I watch her.

"Go on," Hildebrand says, patting her hand. I have a visual of her on her knees at his feet sucking his old dick. I throw up a little in my mouth at the image.

She turns to us, looks at me first, then Isabelle, her features schooled perfectly to show concern. Uncertainty. Vulnerability even.

"I was going through some files in Carlton's desk and I came across something that seemed strange." She stops, focuses on Isabelle. "I don't want to hurt you, honey."

"What is it? You're scaring me," Isabelle says.

"I feel sick to say it," she says, turning to Hildebrand.

"I'm sure." I look to Hildebrand. "This is a waste of my time."

He puts up a hand for me to be patient. Julia clears her throat, sighs deeply.

"Danny Gibson's name was on a file in one of his drawers."

"Danny Gibson?" Isabelle asks and I know what Julia fucking Bishop is about to do. I know exactly.

And I have to admit. She's clever. More clever than I assumed.

She nods. "I was surprised. I mean, I thought at first he'd just tracked the trial or something but," she pauses, shakes her head, wipes away an imaginary tear. "It was a payment schedule."

I don't have to look at Isabelle to know her reaction. I feel it. I tried to tell her the same thing just days ago. It's just being confirmed. But Julia's going to put her own spin on things.

"He tried to... Danny Gibson being at your house wasn't an accident, Isabelle. Carlton wanted you out of the picture. He hired that man to do it."

I turn to Isabelle now who sits still as stone, and as pale.

"I'm sorry. I'm so sorry." Julia starts to cry and I have to admit, she's good. Isabelle is on her feet in an instant hugging her. Comforting her.

I watch from my seat, wrapping my left hand around the bruised knuckle of my right fist. I have to stop myself from attacking. Because I want to attack.

"He used my account at the charity to make the second payment. Used my name, Isabelle. I didn't know. I had no idea. I'm so sorry. I'm so, so sorry."

"It's not your fault. How could you know?" Isabelle is crying too and rubbing Julia's back.

When I turn to Hildebrand, he's watching me. "Well, it turns out Mr. Bishop wasn't very smart if he left a paper trail. Considering his other offenses, I'm not sure at all whether this funeral service should be held at the cathedral. If he were alive and Ms. Bishop came to me with this, the Tribunal would have no choice but to take action." It's bullshit because he could have done that with the information I had on Bishop. But he is also playing a part. Covering his ass.

"He's dead now," Julia says. "And it would only bring shame on us. On his son and myself. So, I'm asking for leniency, Councilor. I'm asking that this information be kept between us. There's nothing to be gained by going public either within The Society or outside of it. Christian is dead. Carlton is dead. There's just you and me, Isabelle. And Matty." She tacks on her son's name as if it were an afterthought.

I could mention her visit to Danny Gibson's brother but decide to keep it under my hat. Let her think I don't know. I'm curious if Isabelle will give it away. She doesn't want it to be true. I watch my wife.

"You're right. We don't want anyone else hurt by what he did," Isabelle says.

"Thank you." Julia squeezes Isabelle's hand. "I loved him. Through it all, I loved him."

Isabelle smiles warmly. My sweet wife. She is no match for this pariah.

I get to my feet and draw Isabelle to my side, keeping her close.

"You said you had a request for coming forward

with this information. Surely keeping it quiet isn't all you want."

Julia's gaze is cooler when it falls on me. I wonder if Isabelle sees that. She glances to Hildebrand then back to me. She licks her lips before speaking.

"I ask you to withdraw your request for a second autopsy," she says.

I want to look at Isabelle. See her face. But I don't. And I want to smile the victor's smile. But I won't. Because I meant what I said to Isabelle earlier. This isn't about winning. There can be no winner.

"Why would I do that?" I ask.

Isabelle remains conspicuously quiet. I wonder if Julia is expecting her to jump to her defense.

"Well," Julia says, faltering as she glances from me to Isabelle to Hildebrand. I get the feeling she was counting on Isabelle to take her side. "There's no sense in dragging us all through that, is there? Delaying the funeral. Making people wonder why. Asking questions."

I shrug my shoulders. "I could give a fuck."

"What about my son. Do you give a fuck about him?" she snaps.

"Do you?" I ask.

She looks appropriately affronted.

"Mr. St. James," Hildebrand starts, stands. "Perhaps we should leave what little dignity Mr. Bishop has left intact."

"What dignity would that be?" I ask him. "He died fucking a whore while his supposed beloved, the mother of his child, was at home warming his bed. Or at least that's what I'm being told I should believe," I address her with this last part.

Hildebrand clears his throat. "There's no need for cruelty, St. James."

"I didn't have to share this information," Julia says, appealing to Isabelle. "But I wanted to make an effort. For our families' sakes. For Matty." She turns to me. "For Angelique."

My jaw tightens at the mention of my daughter. I quickly consider something. I think maybe it would be a good idea to send Angelique away for a little while. Until this is finished. Until Julia Bishop is no longer a threat.

"What are you afraid of?" I ask. "What do you think will be discovered?"

"Nothing. Of course. It's just a waste of time. I'd like to put this behind myself and my son and start over. God knows Matty deserves that. Doesn't he, Isabelle?"

"He does," Isabelle says and takes Julia's hand. "But for there to be peace between our families, and there must be because we are joined for better or for worse, all of us, let Jericho have his second autopsy. And when nothing is discovered, then it will be behind us. All suspicions erased."

Julia looks at her with a moment of what I swear

is hate on her face. Does Isabelle see it? It's there and gone in a split second. Then Julia smiles, nods.

"You're right, cousin. You're right."

She meets my eyes momentarily and I wonder if she sees the small upward curving of my lip. That's for her eyes only. The autopsy is scheduled for tomorrow. And my wife is on my side. Now those are victories. Especially the latter.

I squeeze Isabelle's hand.

## 36

## ISABELLE

I'm wrapped up in my own thoughts on the way home and once we're back, Jericho goes into his office. I place a notebook and pencil into my backpack, pull on an oversized sweater and walk to the chapel.

I need to be alone. To think.

There's just one thing that doesn't add up.

Once I'm at the cemetery I can't help my glance to Nellie's grave marker. The shovel is gone and the ground doesn't look disturbed. I look in the direction of where I'd seen what I thought was the end of a cigarette, but the sun is shining and there's no one out here.

I walk into the chapel and replace the tea light in front of Christian's photo. I then take a seat on the front pew, resting the notebook on my knees, my feet on the seat. I tug the sweater closer. There's always a chill here. All that stone never warming up. I open my notebook and hold my pencil, but can only stare at the blank page as I think. As I go over what happened at Councilor Hildebrand's office again.

What Julia said makes sense. Maybe it was all Carlton. It fits. It would work. He hired Danny Gibson to hurt me.

No.

Not just hurt me but to kill me. To ensure the inheritance wouldn't go to me or to any child I would bear in the future.

Christian paid the heaviest price for his greed. I don't feel sad for the loss of Carlton. I don't feel it as a loss. And I don't know what that says about me but it's the truth.

The way Carlton paid Gibson. Using Julia's account. Her name. He could easily do that. It's absolutely possible and even without questioning it, I'm still here. Still trying to line things up.

There are two things about today that have me thinking.

Jericho claimed that Julia had gone to see Gerald Gibson, Danny's brother, the night she left me at the theater. He claimed the van that almost ran me over was in his garage.

He didn't bring it up today. He could have confronted Julia, but he didn't.

So, does that mean he's lying? That he lied about Gerald Gibson? Is there even a Gerald Gibson?

But if Gerald Gibson does exist and if Julia went to him after seeing me at the theater, then what he's saying is true. Because she claimed to only have discovered the truth about Carlton's connection to Danny Gibson in the last day or two.

If she's lying about that, then she was involved in Christian's death. In the attempt on my life. Because it wasn't an accident. I think some part of me always knew that.

I shake my head and doodle in a corner of the page. She and Jericho have one thing in common. They both think I'm a good person. But I get the feeling when they say that what they mean is that I'm not very smart. Because I know the level Jericho is playing at. And if Julia's playing on the same field, well, I am nothing more than a pawn to them both. And the knowledge hurts.

The door opens then, startling me, and I turn to find Jericho exhaling when he sees me. He smiles as if relieved and I sit up, close the notebook.

"There you are," he says.

"What did you think? That I ran away?"

He raises his chin just a hair at my comment and steps inside, closing the door behind him.

"With all the guards on the property I doubt I'd get to the front gate."

He walks to my pew, lifts my legs and sits down beside me. He's hooking my legs over his lap and looking straight ahead at Christian's photo and the candle burning on the altar.

"Do you want to run away?" he asks, surprising me with the question.

I study his profile, the hard, uncompromising line of his jaw. The straight nose. The little bit of graying hair at his temple. He turns to me, and my heart skips a beat. He's so beautiful especially when he lets me see him. When he lets me see into his soul.

My eyes mist and I shake my head.

I want this thing between us to be true. To be real. I want him to mean what he said. That he wants me. No matter what. I want him to choose me because I have chosen him. He's a part of me. Inside of me. Inside my heart.

And he can break mine. Does he know how easily he can break mine?

"Why didn't you confront Julia about her visit to Gerald Gibson?" I ask.

"Why didn't you? That's the more interesting question, don't you think?"

I sigh, rotating to put my feet on the ground, to face the small, flickering flame. "I don't know."

"Yes, you do. I've underestimated you."

I turn to him. He smiles a weary smile.

"Her story was good," he says. "Believable. She's clever."

NATASHA KNIGHT

"Like you," I say. "I don't think I'm as clever as either of you."

"You are. And you're kind, Isabelle. That's something neither of us are."

"But I'm not clever."

"You are."

I shrug. I'm not saying it for him to feel sorry for me. I'm saying it because it's the truth.

"Does that mean you believe me about her?" he asks.

I look down at the closed notebook on my lap. I've had it forever. I keep all my notebooks with their random doodles and notes and poems and anything else that makes me feel.

I turn to face him. "What happens if your autopsy doesn't reveal anything else?"

"It will."

"What if it doesn't? What then?"

He grits his jaw, looks away.

"And what if your DNA test proves what Julia claims. That Matty is Carlton's son and the rightful heir to the Bishop throne."

"Throne." He snorts.

"What will you do, Jericho? What happens then?"

He sighs, turns to me. "I'm sending Angelique away with my mother and Dex. You should come in and say goodbye." He stands.

"Why?" I ask, standing too. Surprised by this

turn of events.

"Because I trust my instincts."

"For how long?"

"Don't know. Until this plays out. Until Julia Bishop makes her move."

"What if there is no move to be made?"

"There is, Isabelle. You can trust me on that one. There is."

The door swings open then, and we both turn to find Leontine in the doorway, an expression on her face I haven't seen before. She's flushed and out of breath.

"What is it?" Jericho asks, instantly on alert as he rushes to her.

She looks at me over his shoulder in a way I don't quite understand. Not right away. Although I've never really had a great read on Leontine, I know she wants what's best for Jericho and Angelique. I thought as far as Angelique was concerned, she knew of my love for her. She knows we want the same thing. Jericho and I, well, we're more complicated.

"Mother?" Jericho asks, giving her a small shake.

She drags her gaze from me and doesn't say anything. I realize she must be showing him something because Jericho looks down. There's a moment of heavy silence before she finally speaks as they separate. Jericho turns to me studying whatever it is he has taken from her hands.

"Angelique found them. She wanted to surprise Isabelle with a drawing she'd made. She was hiding the drawings in Isabelle's room. I didn't realize or I wouldn't have allowed her in there, of course. But they were in her violin case. Hidden in a pocket."

I feel the ground beneath my feet shake or maybe that's my knees wobbling as a wave of cold makes me shudder and sweat at once.

I know what she found.

And I can guess what they are thinking.

When Jericho drags his gaze from the packets in his hand to me, I feel myself back up a step. My mouth falls open. I want to explain. To tell him I never intended to use them. Tell him I'd forgotten about them. But no sound comes. Just my mouth opening and closing like a fish out of water.

"Go." His voice is low and dark. It's how he sounds when he's the angriest.

"I..." I start but nothing else comes.

"I said go." The command is for Leontine but he's looking at me.

"Should I have Angelique wait? She'll want to say goodbye—"

"Make up an excuse. I won't be letting her near my daughter."

My hands are clammy as the notebook and pencil drop to the ground. An audible breath comes from me. The sound of dread.

"Jericho," Leontine starts. "Perhaps—"

"Get out!"

She glances once at me then hurries out. Leaving me alone with him. My husband. My devil.

"I wasn't... I forgot." I shake my head, push a trembling hand into my hair. I swallow hard to gain some control over my vocal cords. "Jericho—"

He's on me in an instant, hand around my throat, pushing me backward, bending me at a painful angle over the altar. I'd scream if I could, but I can't inhale any air. I grip his forearm but he's too strong and he's too angry.

"You fucking liar!" He brings his fist with the pills in front of my face, crushing them, the packaging bending, pills popping out of their pockets. "You fucking liar!"

I slap at his face, scratching it. He eases his grip on my throat enough that I gulp down air. He captures my wrist to stop my attack and leans over me, face so close to mine I feel his breath. Feel the rage in his eyes, the abyss behind them.

"You would have killed my baby?"

"No," I croak, gasping for breath. "No!" If he'd just let me explain. If he'd let me tell him what happened. I forgot about them. It's true. I forgot they were even there.

"Have you taken any?"

"I can't—"

"Have you taken any!" he roars.

I try to shake my head, but I can't. I can't speak to

answer him either. I think this is it. I think he's going to kill me. Does he realize it? Does he realize how strong he is? How hard he's squeezing?

But just as my vision begins to fade, he's off me, his attention diverted. I drop to my knees and gasp for breath, clutching my throat as I try to breathe. Try to speak. To tell him.

"You'll kill her!"

I look up to see why he released me. To see who saved my life. Ezekiel. The brothers caught up in a whirl of fists and fury while I watch, helpless, powerless.

"She tried to kill my baby!" Jericho roars.

"No!" I scream. Or try to scream but my throat is too raw and it comes out a whisper. This is my baby too. Our baby. I wouldn't. I just forgot them. Forgot all about those pills.

In an instant Jericho is standing over me again and I scramble backward on my butt. He crouches down, fists a handful of hair, and tugs my head back.

"Where did you get them?"

"Jericho!" Zeke tries to dislodge him, but Jericho holds tight.

"Where?"

"You're going to hurt her you fucking idiot!" He yells but Jericho only has eyes for me. Only has rage for me. "The baby, Jericho. The baby. Think."

That makes him stop. Makes his hand loosen just a little. I'm sobbing. Terrified and sobbing.

"I wouldn't," I start but can't get enough air to get the words out. "I—" A sob has me hiccuping.

"Let her go, Jericho. Let her go and get yourself under control."

"I didn't... I wouldn't hurt..."

He lets me go, straightens to stand. They both look down at me, Ezekiel with concern, Jericho with hate.

"You have to believe me," I try. "I didn't take them."

"Up!" Jericho commands.

"I swear."

"Up!" he roars, gripping my hair and dragging me to my feet. I scream this time. I find enough breath and voice to scream as he drags me from the chapel, through the woods and into the house. Everything is a blur as I try to keep up, as I try to beg him to stop. To listen to me. To hear me out. But he won't hear. He can't.

When he unlocks that steel door, I think he's going to throw me down the stairs. Instead, he grips my arm and catches me as I stumble once, twice, dragging me down the hall away from the suicide room. To the one where I spent my first night in this house. He pushes me onto the bed with its creaking springs and steps away, rage barely controlled as his hands clench and unclench. I know if I wasn't pregnant, he'd kill me. I know it. I back into the farthest corner I can and grip the rungs of the headboard, sobbing.

"You'll stay here. You'll spend the rest of your wretched days here. You fucking liar. You fucking lying Bishop! And once you give me my baby, you'll go by way of Nellie Bishop. I'll bury you after I squeeze the breath out of you, you fucking deceitful bitch!"

My lips tremble as tears spill down my cheeks. My head hurts and my heart aches at his words.

He leans in close again and I scream once more.

"Stop it. Stop the fucking tears. You're a liar. You're a Bishop. I know the truth. I know you. And I won't be fooled again. Not as clever as us?" he snorts. "You with your sweet, innocent act. You're the worst of them!"

He reaches for me but Ezekiel grabs him from behind and drags him away. They're out of the room and into the corridor and all I hear are the words *think* and *baby*. It's Ezekiel who closes the door with one glance at me. I think it's Ezekiel who locks it. But at that point, it doesn't matter. Because it's over. I'm locked in and the room is so dark, but I can't even move to turn on the light. I can't stop myself shivering and can't make my legs work. As all sound vanishes and the air settles and I wish Zoë's ghost was here to keep me company. I wish Zoë's ghost was here so I wouldn't be so alone. So afraid.

## 37

# JERICHO

"You can't leave her down there."

I disconnect the call and look up at my brother. "Ever hear of knocking?" He's got a bruise along his temple. I have a matching one and a cut on the bridge of my nose to rival the one he has on his cheek.

"I'm serious, Jericho." He takes a seat. "She's pregnant. You don't want to endanger the baby."

"She'll be fine. She has shelter. I'll get her a blanket. She'll have food. What more does she need?"

"Sunlight? Fresh air? Not to feel terrified?"

I set my forearms on the desk and lean toward him. "She would have killed my baby. How do I know she hasn't tried? Maybe succeeded? Barnes will do a blood test so we'll know for sure."

"Did you see her face when you were attacking her?"

I sit back, lift my chin and keep my mouth shut. Because yes, I saw her face. In fact, I can't get it the fuck out of my head. That or the way my hand wrapped around her throat. The panic in her eyes when I squeezed.

How close I came to killing her.

"She's safest down there," I tell my brother, swiveling on the chair to get up and pour myself a whiskey from the sideboard.

"Safe from you?"

I drink it, push my hand into my hair, consider another.

"Haven't you had enough?" he asks.

I snort, pour another and look at him as I swallow it down.

He shakes his head. "At least get me one."

"That's the spirit," I say, pouring him one then resuming my seat behind the desk.

"At least talk to her. Hear her side then decide what you believe."

"She betrayed me."

"You don't know that."

"Yeah, I do. Pretty sure she got the pills from her cousin. Which is in and of itself a betrayal. I'd guess that happened the night they met at the concert. Hell, what do I know? Maybe it was planned all along."

"You know Isabelle, don't you? At least a little?"

I grin, drink a sip of whiskey. "She fooled me. Like any Bishop, she's a good liar."

"You don't believe that. I see it on your face."

"Then you need to get some glasses."

Zeke sighs. "Look, either you talk to her or I'm going to go down there and get her out myself."

"You will not go near my wife."

"Talk to her. You've let her sweat long enough."

"Will it get you off my back?"

He considers, nods.

"Fine." She betrayed me. After all that we talked about, all she asked, she betrayed me. Played me for a fucking fool. And the thought of it tightens something inside my gut. Inside my chest. Makes it fucking hard to breathe.

"I spoke with a couple people from The Cat House," Zeke says.

"And?"

"Carlton Bishop was fine. A little under the weather the few days prior but he'd said he was feeling better. They drank a lot. And when the activity began, he dropped dead."

"He'd been at lunch with Joseph Sawyer yesterday. Sawyer said he looked gray. Thought he was working through a bad cold."

"Did you instruct your man doing the autopsy what to look for? Unless he knows the signs, he won't find anything."

"Told him what I learned. Told him about the penchant Society folks have with poisons. He's good. Came highly recommended by the doctor who saved Santiago De La Rosa's life after he was poisoned."

Zeke nods.

"Should have preliminary results tomorrow."

"Angelique was pretty upset she couldn't say goodbye to Isabelle."

Shit. I push a hand into my hair again. What a mess this is. What a fucking disaster. "She'll have to get over it."

"She loves her, you know. Angelique loves Isabelle. She's the closest thing to a mother she's ever had."

I close my eyes. The thought hurts because some part of me thought Isabelle would be something like that to her. I never wanted her to replace Kimberly, but she was fast becoming someone I could trust with Angelique. Someone who loved her as much as I do. As much as Kimberly would have. Was that a lie too? Was she acting then too?

Zeke finishes his drink and gets to his feet. "Go downstairs. Talk to her. Get her out of the cellar, brother. I'm telling you, you're wrong about her. And you don't want to find that out too late."

I nod, set an elbow on the desk and put my forehead in my hand. What a shit show.

A few minutes after he's gone, someone knocks on my door.

"Yes?"

"It's Catherine sir," Catherine says and opens the door a crack. "The room's ready."

I get to my feet.

She hesitates.

"What is it?" I ask.

"Are you sure you want things this way? She's your wife. She's going to be the mother of your child."

I close my eyes.

"I'm sorry, sir. Just… Wouldn't feel right if I didn't speak out on this. I hate to see something terrible happen. Isabelle's a good girl."

"I don't pay you to speak out, do I?"

"No, sir." Her cheeks flush red and she hangs her head, walks out of the office.

Fuck.

I get up, go to the door. "Catherine. Wait."

She wipes her face with her apron before turning but I see how red her eyes are. God. I'm an asshole.

"I'm sorry. I didn't mean that."

She nods. Tries to smile. What must my own staff think I am? I know the answer to that. Isabelle has said it often enough. I'm a devil. Satan incarnate.

"Can you bring up some food for her please."

"Of course. I'll warm up some soup for her. She likes those dumplings. Keeps asking for them."

Why didn't I know this? "Thank you."

Catherine disappears toward the kitchen, and I walk down the corridor toward the cellar. I push the key into the lock, open the heavy door and begin my descent, unsure what I'm going to do just yet.

## 38

## JERICHO

S he's been down here for the whole of the afternoon. I unlock the bedroom door and open it to find her lying on the bed, asleep. I take a moment to watch her. She's small, curled into herself under the oversized sweater she had on. Her hair is matted to her face. She must have cried herself to sleep.

It takes all I have to steel myself against her. She looks so innocent. So incapable of doing what she's done.

She makes a sound as I watch. Her forehead wrinkles. I push the hair that's sticking to her face away. She's sweating.

I say her name quietly, but she doesn't wake up. She just makes that sound again. Like she's fighting something. Someone.

Danny Gibson comes to mind. Danny Gibson

on top of her. And I remember what she told me. How her nightmare isn't Christian being murdered but Gibson's near rape of her. Remember how she described what she felt in her nightmare years later.

"Isabelle," I say louder, and she rolls onto her back. She's moaning now, it's like an unbroken wailing sound.

"Wake up Isabelle." I put my hands on her shoulders, squeeze. "Wake up."

She blinks rapidly but then her hands come to my arms and she's trying to push me away. Does she think I'm him? Is she seeing his face?

"Isabelle, wake up. You're having a nightmare. Isabelle!" I give her one hard shake and release her when she bolts upright, sucking in a gasping breath, hands out in front of her as if to ward something or someone off.

I catch her arms, stop the momentum. It takes her a long minute to process where she is. To remember what happened. When she looks at me that same expression from earlier darkens her features. I remember her face when I had my hands around her neck. When I was choking her. But I shove the guilt away. She had those pills. She may have taken some of them. As far as I know, she has already miscarried.

But then her face softens, her forehead furrows and she hugs me.

And it takes me out of the moment completely. Out of my head.

"You came back for me," she says against my neck, fresh tears wet on my skin.

I don't know what to do as I feel her body surrender against mine, molding to mine. She hugs me tighter, pulling herself closer, repeating those same words. My arms move of their own accord and wrap around her. Instinct? No. More than that.

Want.

Need.

I hold onto her and try to process what the hell is happening. What I believe. What is true versus what I want to be true.

"I didn't take any. I never intended to. I should have flushed them down the toilet the night she gave them to me. I just forgot about them. So much has happened and I forgot."

She draws back and looks at me with those big, sad blue eyes. Like broken glass.

Shards of sharp, cutting glass.

She feels me stiffen. I see it in her eyes. See it in the way her forehead furrows, the way she curls into herself.

"But that's not why you came back, is it?" She hugs her arms around herself protectively.

"No."

"What do you want then?" She shivers, looks for the sweater that has slid off her.

I stand up, push my hands into my hair.

"I didn't take them," she starts as if we're still having that conversation. "I wasn't ever going to. You have to believe me. I wouldn't hurt our baby. I would never do that."

It takes all I have to swallow the lump in my throat. To harden my heart. Because when I see the look in her eyes, it fucks with me. It makes me want to take her into my arms and hold her and believe her.

*She's a Bishop. Remember that.*

"Stop talking and get up."

"Please, Jericho, you have to believe me. Please."

"I said stop talking and get up. I'll fucking gag you if you don't shut up."

"Why are you being like this?"

"I won't fall for your tears. Up. Last chance."

She slides across the bed and gets up, pushing her arms into her sweater.

"Walk."

She walks ahead of me all the way up to her bedroom where once she's inside, she stops. I close the door behind us and watch her as she looks around. Takes in the state of things. She turns to me.

"Where are my things?"

"You won't need them. But I thought this room would be more comfortable than the cellar, considering the child."

The room is stripped bare. Only her bed

remains. One pillow. No books. No clothes apart from essentials. Her violin. That is the one thing I will allow for her comfort.

She tests the door between our rooms. It's locked. She's no longer welcome in my bed.

On the desk is her violin case. She opens it, exhales in relief. She touches it, then turns to me and I see the tiniest spark of hope in her eyes.

"Did you order this?" she asks, gesturing around the room.

I nod.

"And this too?" she asks about the violin.

"Yes."

She walks toward me. I stand still as stone unsure what she's going to do. When she reaches up to touch my cheek, we both flinch at the spark of electricity.

"Then there's hope," she says and I'm more confused than I've ever been in my life.

She stands on tip toe and touches her lips to mine. I don't respond. I don't kiss her back. But I also don't push her away. I guess that encourages her because she kisses me again. Longer this time, holding my face with both hands.

I take her lower lip between my teeth, snaking my hand up her back and into her hair to hold her still as I bite down, drawing a cry from her. I taste the copper of blood.

She tries to draw back but I keep her close and

look down at her. "You want to be fucked? Is that what this is about?"

Her mouth opens but before she can speak, I close mine over it, walking her to the bed. I spin her and hold her back to my chest as I slide one hand down to undo the button and zipper of her jeans. Bending her over the foot of the bed, I push her jeans and panties down.

"Jericho—"

"Stay." I place my knee on her lower back to pin her and undo my belt, my slacks.

She turns her head to watch and doesn't fight me. I grip her ass and lift her hips a little, splaying her open to see her. All of her.

I'm not gentle when I take her. Take what's mine.

Isabelle gasps, fists the blanket, her body stiffening.

"You want to be fucked?" I repeat, thrusting into her. "You think you can turn my head? I'm not so simple as that but I will oblige you only to take what I want from you."

I nudge her knees apart and fuck her hard, forcing the breath from her with each thrust, laying myself over her as sweat collects along my forehead.

She tries to turn her head, but I grip a handful of hair to stop her. I don't want her eyes on me. I won't be able to do this if I see her eyes.

"Not like this," she says. "Please."

I bite the curve of her neck bring my cheek to

hers as I near my finish. She's meeting my thrusts, arms curled back so she can hold onto me.

"Please, Jericho. Kiss me. Please kiss me."

"Fuck." I tilt her head back, kissing the corner of her mouth. When I loosen my grip on her hair, she turns to kiss me like she wants and that takes me over the edge. That is the thing that has me moaning as I release, giving her all my weight. I spend my seed before we slide to our knees on the floor, me crowding her back, panting. Her turning herself so she's curled into me.

"I love you," she whispers into my chest, my neck. Her hands on my face. "Do you know that I love you? Devil or not, St. James or not, baby or not, I love you."

I look down at her earnest face, her huge eyes, small hands holding onto me as if afraid to lose me.

"And I'd never hurt our baby. How can I hurt a piece of you?"

She smiles a small, sad smile. I try to process her words, a part of me wanting to see the lies. The liar. But I don't. I see Isabelle. I see the Isabelle my own heart has been growing more and more tender for. And I want to believe her like I've never wanted to believe anything before.

"You know that though," she says. "I know you do. You won't lock me up in here. You won't."

I close my eyes. Force her face from my mind. Remember the pills. Remember my rage. But it's getting harder and harder. I pull free of her and get to my feet, zipping my slacks, leaving her on the floor with her jeans tangled around her ankles.

"Jericho?"

Shit. I need to think. I take a step to the door. Stop. Turn back to her.

"Was it the same one?" I ask, not sure why I care.

"Same one?" She's confused.

"The nightmare. Downstairs. Was it Gibson?"

She blinks, her expression changing, worry etching a fine line in the space between her eyebrows. She pulls her knees up, wraps her arms around them and shakes her head, shifting her gaze down.

"What was it then?"

It takes her a minute before she answers, and I can see whatever it was terrified her.

"Tell me," I push.

She looks back up at me. "The grave. The place next to Nellie's. It was dug up. It was ready for me."

Fuck.

Jesus.

I push my hands into my hair. Squeeze my eyes shut.

Fuck!

"It's just a dream, isn't it?" she asks, voice small. "You're not going to do that to me, are you?"

I look at her. I can't help it. It's a mistake though. I know how fucked I am when my chest tightens and

I can't breathe. When it takes all I have to turn away from her. To walk the hell out of that room. Because after all of it, all that's happened, I can't do that to her. Not even close. I'd kill anyone who tried. Because I love her, too. I fucking love her.

## 39

## ISABELLE

I see the empty space where he stood. Hear the lock turn on the door. I shudder, looking down at myself. My jeans and panties around my ankles, my inner thighs and between my legs wet with him.

My chest aches and even though my stomach growls with hunger, I don't think I could eat right now.

I force myself to my feet, slip off the jeans and panties and walk into the bathroom. My gaze lands on the violin and I remind myself there's hope in the fact that he left my violin. If he hated me, he'd have taken that from me. If he hated me, he'd have smashed it to bits and left the pieces for me to find.

I walk into the bathroom and close the door behind me, strip off the rest of my things and switch on the shower. I need to warm up. I'm cold from the inside. I step beneath the flow and stand there for an eternity.

My mind is working hard to process what just happened. I told him I love him and I'm painfully aware that he didn't say the words back. That he looked lost. Confused. Not at all the devil I've come to love.

I move through the motions of washing my hair, my body. I look down at my stomach. It's still flat. I lay both hands over it. I meant what I said. I would never hurt this baby. And the fact that it's his, that it's a piece of him, just makes me feel even more tenderness toward him or her. I think it's going to be all right. It has to be. It will take time for him to trust me, and I understand that. I have to. But we will be all right. He and I. And we'll be a family, all of us.

Strange that I can't imagine a life without Jericho or Angelique in it. All I feel at the thought is emptiness.

My mind wanders to Julia. To how she gave me the pills intending for me to abort this child. Wanders to what she told us in Hildebrand's office about Carlton and his role in Christian's death. She seemed so earnest. So upset.

But she never mentioned Gerald Gibson. And neither did Jericho. It's the one piece that gives me pause.

When I switch off the water, I hear humming in the other room. I wrap a towel around myself. It's

Catherine. I smile and walk into the bedroom to find her laying a table for me. Well, it's a roll-in table she's set at the window. She's arranging a single, bright red Gerber daisy in a small glass vase.

"There you are, dear," she says when she sees me. "I hope you don't mind that I came in while you were showering. The soup's warm and I thought you'd be hungry." She's trying to smile but her expression falters. She knows what he did. Where I've been. I'm sure the whole household knows.

I feel myself blush, embarrassed at it. At his treatment of me. At my powerlessness.

"Thank you," I say, pushing through the emotions. "I am always hungry for your soup and dumplings."

"I brought extra," she says. "You need to eat for two now. And there's some juice and a small dessert." She lifts the lid on a plate with a hunk of chocolate cake on it.

"Small?" I ask, moving toward the table.

"Well, like I said, it's for two and we need to put some meat on your bones. You're too skinny if I may say so."

"I just haven't felt well," I say as she opens a dresser drawer and takes out some clothes for me. She's almost like a grandmother to me. Always kind and looking after me like she cares about me.

"Now you get dressed and sit down to eat. If

you'd like anything else, you just let me know, all right?"

"This is perfect, thank you so much, Catherine."

She smiles, looks like she wants to say more but then nods and leaves. I hear the lock turn. Sighing, I get dressed and I sit down to eat. I watch the lights come on out on the patio, the pool lit up, red leaves scattering in the cool breeze. Fall has properly arrived.

I avoid looking into the woods. I'm nervous I'll see that cigarette light again although I know that would be a stretch from up here. I should tell Jericho. I will the next time I see him.

But I don't see him for the next three days. Catherine delivers my meals, three a day, but other than her I don't see anyone. I don't even know if Jericho sleeps in his room, it's so quiet but I remember it's sound proofed. Even when I press my ear to the door, I hear nothing.

And I miss him. When I ask Catherine if he's home, she gives me vague answers and I can see she's uncomfortable, so I've stopped asking. I wonder when Carlton's funeral will be or if it's already been and past. I wonder about the autopsy and the DNA testing for Matty. Is he really Carlton's son?

As I sit by the window and play my violin, I think about Christian. I may not be able to go to his grave on the anniversary of his death this year. It will be the first time since he died if that happens.

It's just as I'm thinking about that, that I hear the lock on my door followed by a knock. I turn, surprised. I just had lunch so it's not Catherine.

"Isabelle?" Ezekiel asks, knocking again.

"Come in," I say, standing.

He walks into the room, takes in the surroundings. It looks so bare. Nothing on the walls, the bookshelves. Like a prison. It is a prison after all.

I move to put the violin in its case. It's good he sees it. Because this isn't right. I don't deserve to be locked up in here and I'm glad Ezekiel bears witness.

He clears his throat. "How are you holding up?"

I close the case and turn to him, shrug a shoulder. "How much longer will he keep me in here?"

His jaw tenses. They have these little tells, the brothers. If you watch them closely enough you get to know them. They're so similar in some of their traits.

"I haven't talked to him in a few days," he says. "He has a lot on his mind."

"The autopsy or the DNA test?"

"Both."

"What's going on? Has Carlton been buried?"

"Service is this evening."

"So the autopsy is over?"

He nods.

"The result?"

"I don't know that just yet."

"Would you tell me if you did?"

"I'm not sure, honestly," he answers after a moment, and I appreciate the honesty. "You have a visitor, Isabelle."

"A visitor?"

"Megs. From the café, I believe."

"Megs is here?"

He nods. "She was worried about you. Says you usually see each other more often this time of year."

"It's almost the anniversary of Christian's death."

"I know. Come," he says, gesturing to the open door.

"Does Jericho know?"

"Don't worry about my brother. I'll take care of him."

I remember how he fought him at the chapel. He probably saved my life. "Thank you for what you did at the chapel," I say.

He opens his mouth, then closes it and just nods. "Come, Isabelle. Your friend is waiting."

"Thank you," I say again and walk out into the hallway, looking around the house like it's foreign to me. I wonder if this is how prisoners feel when they're set free. But then I remind myself it's only been a few days. Jericho will come around. He has to.

"She's in the library," he says once we reach the landing. I can already hear Catherine and Megs talking through the open door. When I get there, I smile wide at the sight of my friend.

"Megs!" I run to her, hug her.

Catherine straightens from where she's laying out everything for tea and smiles too, then quietly retreats from the room and closes the door.

"Hey," Megs says, drawing back. I realize I'm crying when she wipes my face. "What's going on? Why are you crying?"

I straighten, wipe the backs of my hands over my eyes. "It's just good to see you again. I'm so glad you came."

"Why haven't you been in touch? You don't answer your phone. It just goes right to voice mail. You've been MIA, Isabelle."

I sigh and we sit down on the couch. I notice the pastry box and open it but even the gorgeous cake inside doesn't elicit much response. "I don't have my phone anymore," I say, not quite looking at her because how do I explain this?

"Did you lose it or something? Or get a new number you aren't sharing with me?" she teases.

I decide I'm not going to lie to her. I'm not going to cover up this strange situation. "He took it. He hasn't given me a new one."

Her eyebrows furrow together as she processes this. "What do you mean?" she asks slowly.

I slice two pieces of cake and set them on the plates Catherine left but neither of us picks them up.

"My situation right now is...strange. Jericho is..." I draw in a deep breath and consider how to tell her. But I don't have to because she speaks next, and I'm surprised.

"Julia wasn't lying, was she?"

"Julia?"

She glances at the closed door and leans in closer. "She came to see me a couple of days ago. She said she was worried about you. Said your husband wouldn't let you talk to her. That you're a prisoner in this house. Is that true, Isabelle?"

My face flushes with heat and more tears threaten, but somehow, I hold them back. My heart races. I'm embarrassed and I want her to understand. It's just too much.

"Honey, what the hell is going on?" She pulls out her phone. "I can call the fucking cops here right now."

I shake my head, feeling the lump in my throat I'll need to swallow before I can form words.

"There's a lot of history between our families, Megs. And Jericho... The police won't be able to do anything."

"What do you mean they won't be able to do anything?"

"Nothing. It's..." I draw in a deep breath. What do I do, tell her about The Society? About the power they wield. About the strange traditions and rituals. She'll think I've gone mad.

"It's not nothing if he's got you locked up in here. What the hell, Isabelle? I don't like Julia," she says, standing, pacing. "But fuck. She was telling the truth, wasn't she?"

"I don't know what she told you but I'm sure at least some of it is true."

"Shit." She sits down and I get an idea. Because there is one thing Megs can help with.

"Listen, can you do something for me?"

"Anything. What can I do?"

"Can you find out if there's a man named Gerald Gibson who lives somewhere near here, I guess? I'm not sure exactly where. New Orleans though. Or near it. He'd have a brother named Danny Gibson." Saying his name takes something from me and it's a moment before I can continue. "Don't go to his house or anything. I just want to know if he exists and where he lives. And if you can find out if he owns a white van." I add that last part uneasily.

Megs studies me. "Who is he?"

"Just find out for me, will you? Maybe you can come see me again and tell me. But don't tell Julia I asked."

"What the hell is going on, Isabelle?"

"I'm pregnant," I tell her. She looks surprised. "Julia didn't tell you that part I guess?"

"No, she didn't. How far along?"

"About two months."

"Shit. Is that why you got married?" she is doing quick math.

I shake my head. "No, that's a lot more complicated. But the reason I'm locked up in here is Jericho found something I forgot I even had. And he thought I'd hurt our baby." God. It sounds terrible to say that to her. To hear myself say it out loud to her.

"Jesus."

"It's going to be fine, I know it is, but there's just a lot I'm trying to figure out. If you can tell me about this Gerald Gibson, it would help."

If he doesn't exist, then Jericho was lying and I have to be ready for that. If he does, and he owns a white van, then I have to be ready for that. Especially if Julia was somehow involved. Either way, I lose, but I have to know the truth.

"Listen, if this guy exists, you need to stay away from him. Just tell me if he is real or not and where he lives."

"And if he owns a white van."

I nod.

"All right. I'll see what I can dig up. I'm guessing you won't be visiting the café anytime soon."

"I doubt it."

"It's okay. I'll come back and see you. His brother let me in, but do you think Jericho would?"

"I don't know."

"You know what, don't worry about it. I'll figure it

out," she says and gets to her feet. I get up too. "What else can I do for you?"

"Just that. That's enough for now. Thank you, Megs."

She nods, comes to hug me. "I wish I could stay longer but I have school pick up."

"No worries. I'm so glad you came."

She pulls back, looks down at me. "At least eat the cake. You need to put on weight if you've got a baby in there." She hesitates for a moment. "Isabelle?"

"Yes?"

"Do you want the baby?"

"I do. I didn't at first, when I found out, but I do."

"Okay. And one other thing," she says, just before releasing me. "I almost forgot because Julia's so fucking cryptic. She told me to tell you that you have a friend in the woods. I don't know what the hell that means, but there it is. It was just weird enough that I remembered, and I had to say it exactly that way." She studies me, eyes shifting between mine. "And you clearly understand what she meant. I guess that's good."

I nod, because yes, I do understand. The smoker I thought was out there. The one who didn't answer when I called out. He's real.

"Don't tell her I asked you about Gerald Gibson, okay?"

"I won't tell her anything. She may be worried

about you, but it doesn't change how my hackles go up anytime she's around. There's something not right about her."

I don't answer that but when she leaves, I go out to the patio and sit in the cool, fall air. I'll wait for someone to come and escort me back to my cell as I search the woods for the red light of a cigarette, not sure if he's friend or foe.

## 40

# JERICHO

"Are you sure? There can be no doubt," I repeat.

Dr. Rosseau sighs. "There is no doubt. This evidence will stand up in any court of law, including The Tribunal."

I find I can't quite smile at this news although it is good news. Exactly what I was hoping to find. But there's also bad news.

"And on the DNA?"

"That's not my area of expertise, as you know, but I trust my team and have used them multiple times. The boy is Carlton Bishop's son." And the rightful heir.

I nod, eyes on the autopsy report. "The previous coroner was quick to rule it as cardiac arrest. Why?"

"Unless he knew to search for specific traces of any number of poisons, he wouldn't find it. And that's one of the beauties of Oleander. It's as unde-tectable as it is deadly. The makings for a perfect crime."

I look up at him. Santiago referred me to Dr. Rosseau. He is a specialist in poisons and a member of The Society. He saved Santiago's life a few years back. And this evidence will destroy Julia Bishop.

"Although considering Carlton Bishop was in excellent health, it should have raised some flags."

"Are you suggesting he was incentivized to draw the cause of death as quickly as he did?"

"I'm not suggesting anything of the sort. I wouldn't, of course. But knowing what we know, it's a question."

"And the miscarriages Bishop's wives suffered, is there any way to know if they weren't purely natural occurrences?" I ask. I know I'm pushing.

"That I can't tell you." He sits back, studies me. "But you should have enough evidence to draw Ms. Bishop to the negotiating table at least."

"I won't be negotiating," I say, standing. I check my watch. "The files?"

"All in your inbox but you're welcome to take these as well. They're yours," Dr. Rosseau says, standing. He tugs at the sleeve of his shirt. He's dressed elegantly with diamond cuff links, a Rolex watch, a custom-made suit. His office is opulent, lavish, as is the rest of his home.

"Thank you, Dr. Rosseau," I say, collecting the folders and extending my hand.

He shakes it. "You're welcome, Mr. St. James. And I'll of course be available should Hildebrand or any of the Councilors need my testimony."

"I'm betting it won't come to that." For Isabelle's sake but also for the little boy's. Matthew Bishop. Matty. No four-year-old needs to see his mother dragged off to prison, or worse, for murder.

I haven't seen Isabelle since the night I left her locked in her room. Since she told me about her nightmare. Since she told me she loved me. I wonder if she's had the dream since, but I stop my mind from wandering there. I can't think about that. About her.

"Home, sir?" the driver asks as we merge onto the highway. He's new. A young guy.

"What's your name?"

"Anthony, sir."

"Anthony." I vaguely recall the name Dex mentioned. His replacement for the time being. "No, not home." I check my watch, reread the text Zeke sent not half an hour ago. The one about the grieving Julia Bishop. "Take me to the cathedral." He knows which one.

"Yes, sir."

I text Dex to check in on Angelique and my mother. He sends back a photo showing me they're more than fine. Enjoying the indoor swimming pool at the house I rented in the Adirondacks. Angelique apparently loves it. Loves the fall colors and the adventures she's having with Dex on their daily hikes. She should be having those with me. But instead, I'm in New Orleans dealing with a pariah who murdered her lover and who knows how many others. Who attempted to run over my wife and gave her the means to end her pregnancy.

Isabelle's words come back to me. She loves me. How can she hurt a part of me? Her face is next. Her eyes. Too often wide and frightened. Too often of me. And yet she loves me. And what have I done but make her life hell?

"Sir, we're about five minutes out."

"Thank you." I start to put my phone away but change my mind and type out a text to my brother.

Me: *How is my wife?*

The dots appear as Zeke types his reply: *She's a prisoner. How do you think she is?*

Shit.

Me: *I'm almost to the cathedral. Is the boy there?*

Zeke: *She sent him home a while ago. It'll be her and the priest. I'm on my way to visit the coroner. I'll let you know what I learn as soon as I can.*

Me: *Thank you.*

The driver takes me to the front entrance of the cathedral where Mass was just said for Carlton Bishop's soul to be welcomed into Heaven. Best I can hope for him is that he's burning in hell, but at least she gave him what he deserved. He'd have suffered in the days leading up to his heart attack. It's not enough for what he did to my family but it's all I have. As I step out into the cool fall night, I know it has to be enough because there are more lives at stake now. And I can't bury another woman I love.

Two IVI guards stand sentry at the cathedral doors. They open them upon my approach and I'm happy to see Zeke was right. The place is cleared out apart from Julia Bishop and the priest, with whom she's speaking as she adjusts the lilies decorating Carlton Bishop's coffin.

The door closes loudly and my steps echo making them both turn, the priest's face a mask of equilibrium. Julia's flashes with surprise, then anger.

She faces me fully, folding her arms across her chest, standing between me and the coffin as if to keep it safe from me. Bishop's dead. I don't have to desecrate his corpse. It's her head I want now.

"Am I late?" I ask, stopping a few feet from them.

The priest clears his throat. "The ceremony is over, but the body will remain until the morning for burial."

"Then I can pay my respects," I say, only glancing at the priest. "A word, Ms. Bishop."

"I don't have anything to say to you."

"But I have something to say to you. And I believe you will want to hear it." I glance to the priest. "Alone."

She studies me. I smile faintly although nothing about this is making me happy. Because no matter what, Isabelle will be hurt. So will an innocent child. And he doesn't deserve that even if he is a Bishop.

The priest looks nervously between us. "Ms. Bishop, I can stay—"

"No, thank you," she says, turning to smile to him. "I'll be fine."

He glances at me once more before nodding and walking toward a small door at the back of the cathedral. His steps echo in the cavernous space and I wait to speak until the door is closed.

"Are you satisfied with yourself? Delaying his service? His burial?"

"I could give a fuck," I say, walking around her to look at the stupid face of Carlton Bishop in the framed photograph. I pick it up, study it. "Was he your puppet all along?" I ask, slowly turning back to her.

She's cold as ice, this one. Doesn't break a sweat. "I don't know what you mean. What I learned the other day..." she drops her gaze, her forehead creasing, eyes sufficiently wet when she turns them back up to me. "It broke my heart to learn he had anything to do with Isabelle's brother's death. Shattered me to see her face when I told her the truth."

"M-hm." I put the photo down. "The boy is his. Congratulations. That was well-played."

She lifts her head, tilting it a little, any false

sadness gone. Replaced by a cool, unreadable beauty.

"I wasn't playing at anything. I loved him. Matty is a product of our love."

"Oh, I almost believe you."

"What the hell is wrong with you?"

"I think you're a liar, Ms. Bishop."

"Go to hell, Mr. St. James." She turns to walk toward the front pew where her coat and purse are. "I'm going home to my son."

"Oleander," I say. She stops dead. I watch her narrow shoulders stiffen. "Clever, again. Undetectable. Unless you know what you're looking for, that is."

She resumes walking, albeit stiffly, toward the pew.

"And of course, he'd suffer first. It's what you wanted, isn't it? For him to suffer at least a little?" She bends to pick up her purse and coat then straightens to face me. "All those visits to the Cat House must have hurt."

"I don't know what you're talking about."

I take two steps toward her. "I'm not stupid, Ms. Bishop."

"No? I'm not sure I agree." She grins. Bitch. "I mean, taking the inheritance out from under your nose wasn't that hard. And poor Isabelle. Pregnant with your spawn." Her lips curl making her ugly as she looks me over. "I tried to fix that for her, but she's not very smart either. Never was."

Blood rushes in my ears and every muscle in my body tenses.

"Or maybe it was just the sex that turned her head," she says, studying me, licking her lips seductively. She lets her gaze move over my shoulders, my chest, lower. "I mean, I get it." Her eyes meet mine. "I'm sure you're a good fuck and if it was the Bishop fortune you wanted, well, Isabelle was your only option. But things can change, Jericho," she says, reaching out a hand to adjust the lapel of my suit, letting it linger on my chest. "In fact, they have."

"You make me want to vomit, Ms. Bishop. Isabelle is a hundred times the woman you could ever be."

Her face contorts, her guard down for a moment. "Well, isn't that romantic." She drops her arm and narrows her eyes. "I had him cremated you know. The body's gone."

Cremated? I glance at the coffin.

"Just ashes in there. I mean, what does it matter, burying ashes or burying a body that will turn to ash in time anyway?" She walks around me toward the coffin, picks off a lily, dropping several to the floor in the process. "And oleander," she starts, turning to me after tucking the flower into the pocket of her mourning dress. "Well, that's a bit far-fetched, don't you think? I mean, what year is this?"

"Tell me something," I start, standing in the middle of the aisle to block her path. "Did you kill the babies?"

She blinks, surprised, and although I have no proof, I think she did. I think she must have. Miscarriage after miscarriage, wife after wife.

"Those miscarriages, awfully convenient. And here I thought it was Bishop's faulty sperm."

"Get out of my way."

"The Tribunal will hang you," I say, and watch her face lose a little color. "He was a Sovereign Son. And at least two of those children were male. You know how important a male heir is to The Society. Pure blood and all, as old-fashioned as the idea is. As old-fashioned as poison which our members do seem to love."

"There's no proof. Your word against mine. I have an autopsy report."

"So do I. And a coroner who was bribed." I don't know that for sure but I'm willing to bet on it. Zeke will confirm soon enough. From the way her eyes shift between mine, I know I'm right. "You'll hang, Julia."

"You'd destroy Isabelle."

"Tell me something, did you pay Gerald Gibson to run her over? And when he fucked up, did you drop by to rip him a new one the night you gave my wife those abortion pills? Or was it to devise another attack?"

She blinks hard. "I don't know what you're talking about."

"No? Well, I'll ask you an easier question then. The pills. How many did you give Isabelle?"

She doesn't answer right away and there's that mask again, that arrogance. That cold, calculated snake rearing its ugly head. "Didn't she tell you? I thought you two love birds would have no secrets from each other." She steps toward me so I can smell the stench of her perfume. "Although a man like you will always keep secrets, won't he? Like why you were in Mexico on that ill-fated trip to meet with the leader of a cartel. Your poor fiancée. Did she have any idea?"

My hands fist at my sides and it takes all I have to fight the urge to wrap them around her neck and commit murder here on this sacred ground. Blood pumps so hard it's a wonder I can hear her at all over the rush of it.

"Wrapping up work for dead daddy, isn't that right? I mean, isn't the cartel where you made at least a chunk of your fortune? It was when he was alive." She smiles wide, shifts her weight to set her hand to her hip. "I have all the paperwork. I could share it with you if you weren't sure. Hell, I could share it with all the world, the work you were doing down there while playing doting husband to be, daddy to be. And poor, poor Kimberly. That was her name, right? As gullible as Isabelle. You have a type. But—"

I whip my arm out, clutch her throat, and walk her back so fast one of her shoes falls off her foot. The coffin almost tips off its pedestal when I bend her over it backward. I lean into her face.

"For Isabelle's sake, for your son's sake, I'm going to give you an out. One chance, Ms. Bishop. Walk. Away. Disappear. Take the boy and go. And none of this comes to light. And you don't hang. Because whatever you think you can do to me, you are the one who will swing at the end of a rope. And when you do, I'll take that boy of yours and raise him as my own. I'll make sure to erase any memory of you. For his own good, of course. You have three days to decide. Three days. Do I make myself clear?"

Her hands are around my forearm trying to tug me off. I'm pretty sure I could kill her right here. Right now. I remember how I'd held Isabelle in a very similar fashion days ago when I thought she tried to kill our baby. Something heavy and dark settles around me, inside me. How could I have done that to her? How could I have hurt her like I can hurt this pariah. Because Julia Bishop isn't lying about my visit to Mexico. I was there doing business. I knew who Felix Pérez was. And I completed one final deal on my father's behalf with him.

I can tell myself it was my duty to my father as long as I want, but I chose. I chose to go. Even before

I knew what he'd done to Zoë. Before I knew what a vile human being he was. I'm still the one who flew to Mexico to meet with Pérez in his name. To ensure one last transaction with men my father never had any business dealing with and close that chapter of St. James history.

I'm still the one who took Kimberly. I'm still the reason Angelique never knew her mother. Never even saw her face.

"Six," Julia gasps out, her eyes red and huge, popping out of her head.

I blink, come back to the present.

"Six. Pills," she manages.

I loosen my grip around her neck. Six pills. It's how many I counted when I confronted Isabelle. She wasn't lying. She never took them. And still...what I did to her. Fuck. How I keep hurting the people I love.

Angelique's sweet face floats into memory. Her growing up with a bodyguard instead of her own father. My innocent baby girl. What will I do to her? How badly will I damage her?

Julia drops to her knees the instant I release her. I don't bother to stop and look. I don't bother to do anything but walk to the door, my steps echoing, loud, drowning out her gasps for breath. But not loud enough to drown out my guilt. My very real knowledge of who I am. What I am.

A devil.

# 41

## ISABELLE

I'm woken in the middle of the night by something falling to the floor near me. Startled, I bolt upright, my eyes taking a minute to adjust to the darkness. A shadow bends to pick up the violin case. Set it against the wall. Then straighten.

"Jericho?"

He turns to me and from the little bit of light filtering in between the curtains, I see his face and know something happened.

"What is it?" I ask, pushing the blanket off to get up and go to him. I smell the liquor before I'm close. When I reach him, he looks down at me and sets one hand at my lower back.

He says my name and sways a little.

"You're drunk, Jericho."

"No."

"Yes." I take his hand and lead him to the bed, switch on the lamp on the nightstand and sit him down. I push his suit jacket off his shoulders. It's wrinkled and looks like it's been through a very long day and a longer night. I toss it aside and look at him. He sits there looking up at me. His hair's messed up like he's run his hands through it a thousand times. I'm not sure when he last shaved. The five-o'clock shadow is fast becoming a beard.

"Isabelle." He reaches up to touch my face, caresses my cheek then the length of my hair before letting his hand come to rest at his side again.

"What's happened?" I ask again as I kneel to unlace his shoes and slip them off one by one, then his socks. I straighten, start to unbutton his shirt. He just sits there and watches me. Every time I look at his eyes, I see a sadness that seems eternal.

"Why are you good to me?" he asks, sounding tired. Worn out. "After everything I do to you."

I tug his shirt out of his slacks and open it, touch the skin of his chest, then cup his cheek. "I already told you that. Don't you remember?"

His eyes flutter closed then open again. I shake my head and pull the shirt off his arms.

"Tell me what happened," I say, then pause, alarmed. "Are Angelique and your mother okay?"

He appears confused, then nods. "Fine. She's having fun with Dex. He's more a father to her than I am, you know that?"

"That's not true. Lie down."

He does without a word, and I look at him with his head on my pillow, big body on my double bed. His is a king. He looks like a giant here. And at the same time, he looks vulnerable. Because I see his exhaustion.

"What are you killing yourself for?" I ask myself more than him as I undo his belt. I strip off his pants, then tug the blanket out from under his legs and lie down beside him. I pull the covers over us both and use his arm for a pillow. He holds onto me and when I hear his breathing level out, I close my eyes. I'm not sure if I fall asleep or if we're both asleep for a time before he speaks, the deep quiet of his voice waking me.

"It was my fault she died."

It takes me a minute but I realize he's talking about Kimberly.

"I knew what I was doing, who I was dealing with when I went down there. I should never have taken her. Never."

I lean up to see his face in the shadowy light. He's looking up at the ceiling.

"My meeting with Pérez, it was business. My father's business."

"What do you mean, business?"

"My father dealt with that bastard. He was the one who put Pérez in touch with suppliers on this side. Brokered the deals. Made the family a lot of money."

"Your father did business with a cartel?"

He nods. "Zeke doesn't know. Shit. We're so good at keeping secrets and look where it got us."

"What did you do? What was your part?"

He sighs deeply and I know he's holding himself accountable now. This is his confession. "I finished his business with the agreement it would be the last. I am sure that's why Pérez agreed to the hit Bishop arranged with him. Had agreed to it even while he sat with us in his living room, that smug smile I hated on sight. It's why he didn't push back when I told him this was it. I was severing ties."

"Oh, Jericho."

"And then she took the bullet meant for me."

I don't want to be hurt or jealous. This is his past. She is his past. I know this. And she'll always be a part of his life and in turn my life and that's as it should be. She was Angelique's mother. And he loved her.

He turns his head toward me, touches my cheek. "How many people will I hurt? I'm cursed, Isabelle. I hurt everyone I love. Or worse."

I blink and he wipes a tear away with the pad of his thumb.

"See?" he asks.

"No. What happened to her wasn't your fault. That blame isn't yours to carry."

"It is, sweetheart."

"Jericho—"

He cups my head and pulls me into his chest, quieting me. His big hand rests on my cheek, my hair, his other arm wrapped around my waist.

"And I do love you, Isabelle. I do. If I were a better man I'd let you go before I hurt any more than I already have but I'm not. And I can't." He turns his head and presses his lips against my forehead. He just holds me like that, tight to him, so tight, kissing me like that. I think about his life, the burdens he's carried, he's still carrying. The guilt. And I hug him closer, hold him tight to me, too.

42

---

## ISABELLE

When I wake up, I am alone. It's like the night before didn't happen. And maybe he was so drunk he doesn't remember it. Although my door is unlocked, so after dressing quickly, I go downstairs to find Jericho drinking coffee and talking to his brother in the dining room.

They both grow quiet when I stop inside the arched entrance. Jericho looks me over. He's cleaned up. Shaved. Fresh from a shower. He doesn't look even a little bit like the broken man of last night. It makes me wonder if he remembers what he said. The things he told me. How he said he loved me.

"Good morning," Zeke says to me, smiling. "Good to see you out and about."

"Good to be out and about," I tell him.

He walks out of the dining room and I turn to find Jericho still watching me.

"I didn't hear you leave," I say.

"You were sleeping so peacefully I didn't want to wake you. Come in. We'll have breakfast."

It's awkward, or at least it is for me, as quiet settles around us. He makes me a plate of food, remembering to skip the bacon. He places it in front of me, then sits down himself with a similar size dish.

"You slept well after I woke you up?" he asks.

"You were really drunk," I say instead of answering his question.

"And you took care of me. It's becoming a habit." He eats another mouthful.

"You said some things."

He smiles. "I did."

"About the cartel," I say after a glance to the hall.

He nods, no smile this time.

"About you and me," I add after clearing my throat and turning my attention fully to my plate.

"I remember, Isabelle." I glance his way quickly. "I meant it, in case you're wondering."

I put my fork down and study him. There, buried deep beneath the surface, I think I glimpse that man of last night. Just a quick sighting of that other, vulnerable creature. "I meant it too when I said it."

"I'm sorry about what I did to you at the chapel.

I'm sorry I scared you. I know you didn't take those pills."

"You believe me?"

"Your cousin confirmed the number she'd given you."

"Ah." I wipe my mouth with my napkin, suddenly having no appetite. "You believed Julia over me. That's nice. Doesn't sting at all considering you hate her."

His expression darkens. "No, I don't believe her over you. I just had corroborating evidence."

"Do you hear yourself?"

He wipes his mouth, clears his throat. "You know what, I do."

His phone buzzes in his pocket, he reads something on the screen, then tucks it away and stands. He walks behind my chair, wraps a hand around my cheek and leans down so his mouth is at my ear. My heartbeat picks up at having him so close. His hand is warm, his big body at my back makes me shudder with conflicting emotions. I want this man like I've never wanted anyone before, but he is both vengeful and broken. And as much as he may mean it when he says he loves me, he also warned me last night, didn't he? He's cursed. Everyone he loves gets hurt. I need to be careful.

"I can't change overnight, but I'm trying," he says. He's so close his breath tickles my ear making me shudder. He kisses the corner of my mouth, then turns me and kisses me deeply. "We both have to learn to trust each other. Okay?"

I nod because I can't really speak. My heart is hammering against my chest. I don't know if it's pregnancy hormones or what, but I don't think I can form words right now.

He smiles, draws back. He must see all those things on my face.

"Eat your breakfast. I have a surprise for you this morning."

"What surprise?" I ask as he takes his phone out of his pocket and heads out of the dining room.

"After breakfast we'll go to Dr. Barnes's office for your first ultrasound."

"Ultrasound?"

"We'll see the baby today, Isabelle. You want that, don't you?"

I smile and nod. Because yes, I do want that. I would love that, actually.

---

WE ARRIVE AT DR. BARNES'S OFFICE AT A LITTLE before noon and are immediately shown through the lavish waiting area into his office. It's large and as comfortable as can be, I guess, given the bright lights and sterile setting. The men shake hands and talk while the nurse shows me to a small room where I change into a gown. Once I'm ready, she leads me back to where the doctor is explaining something about the ultrasound machine to Jericho.

"Hop on up here, Mrs. St. James, and we'll get a first glimpse of your baby," Dr. Barnes says, smiling, appearing a totally different man than the one who was at the house when I found out I was pregnant. The moment I knew what Jericho had done. How everything has changed in such a short amount of time.

Jericho stands at the head of the table as I get situated, the gown covering me as I set my socked feet in the stirrups.

"This will be a transvaginal ultrasound," Dr. Barnes explains, rolling himself toward the lower half of the table. Jericho takes my hand, surprising me, and I glance back at him. I'm nervous. I have no idea why but I'm nervous. And he looks a little like I feel, too.

He meets my eyes and squeezes my fingers. I remember what he said this morning. About how he's trying but it will take time. About learning to trust each other. I squeeze back just as I feel the wand enter, the gel so cold it makes me shudder.

But I don't have a chance to consider the discomfort or anything else, because I hear it. The first sounds of our baby. Before I turn my head to look at the monitor, Jericho's hand tightens around mine and my eyes fill up with warm tears. My chest swells as I listen to the quick, strange echo of my baby's heartbeat.

"There he or she is," Dr. Barnes says. "We won't know the sex just yet, if you want to know at all."

"No," I say quickly, glancing up to Jericho to find his eyes locked on that monitor. "We don't want to know the sex."

Jericho glances down at me. Nods. "As you wish." He shifts his gaze back to the monitor as I do too, and we watch this tiny blob that doesn't look exactly like a baby. Dr. Barnes measures this and that, explaining things I don't hear because I'm too busy listening to that little heartbeat. Watching the tiny life on the screen. Wholly enthralled.

We leave an hour later and, in my hand, I'm clutching about two dozen photographs of the baby.

"Angelique will love to see these," I tell him absently as we climb into the backseat of the car. I don't know this driver. He's new since Dex is gone. I glance to Jericho as he closes the door behind himself. "When will she be back?"

"I'm not sure yet."

His expression darkens and I remember the other part of our lives. The one where we're not a normal couple who just had the first glimpse of their baby.

We're a couple dealing with people who mean us harm. Where the threat is real enough to Jericho that he sent his little girl away to keep her out of danger.

"What did you find out in the autopsy?" I ask, the happy mood vanished almost as if it wasn't even there at all.

He looks at me. "I'll deal with that. You don't have to worry about that."

I study him and I think he means well. I do. But this is about me too.

"There is something then?" There is. I don't know how I know, but I do. "He didn't die of a heart attack, did he?"

He sighs, but neither confirms nor denies, at least not verbally. He just keeps his gaze straight ahead as we get to the next place. The next surprise, I guess. The car pulls up in front of Cotton Candy and I can see from the windows that it's completely empty inside. The lights are on and I see Megs at the counter typing on her laptop, a mug at her side.

"Second surprise," Jericho says as he opens the door, climbs out and extends his hand for me.

I'm still clutching the photographs, so I unzip my purse, putting them inside, then take his hand and step onto the sidewalk. I can't help my glance down the street where that van had come from and he must see it, because he tugs me closer.

"It's fine. I wouldn't bring you here if you wouldn't be safe."

I smile up at him but my question of moments

ago lingers, a shadow on what should be a bright day. He found something in Carlton's autopsy. Something that makes his death not a natural one.

*Julia.*

No. I don't let myself go down that road. Not yet.

"Why is the cafe empty?" I ask as we walk inside, the driver standing by the door.

"Key's in the lock," Megs says to Jericho then rolls her eyes at me when he turns his back to lock it.

"What's going on?" I ask anyone who will answer me.

Megs comes around the counter to the single table that is set with pink and blue balloons and two place settings. On the table sits a silver carafe of coffee, a pot of steaming tea, and a gorgeous cake, also pink and blue, rests between them.

"Your husband rented the place out for the day," she says, gaze shifting to Jericho as he smiles, wrapping an arm around me. "Because he's crazy," she adds before gesturing to the table. "The seat with the gift is for you," she adds as Jericho pulls out the chair.

"You rented the whole place?" I ask him as I settle in.

"Yes," he answers like it's the most normal thing in the world to do. "The balloons are a little overdone, don't you think?" he asks Megs.

She juts one hip out, sets her hand on it and

takes his measure. It's a look that would have most men cowering, but my husband isn't most men.

"No, I don't think it's overdone at all. And if you like those so much, you're going to love the inside of the cake."

He shifts his gaze to the brightly colored pink and blue cake. "Christ," he mutters and sits down.

"See now, that just made my day that much happier. Oh, and of course earning about five times more than the café being open would have brought in. Thanks for that by the way," she says to him then turns to me, smiles. "You. Open your gift."

Her face gives nothing away about what I told her on her visit to the house. And I'm not actually sure how she feels about Jericho, this banter between them not unfriendly but also not quite friendly.

"I love gifts," I say, and she watches as I tear the package open. It's a book about pregnancy, what I can expect, a week-by-week guide. "It's perfect! I don't have one."

"I'm glad you like it. But it's just the beginning. If I'm going to be an aunt and godmother—"

"Godmother?" Jericho cuts her off, eyebrows rising high on his forehead.

Megs just carries on. "You know I'm spoiling him or her. I've already started a collection. It's been too long since I've held a baby." Megs leans in to hug me. "You good?" she whispers.

I hug her tighter. "Yes. Thank you."

"Page 286," she whispers and pulls back, turns to Jericho. "Are you just going to sit there or are you going to make yourself useful and pour the lady a cup of tea?"

I look down at the book on my lap tempted to turn to page 286 now. In fact, it takes all I have not to as I set it aside and listen to their back-and-forth. Jericho makes a comment of "…isn't that your job? I thought for what I paid I'd at least get halfway decent service."

But even in his tone, I get the feeling he might like Megs. At least not hate or completely distrust her. It's when we're cutting into the cake that his phone rings. I pause with the knife just touching the icing and watch as he takes the call, getting up to speak in a lowered voice.

"Does he think he's some sort of spy?" Megs asks, watching his back for a moment before turning to me. I notice the glance she gives Anthony at the door. "He was sweet to rent the place out for you. You should have heard him when he called me." She shakes her head. "If I didn't know the other side of him, I'd think he was just a big teddy bear."

A teddy bear. Jericho. That's twice someone's called him that.

"I have ultrasound pictures," I say, changing the subject as she pulls up a chair. I set the knife down and take out the photos to show Megs. A glance at

Jericho tells me that whatever is going on it's got him worked up.

"Oh, my goodness! Looks just like dad," she says once Jericho disconnects the call and returns to the table, his mood visibly darker.

He glances to Megs. "Aren't you supposed to serve and leave?"

She rolls her eyes and hands me back the photos. "Well, let's just hope she inherits mom's personality or that kid is doomed."

"For fuck's sake," Jericho starts.

Megs laughs and walks away. I cut a slice of the cake only to have about a million pink and blue sprinkles spill out onto the dish and over the table, the sight so gorgeous all I can do is laugh. I think how much Angelique would love this. How much I love it.

But before I can ask Jericho to take a picture of it, before he can even enjoy the spectacle or be irritated by it, his phone rings again. This time when he answers his tone is sharp. There's a long silence while the person on the other end responds. I glance to Megs who is watching from the counter. When I look back to Jericho, I hear his muttered curse before he shoves the phone back into his pocket and returns to me, body tense, legs stiff.

"We need to go," he says.

"What? Why?"

"I need to take care of something. It's urgent." He

picks up the book and my purse and gestures for me
to get up.

"What's going on?" I ask without standing.

"Nothing to upset you. We just need to leave."

"Remember what you said this morning? About
trust?"

"Yes, that I'm working on it, and it will take us
both time to trust. Let's go, Isabelle."

"You go. I want to eat my cake."

"I'm not leaving you here."

"Why not? The door is locked. Anthony can take
me home when I'm done. You're busy anyway."

"Isabelle—"

"Tell me what it is then. Tell me why you're angry
again. And tell me what you found in the autopsy."

He grits his jaw, hands tensing into fists. He
closes his eyes, then, ten seconds later, opens them
and takes a deep breath. "Okay. You'll stay here.
Anthony will stay with you. The door will remain
locked. Anthony," he calls out and Anthony is at the
table in an instant. "I need to take the car. Call for
another one to be brought around. Once it's here
and my wife has enjoyed her cake, take her home.
No one comes in. No one goes out. Is that clear?"

I roll my eyes and pick up my fork, no longer
interested in them. Angry at this turn of events.
Disappointed by it, by his words about trust because
they're empty.

"Yes, sir," Anthony says like a good puppet.

"Good." Jericho lays his big hand on my shoulder. "I'm sorry."

I shrug it off and put a bite of cake into my mouth, but as delicious as it is, I can't stomach it.

A moment later, Jericho is gone and Anthony is back at the door. Megs joins me at the table.

"Shit," she says. "Waste of good cake." She cuts herself a slice as she glances at Anthony. "But at least we get to talk."

"Page 286?"

She nods and takes a bite. "Fuck, I'm good." She says louder than necessary, then lowers her voice. "I found a house in the Seventh Ward that belonged to a Marjorie Gibson who is deceased."

"What?"

"The address is on page 286. She has a son named Gerald who has a rap sheet about as long as my arm, and another named Danny who is currently serving time for the murder of one Christian York. That's thanks to my detective friend. What the fuck is going on, Isabelle?"

"Shit. He's real."

"And he is not a nice man."

"No, his brother wasn't nice either. Does he live at the house?"

"Last address was out in Vegas."

"Vegas?"

She nods. "But it doesn't mean he's not here and just hasn't changed his address."

"The van?" I ask, not sure I want to know. Not at all.

"He owns a white van. What does it mean?"

"I'm not sure. If he's out in Vegas, nothing. But if he's not..." It means Jericho is telling the truth. At least some of it. And possibly that Julia isn't. "Do you have your car here?" I ask, hating the idea even as I ask but unsure what else to do.

"My car?"

I nod.

"Out back." Her eyes narrow. "And no, you're not taking it to pay a visit to that shithead."

"I'm not planning on visiting him if he's even in town. I just want to see the house. See if the van is there." See if it's the same one.

"Isabelle, no."

"I won't have another chance like this. I can't leave the house without Jericho. I can't call you or anyone else. I can't do anything without his permission."

Megs swallows, glances at Anthony. "What about him?"

"Cake?"

She slips her hand into her pocket and takes out the keys. "This one will unlock the door at the end of the hall past the ladies room. You'll see the car out back." I close my hand over it, glance at Anthony who is smiling at something on his phone. I slip the keys into my purse and Megs quickly shoves her phone in there too. "You know the code. You're just driving by, right?"

I nod.

"It should take you twenty minutes to get there. If I don't hear from you in twenty, I'm sending cops to Gibson's address."

"No. I need more time."

"Fine. Twenty-five. Then you're straight back. Agreed?"

I nod, get to my feet. She closes her hand over mine. "Don't do anything stupid, Isabelle. You hear me?"

I nod, smile and turn to Anthony. "Can you get the cake packed up? I need to use the lady's room."

"Sure thing, Mrs. St. James."

"You may as well have a slice first," Megs says and gets Anthony a slice, making him sit down as I slip through the door and toward the exit.

# 43

## ISABELLE

I understand why she named her car The Potato. It's a clunky old Mustang and it sputters to life, hiccuping all the way, making me wonder if it'll run at all. But then the rumbling settles and I shift to drive, the gear sticking momentarily.

The car itself is spotless even though the scent of gasoline permeates the interior. Megs loves the old thing. It was her father's. It's why she keeps it. He loved it too.

The Seventh Ward is not the best neighborhood. I know that. But during this time of day, I should be fine. I think about what I'm going to do when I get to the house where Gerald Gibson could be living. This is Danny's brother. The man who tried to rape me. The man who killed Christian. Can I even do this?

I have to.

Because I have to know the truth about Julia. And if the van that tried to run me over is at the house, then it can't be coincidence.

Carlton's cause of death was not natural, I know that. And Jericho believes Julia is at the root of all of this. His death. The attack on me.

Possibly the attack that killed Christian.

The light a few blocks from Gerald Gibson's house turns red. I stop, rub my face. Am I ready to know this? Am I ready to know that Julia, my cousin whom I trust, with whom I have a relationship, whose son I love, could have tried to hurt me? Could have had anything to do with Christian's death? She explained it all so easily the other day and it makes sense that Carlton could have used her name and email address for the payment. But why would he leave a paper trail? That makes no sense. Why keep a record of your crime?

But it could be true, too, and Jericho is too angry to see it. With Matty being Carlton's son, the inheritance is settled. Jericho must see red at that and Julia would become his natural target.

Someone honks their horn, startling me. The light has turned green. I take my foot off the brake and drive, looking at the street names. I'm a few blocks out and my anxiety grows as I drive slower than the speed limit, the car creeping along once I turn onto Marjorie Gibson's street. I see the house at the far end. It's nondescript, blends in with the others on this street, the houses worn down, a neighborhood forgotten. They're all single-story homes with curtains pulled closed over windows. The cars parked along the street and on driveways are older, unloved models.

The driveway is empty. The house dark. It, too, looks empty. Like no one lives there. There's a garage at the end of the driveway and the door seems to be stuck. I drive by slowly, peering toward it and although I'm too far to be sure I see there's a vehicle inside. A truck or a van. And I can see it's white.

At the end of the street, I make a U-turn and creep toward the house. I park Megs's car and kill the engine. I sit inside for a long minute, my hands sweaty around the keys.

I just need to look at the van. I'll recognize it. The day is a blur but there was one thing that I remember. And it's distinct.

I check my watch. I have ten minutes before Megs calls the police, so I dig her phone out of my purse, punch in her code and dial the café. She answers on the first ring. I'm sure she's been waiting.

"Hey," she says.

"I just got to the house."

"And you're just doing a drive-by, remember?"

"I just need to see inside the garage."

"Isabelle—"

"Has Anthony figured out I'm gone?"

"He thinks you have an upset stomach but honestly, he won't buy it too much longer."

"I'll hurry. I just need to see, and the house looks empty. There's no one here."

"Please don't make me regret this."

I don't have anything to say to that, so I disconnect the call. With clammy hands, I open the car door and step out. I tuck the keys into my purse, walking down the sidewalk toward the house. Lace curtains that may once have been nice hang in the windows and through them the rooms are dark. No one's here. It's fine.

But my heart still races. I'm scared. Scared of what I may find.

I look around the street, see the few pockets of people, hear the sounds from inside other houses. Televisions, a dryer knocking against something as it spins, a woman yelling for her child to get inside. Without hesitating, I turn to walk up the driveway as if I belong here.

The garage door is open to about mid-thigh. It's set farther back than the house. I walk straight up the driveway and when I get closer, I bend to peer inside. My heart rate triples, sweat running down the back of my neck.

It's a white van. But it doesn't have to be the van that almost ran me over.

Except that there are too many coincidences here.

I slip under the open door into the garage. The smell of gasoline and stale cigarette smoke is strong here. I walk around the driver's side of the car. The window is open, and I peer inside to see the mess of old food containers, a packet of cigarettes on the dashboard, the butts and ashes of old cigarettes in the ashtray.

But it's not any of those things that make me hug my arms around myself. It's what's hanging from the rear-view mirror. It gives me a flashback to that day. That moment when I waved to Angelique and turned to find the van coming at me, tires bouncing up onto the sidewalk as if the driver lost control, except that he hadn't. I'd seen his face. His eyes. I'd just blocked it all out.

He hadn't lost control.

He'd been coming at me.

And the ratty teddy bear hanging by a noose from his neck on the rear-view mirror had been the most horrific sight. A child's toy, something meant to give comfort, treated in such a way. I remember it bouncing, hitting the windshield.

I need to get out of here. Clutching my purse to myself when the strap slides off my shoulder, I dig for the keys as I exit the garage.

I haven't even straightened when I crash into something hard. Rough hands close over my arms to still me. And when I look up, it's like I'm staring right into Danny Gibson's eyes. Even though that's impossible.

I see the flat nothingness I still remember. That abyss of emptiness.

And just like that night, my throat goes dry, and I can't make a sound. Not even a squeak to call for help. I'm powerless. Just like that night.

## 44

## JERICHO

"He inside?" I ask Zeke as I walk up the drive to Jones's front door. He lives a little over an hour out of town. Zeke is standing in the open doorway. Jones is the coroner who performed the original autopsy on Carlton Bishop and signed off on the cremation of the body.

"In his office."

The door closes behind us and two men stand guard as I walk in, Zeke falling into stride beside me.

"I guess he's not happy about that," I say as we reach the study. Zeke has a man out here too.

"No. Apparently we interrupted a trip to the Bahamas." Zeke finally caught up with Jones last night just as he was to board a private flight. He'd all but vanished off the face of the earth the last couple of days and I wondered if he hadn't met with some terrible end at Julia Bishop's hand.

"Was he alone?"

Zeke nods and opens the office door. "Not very chatty though, are you, doc?" he asks as we walk in.

Abe Jones is sitting on a straight back chair that looks like it was brought in from the dining room. His wrists are cuffed to the legs on either side of him. At his back stands yet another guard. He keeps his gaze on the wall behind us. These soldiers we hire are paid well for both their proficiency and their discretion.

"Were the cuffs necessary?" I ask Zeke. He's in his mid-forties from the looks of him and although he appears fit enough, I have no doubt Zeke could take him. He'd probably enjoy it. Not to mention the men with guns if he somehow got past my brother.

Zeke shrugs his shoulder. "Flight risk. Wasn't taking a chance."

I chuckle. "And the black eye?"

Zeke grins. "That's for wasting my time and sending me all over the fucking city looking for him, isn't that right, doc?" he asks that last part with exaggerated drama.

"I will report you to The Tribunal as soon as I'm freed of these restraints. I will require the full extent of the penalty for what you've done."

I raise my eyebrows and glance at Zeke. "Thought you said he wasn't chatty."

"Maybe he's coming around," Zeke says. He

moves to sit behind the man's desk and starts to look through the drawers.

I sit on the end of the coffee table facing Mr. Jones. I take in his disheveled appearance. He's not a member of IVI but he is on their payroll. He comes from a long line of coroners and over time IVI has made use of his family's services.

"I doubt The Tribunal would hear your argument, but you're welcome to try," I say, adjusting the collar of his shirt. "Take those off," I tell the guard, gesturing to the cuffs.

"Yes, sir," he says while Zeke tsks behind me. I hear the squeaking of the chair as he rocks back and forth on it.

Once Jones is freed, he rubs his wrists and I see the shiny Rolex on one. It's possible it costs more than all the furniture in here combined.

"New?" I ask, gesturing to it.

He smiles, rubs off a smudge of non-existent dirt, then nods.

"It's very nice. A gift from Julia Bishop?"

His face loses some color. "She was very grateful to have had me perform the autopsy on Mr. Bishop so quickly."

"I bet. And what did she pay you to sign off on the cremation certificate?"

His eyes grow wider and skip around the room, settling on the door.

"Please do not make me have to chase you," I say.

"It's been a long couple of days." I stand up, stretch my arms, crack my knuckles.

"Have kids?" Zeke asks. He's found a laptop and is punching something onto the keyboard.

"No," Jones says, then shifts his gaze to me as I move behind Zeke to look at the screen.

"Girlfriend? A pet?"

Jones shakes his head.

"A goldfish maybe?"

"No."

Zeke turns his head, shaking it. "Make this quick and give me the password, will you?"

"Why do you need it?"

"Curious how much you got paid for claiming a man died of a heart attack when he very clearly did not," Zeke says.

Jones's mouth falls open, any remaining color on his face disappearing. "What are you talking about? Carlton Bishop's cause of death was cardiac arrest. I wouldn't have lied about that. I could lose my license. Or worse."

"Password," Zeke says. When he doesn't answer, Zeke gestures to the guard who just uncuffed him. He fists a handful of Jones's hair and tugs his head back at such an awkward angle, the chair falls away and his spine is bent in way that makes even me wince.

"Mexico2020," he rushes to say.

"Any capitals?"

"M. Just the M."

Zeke types it in and voila, we're in. "That wasn't so hard, was it?" Zeke asks and finds the banking app.

I walk toward Jones, pick up the chair and nod for the guard to sit him on it. He does but keeps one heavy hand on his shoulder.

"You've performed autopsies for The Society before. Your family has been providing the service for a long time."

"That's right."

"Tell me about oleander."

He looks at me, forehead furrowed, and I wonder about him. Wonder if he truly thought Bishop died of a heart attack.

"It's a plant," he says.

"And a..." I trail off, gesturing for him to fill in the blank.

"Poison."

"Good. Working for IVI you'd know about those things."

"There wasn't evidence of any foul play," he says. "Mr. Bishop's heart gave out in the throes of a passionate event. There were witnesses. Multiple."

"So I've heard but I'd rather not visualize it if you don't mind."

He grips the sides of the chair and waits for me to continue.

"There was only evidence of cardiac arrest. Nothing out of the ordinary."

"Did you bother to look?"

He doesn't answer.

"Did you bother, Doctor Jones?"

"I was told it would be best to move as quickly as possible and bury Mr. Bishop, considering how he died and the impact it would have on his son."

"By whom?"

He draws his lips into a tight line and his gaze shifts away from me.

"By. Whom?"

"Ms. Bishop. Councilor Hildebrand agreed. There was no reason."

"And who signed off on the cremation?"

He clears his throat. For a Sovereign Son's body to be cremated, a Councilor and the coroner must both sign off. In this case, Hildebrand was said Councilor. Except I've seen his signature.

"Councilor Hildebrand," he tries.

"So, if I were to ask the Councilor, he'd remember the event? He's got a great memory I hear."

He glances away, beads of sweat breaking across his forehead.

"Jericho," Zeke calls out.

I leave the doctor and walk over to stand behind the desk. He points to a deposit in Jones's bank account of $25,000 made from Carlton Bishop days after his death.

"Was Carlton Bishop very grateful for the service of the autopsy you conducted on his dead body or was it the speedy cremation?" I ask Jones.

"That was Ms. Bishop. She took over the account with her son being the heir but obviously so young." Sweat rings are forming under his arms.

"And which was she more grateful for?"

He clears his throat. "I was told it would be better for the boy."

I return to him, sit on the end of the coffee table again and get into his space. "Which was she more grateful for, Dr. Jones?" I ask, leaning close to him, letting him see how far I'm willing to go to extract his confession.

"She said she'd take care of Hildebrand's signature after I signed off. She was going to see him anyway. I wanted to make a call, but it was late, and she insisted it had to be done."

"And you felt it was fine to do after she deposited the money into your account?"

Now he swallows hard and sits very still as sweat runs down his temple.

I get to my feet, turn away to find Zeke watching, posture relaxed. He has a dark side, my brother, one he hides well. And the look on his face is the same as I'd seen on that grainy video in Austria. I give him a nod and he acknowledges the gesture. I then turn back to Jones who shifts his gaze from Zeke to me. I reach for his collar, haul him to his feet and slam him into the wall.

"You've wasted enough of our time. Running. Hiding like a fucking criminal. Booking a private plane to the Bahamas and making us come chasing after you. I'm going to give you a choice. One, answer the fucking question and we'll be on our way or two, waste more of my time and I'll have Hildebrand deal with you. I can tell you a Councilor will not take kindly to having their signature forged in an attempt to conceal evidence from The Tribunal. Which is it going to be?"

"That was her. Not me!"

"Go on."

"She came to my house with two of her men. Big guys. Like you two. Like this one. Mean too. She wanted the body cremated. Said she changed her mind on the burial. And when I explained about The Tribunal, that a Councilor had to sign off, she lost her shit. It took one of those men to calm her down and that's when she paid me the money. I didn't ask for it. I swear. I was just scared. I signed off on what she wanted and when they left, I packed up and left too. I wasn't running from you. I was running from her. From them. I was fucking terrified. She's crazy."

"Got all that?" I ask, not looking away from Jones. Zeke replays the last part of it. "Yep."

"Good. Call Hildebrand. Let's get some men down here."

My phone rings and I release Jones who trips sideways before catching himself. I read the name on the display. It's the man watching the Bishop house.

"Yes?" I answer.

"The woman is on the move. Just left with two men."

I glance at Jones, thinking of his description of the men. "What about the boy?"

"Negative."

"Tail them. Let me know where she goes." The only place she should be going is out of town but to leave her boy behind? That doesn't quite fit.

"Yes, sir."

I disconnect and am about to tuck my phone into my pocket when it rings again. This is an unknown number, but I recognize the area code. It's in the city. I answer.

"Yes?"

"Jericho?" a woman's voice says. It's familiar and I try to place it but before I can, she speaks again. "It's Megs." And the moment I hear her name my heart drops to my stomach because there is no reason for her to be calling me. "I did something stupid."

## 45

## ISABELLE

Gerald Gibson has me inside the house within seconds. He's big. Like his brother. And as mean.

"You scream and I'll fucking knock you out," he tells me as he closes and locks the door behind us.

The inside of the house is a mess of empty food containers, liquor and beer bottles. Cigarette butts overflow from ashtrays. A large, worn-out recliner is set a few feet from the television. I can see cigarette burns on the arms of the torn brown upholstery. Next to it is a half-drunk bottle of beer. There's a couch in about the same shape as the chair against the far wall.

He drags me toward the tv set and switches it on, turning the volume up. It's an old sitcom. The audience laughs as I'm dragged deeper into the house.

Through an arch I see a dining room, set with a round table overcrowded with junk.

That's where he takes me, holding onto my arm. He reaches for a cell phone sitting on the counter between the dining room and a small kitchen.

"Let me go," I finally manage, still somehow clutching my purse.

"I said shut up, didn't I?" he tells me, gripping my arm so tightly, I'll have a ring of bruises.

The phone is one of those older flip phones. He opens it with one hand, pushes a series of buttons, then presses it to his ear.

"She's here," he says into it. I don't hear the person on the other end, but he grins and looks at me. "Yeah, it's her. No doubt." Quiet. Then the grin vanishes. "Ten minutes. And bring the money."

He flips the phone closed and turns his full attention on me.

I take a shuddering breath of air that smells faintly of cat piss. I see the litter in the corner. Over-full. I look all around. Anywhere but at his eyes. Because they're the same as his brother's eyes. Exactly the same.

"Have a seat," he says, lifting a wooden, straight back chair away from the table, setting me on it in the archway between the small rooms. He leans in close to me, his breath stinking, forcing me to close my eyes and turn away. He tells me not to move.

I grip the edge of the chair, not moving. He lets

go of my arm to reach across the table to a pile of zip ties. He turns back to me with a leering grin.

"Good girl," he says. He moves behind me. Taking my arms and bringing them together, securing my wrists with one long, orange zip-tie. He tugs hard so the plastic digs into my skin painfully. "Hurt?" he asks coming to stand in front of the chair, his gaze moving over me.

There's a vibrating sound and his grin vanishes. It's Megs's phone. She must be trying to call me, but I silenced it. Our gazes fall to the floor and he bends to pick up my purse, open it, dig inside. He scatters the photos from the ultrasound all over the stained, filthy carpet. He grabs the phone, looks at the display then throws it against the far wall with such force, I scream.

He checks his watch and turns to me, stepping closer, carelessly crushing some of the photos under his boots.

"We got a few minutes," he says. "Let's have some fun. My brother got a taste, didn't he? Said you were sweet and warm and so wet between your legs." That last part he says so close to me I have to hold my breath. My heart races, as the memory of that night returns. I thought the nightmares were too real. But this, now, being here, seeing this man, feeling him so close, they're nothing.

"The police are on their way," I say as he crouches down and sets his hands on my knees. The feel of him touching me makes my stomach turn. He pushes my legs apart and I wish I'd worn jeans today. But I wore the knit dress Jericho likes.

"They may well be but if there's one thing I know about our boys in blue it's that there's never much rush to get to this part of town. Besides," he says, gaze moving between my legs, to my eyes, then back down as he pushes the skirt of my dress up. "I just want a quick taste of top-shelf pussy." He makes an obscene gesture with his tongue that makes me recoil.

He slides his hands over my thighs and it's just like that night. Just like when his brother unzipped my jeans and slid his hands down my thighs as he shoved my jeans and panties off. I'm going to have a panic attack. I'm shaking so hard. My breath just gasps.

But then my gaze lands on one of the photos of my baby and something stills inside me, something hardens. Without consciously thinking, I act. I bring my knee up, catching him on the chin. His teeth clatter, the hit forces his head back, knocking him onto his ass. I then kick him so hard in the face that he cries out, falls hard, his head hitting the wall. My chair crashes in the opposite direction, my arms trapped beneath it, my own weight pinning me there.

I scream. Twisting my wrists. My shoulders. I hear him curse as he gets to his feet. I lift my head, trying to see what he's going to do, bracing for the worst.

But before that can come, the door smashes open and we both turn to find two huge men entering the house.

Two familiar men.

And behind them, Julia.

## 46

## ISABELLE

Julia's eyes meet mine and for one second, I feel relief. For one stupid moment, I actually feel relieved.

She holds my gaze briefly then takes in Gerald Gibson who is on his feet now. He's cupping his nose with both hands, blood pouring from it.

"She broke my nose," he tells her, moving toward Julia.

One of the men quickly closes and locks the front door, the other steps between Julia and Gerald. Julia puts a hand to his shoulder to nudge him aside.

"Get my cousin off the floor," she says. Even though my mind is cheering, something deeper inside me tells me not to trust it. Tells me she isn't here to help me.

The man moves around Gerald, knocking him back with just his shoulder. He approaches me and unceremoniously hauls me up by the chair. My wrists and shoulders throb with pain.

I watch Julia step toward Gerald, totally unafraid. She's wearing a black pantsuit. Her usual high heels. Her hair isn't quite right. It's in a bun but the bun is falling apart, and her makeup is faded like it's from last night. She's also not wearing her signature red lipstick. Looking closer, the suit looks rumpled. Like she's had it on for a while.

She touches Gerald's face, gripping his jaw with her hand, nails digging into it as she turns it this way and that to survey the damage.

"It's not broken, Gerald. Don't be a pussy." She releases him with a jerk. Gerald wipes the blood from his face on his sleeve.

"You bring the rest of the money?"

Julia loathes this man. I see it in her sneer. She shifts her gaze again to me but only momentarily before returning her attention to Gerald.

"The job isn't quite done, is it?" she asks him, then steps around him, coming to me.

The man who straightened my chair stands at my back, his presence like that of a hulking beast.

"Cousin," she says, looking me over. "Are you okay?"

Something crumples under her shoe before I have a chance to answer. We both look down to see the photos of the ultrasound. She lifts her foot because she's impaled one with her heel. The sight of this, her heel through that photo, is as horrific as that teddy bear hanging by its neck in Gerald Gibson's van. Stupidly, I feel the burn of tears as the knowledge of her betrayal fully settles.

"Was it you all along? Did Christian die because of you?"

She plucks the photo off her heel and studies it, tilting her head as she does. This is a different Julia than the one I know. Than the one she's been careful to show me. She's never been warm but some people are just like that. She is a good enough mother to Matty, although thinking back, there were times she was stand-offish even with him.

She turns her gaze to mine and smiles, all teeth. "Isn't it cute." She looks at the array of pictures scattered at our feet, disgust curling her lip.

"Did Christian die because of you?" I ask again, my voice more forceful.

She seems surprised by the question, or maybe my tone, because she drops the photo onto the floor and looks at me straight, eyes narrowing.

"That really was Carlton. Although I did help clean up his mess."

"Why? Why would you do that?"

"Because there was no way to keep the fact that you're a Bishop secret. Too many people knew, including IVI, and we were backed into a corner. Being that Carlton was married and we were cousins, well, the fact that Matty is his son and the rightful heir could have been contested. Monique knew. She knew her husband spent his nights in my bed and turned a blind eye. After the miscarriages she was a wreck anyway."

Miscarriages. Monique had multiple. I remember Julia telling me about them.

"She was easy to handle," Julia continues. "Stupid. Like all of Carlton's wives."

I feel sick. I always wondered about Monique. But she was just broken. Julia had broken her.

"The miscarriages... Did you..." I can't say it. Even knowing what I know about her, I can't say it. Can barely think it.

"Oh, don't be such an idiot. Matty is the rightful heir. Carlton should have acknowledged him, but he refused. He threatened to cut me off if I did or said anything about us. It's why he gave Monique the house in France. To shut her up about it. I don't know why he cared. It's not like there's anything wrong with him." She walks away a few steps, reaches into her back pocket, and takes something out. "Gerald, come here." She has her back to me, so I don't see what it is she hands him. "You want the rest of the money? I have it. In cash. In that bag there."

She points to a small black duffel sitting beside the door. I hadn't realized she'd brought anything inside. Gerald looks at it too. I watch them. He looks at what she just handed him, then at me, then back to Julia.

"Finish the job, Gerald."

Gerald steps toward me and I can finally see what he's holding. A switchblade. Small but sharp. Deadly.

"Finish the job and we can all live happily ever after. Well, not my dear cousin, but the rest of us."

## 47

# JERICHO

I slam the brakes, the car screeching to a halt half on the overgrown lawn in front of Marjorie Gibson's house. Our arrival won't be a surprise to those inside. In the distance, I hear the sirens of the police cars Megs called. Two of the guards who were with us at Jones's house spill out of the backseat, weapons drawn as I rush toward the front door, Zeke at my heels.

I don't have a pistol. I don't have any weapon. But I don't care. I need to get inside. I need to get to Isabelle. Even though Julia was able to lose the tail I had on her, I see Carlton's Rolls Royce in the driveway. When I get close to the front door, I hear a TV and over that comes Julia Bishop's voice giving the order to kill my wife.

When I find the door locked, I slam my shoulder against it. It doesn't give.

"Finish it! Now!" Julia screams. She knows she's caught. She's out of options. And that makes her even more dangerous.

"Sir!" One of the men shouts, aiming his pistol at the door handle.

I step away and he fires. The door swings open and I'm inside in an instant. In that same moment, a gunshot rings out, a bullet tearing through my shoulder sending me back a step, two, before I regain my footing.

The man who shot the door open enters, firing his weapon. Isabelle screams.

I push deeper into the house, take in the scene. One man on the ground. Another aiming a pistol at the one who took out their guy. Another of my men shoots his way in from the back of the house, Zeke on his heels. He's armed. I didn't know he was armed.

Their soldier takes mine out, a bullet hitting him square in the chest, dropping him. He's got an automatic weapon and as I run toward Isabelle and Julia, he sends more rounds across the living room where Zeke and the last of my men shoot back.

I crouch down, my shoulder burning. And all I see through the pain and smoke is Isabelle. Isabelle bound to a chair, trapped there, unable to run, to take cover. Gerald Gibson is just a few feet from her. In my periphery, Julia Bishop leaps toward him as I lunge to cover my wife from the onslaught of bullets.

I knock her chair sideways, grunting with the force of it, managing to slide my hand beneath her head before it hits the floor. She cries out and I hear the crunching of bone. See the photos of our baby scattered on this filthy floor as gunshots pock mark the walls.

A banshee like scream comes from Julia as she falls on top of me. I turn to her, see the arc of her arm and raise mine to stop her. She slices the dagger toward Isabelle's stomach. I twist my body between her and that short, sharp blade to stop her. To stop the repeating of history and instantly feel the burning pain of the knife plunging into my side.

My body tenses, my arms giving out, unable to hold my weight. Julia jerks away from me, lands on the floor bleeding beside me. Isabelle is trapped beneath me. The photos of our baby are turning red as blood seeps onto the small life captured on that page, ruined.

When I raise my eyes from that photo, the last thing I see are Isabelle's eyes. That too-blue gaze. Shards of glass. Too beautiful for this world. Too beautiful for such an ugly world.

And although I know she's screaming my name, I can't hear her anymore. I can barely see her as my vision fades and the world ends for me like it should have so many years ago.

## 48

## ISABELLE

He dies in the ambulance. I hear the flatline and scream for the paramedics to let me go to him, but they hold me back. The pain in my arm is unbearable as they do.

His face is ashen. Eyes closed. Mouth slack. Blood seeps from his side, his chest. And one of the paramedics is counting, doing compressions, another is giving oxygen.

"Come back to me! You come back to me!" I scream and sob. So close to him but unable to touch him. To hold him. To make him come back. "Please. God. Please!"

We arrive at the hospital and the doors fly open. Nurses and doctors meet us, carrying Jericho's gurney, compressions never ceasing, that count on a loop as I'm lifted out. They race him into the hospital, and I manage to run after them, not caring about my stupid arm when he could be gone.

"Jericho!" I scream his name as they wheel him through doors. Then I hear it. The flat line of the machine changing, beeping in a rhythm.

"He's back!" someone calls out and I want to hug that person. They wheel him through another set of doors and just as someone stops me from following, he opens his eyes. Only for one split second, Jericho opens his eyes and they lock on mine. Time stops for us. Time comes to a screeching halt and the only sound is that of machines and echoes of people close but no longer here. Not in this space with us. This bubble of time. I put my hand to my mouth and a sob escapes me. When he smiles, reaching the hand that is resting over his heart toward me, I know he hears me. I know he sees me. And I know he'll come back to me.

When he disappears through those doors, I'm barred from entering. I sink to the floor and sob, giving myself over to the doctors and nurses. Too exhausted to do anything else.

## 49

## JERICHO

She's asleep on the chair across from my bed. I watch her as machines beep around me. Whatever they're pumping into me makes it hard to keep my eyes open, but I fight it. I want to see her. I need to see her.

Her left arm is bandaged from her wrist up past her elbow. There's a small bandage on her forehead and scrapes on her cheekbone. She's wearing thick socks and that knit dress, but the arm has been cut off and it looks like it's been through hell.

I guess it has. We all have.

I shift my gaze to the ceiling. I died today. I flat-lined for more than three minutes. The last thing I remember before passing out were Isabelle's eyes. The panic inside them.

They talk about your life flashing before your eyes at the moment of death, but for me, I saw that bright, sunny morning in Mexico that turned into the bloodiest day of my life. Now second to what happened this morning. I felt Kimberly dying in my arms. And then I saw her face. Not bloody and lifeless like it had been then. Not gray and slack. I saw her as she was. Young and bright and beautiful wearing one of her happy smiles. She cupped my cheek, oblivious to the blood, then set her hand over my heart and never spoke one word. Just smiled.

Then she took my left hand, her gaze on the wedding band there. She turned it around and around my finger. I swear I still remember the sensation. Before I could attempt to explain things, explain what I'd done to avenge her murder, explain that I'd fallen in love with Isabelle, she laid her hand over my heart and leaned in close to kiss my forehead.

I knew she forgave me then. And more. She gave me her blessing. Said her goodbye.

When I next opened my eyes, I was back in this world, locked painfully in my body. Then I saw Isabelle's face. Heard her scream my name. Saw her stop when our eyes locked for that briefest of moments before I went under again, only to wake up hours later in this hospital bed.

Movement across the room calls my attention. I shift my gaze to my wife who stirs from sleep and blinks her eyes open. She stiffens momentarily and when I smile, she's on her feet and at my side, hands cupping one of my hands.

"You're awake."

"Only for a minute I think," I manage hoarsely, the drugs like hands wanting to pull me under.

"I'll take it," she says smiling, looking down at me and brushing hair back from my forehead. "Sleep, Jericho. I'll be here when you wake up."

---

I DON'T KNOW HOW MANY DAYS HAVE PASSED WHEN I next open my eyes. I'm in the same room but the sounds around me are different. Not so many machines.

"About time," comes a male voice.

I look over to see Zeke get to his feet and approach the bed. He looks like he just walked in from the office.

"You've been out for three days," he tells me.

My throat is so dry I can't speak. I glance at the cup on the nightstand. He picks it up, brings the straw to my lips and I drink. It's heaven. I can drink it down.

When I'm finished he sets it aside and pulls a chair close. "How are you feeling?"

"Been better," I say, although I don't feel pain. Just stiff and tired. "You're good?"

"Not a scratch on me. Our men are fine. Robert needed surgery but he's out and recovering at home. You took the brunt of the damage. Bullet to the shoulder. Knife wound to your right kidney. You're down to one now so try not to get stabbed on the other side."

I attempt a smile. "Isabelle?"

"I sent her home to shower and get some decent food. Apart from a few hours that first day, she wouldn't leave."

I smile. "Good. She's all right?"

He nods. "She's good and the baby's good," Zeke says. "Broken arm, a few stitches, but nothing major. You saved her life."

History repeating? Not this time. "Julia?"

"Took two bullets but survived. She's recovering a few doors down. IVI guards are standing at her door. When she leaves the hospital, she'll be spending her days in a Tribunal cell."

I nod at that, but the news doesn't make me happy. How could it? "Gibson?"

"Dead. Bullet to the head."

"Good. I should have done that when I first learned of his existence."

"It all just went sideways but everyone's all right. Don't beat yourself up. I think you've done enough of that, don't you?"

I remember the dream. No, it wasn't a dream. It was Kimberly.

Then I remember something else. Someone else. "Where's her boy? Matty?"

He clears his throat, studies me for a long moment. "Well, Isabelle brought him home, actually. He was in the house alone, Jericho. That bitch left him there on his own. Isabelle found him in the kitchen trying to make himself a bowl of cereal for dinner when mommy dearest didn't come home."

"Jesus."

"Angelique and mom are watching him. And Catherine of course. She's been stuffing the poor kid and I swear she picks him up to hug him every chance she gets."

"That's Catherine. Angelique and mom are home then?"

"Yeah. I called Dex after your surgery. Angelique has been asking to see you."

"What did you tell her?"

"That some bad people tried to hurt Isabelle and that you saved her."

"Couldn't you tell her I was on a business trip?"

"She's smarter than that, brother. She'd see right through it. Besides, have you seen a mirror?"

"Fuck. Is it bad?"

The door opens before he can answer, and Isabelle peeks her head in. Dex holds the door open over her head.

"Jericho!" She rushes in and just catches herself before throwing her body on top of me. She smiles at me, kisses my forehead, my mouth, then turns to Zeke. "You said you'd call the instant he opened his eyes."

"He literally just opened them."

"And I didn't get a call."

I smile at my brother's expression and reach out to touch her hair. She's left it loose down her back. It's soft and still a little damp from a shower. She's dressed in jeans and one of my shirts with the arm split for her bright yellow cast.

"Is that my shirt?" I ask.

"Oh," she glances down at it. "Yep. I didn't think you'd mind. You have so many."

"Hm."

"And besides, it smells like you."

I squeeze her hand.

"Boss," Dex says. "Hope you're feeling better than you look."

"Good to see you, too, Dex."

"I'm going to go home," Zeke says. "Get some rest myself. You'll stay?" he asks Isabelle.

She pulls a chair up beside my bed. "I'm not going anywhere." She turns to wave Dex and Zeke out but when she looks at me again, her expression is serious, eyes misting. "You saved my life. You almost died doing it. I don't have words."

I study her, see her innocence, her honesty, the good inside her. "How about thank you."

She smiles, wipes a stray tear. "Thank you."

I nod. "You're not off the hook though. You and I have a reckoning coming when I'm out of here."

She flushes, lowers her gaze. Nods. "I know. I'm so sorry I didn't trust you. I'm sorry you got hurt because of me. So many others got hurt because of me."

"You weren't holding the guns or the knife. That's not on you. Julia was going to attack. It was just a matter of time. I'd backed her into a corner."

"Still."

"She used a poison to kill Carlton. She was possibly behind Christian's death."

"I know."

"And who knows who else she's hurt."

"The miscarriages you mean?"

I nod. "Can't prove that but it's too coincidental. Four wives. Never a single child but hers. My guess is their affair had been going on for longer than we know. I wonder if she always had her sights on that inheritance."

"I'm going to talk to her this afternoon."

"Like hell you are. You're going to do as you said and stay put. Your ass in that chair. Am I clear?"

"Jericho, I need to ask her—"

"Your ass in that chair. Am I fucking clear?"

She considers, opens her mouth but I cut her off.

"That reckoning I mentioned? You don't want to add on to what I'm planning."

She flushes red.

"We're going to do things differently going forward, Isabelle. We're going to trust each other. No more secrets. No more half-truths. No more space between us. You understand?"

She nods. "I like that very much."

"Good. Because I like you very much. No. That's not all. I love you."

## 50

## ISABELLE

Jericho comes home a few days later. It's the first time Angelique has seen him since she left the house, and I can see the anxiety on her face as she waits for her dad. Matty is at my side holding my hand and sucking on his other thumb. I think he's still a little bit in shock with the move and not seeing his mom. He's too young to understand what's going on.

But when the door opens and Jericho walks in to the shouts of *surprise*, he stops short. It takes him a moment to take in the balloons and decorations Angelique, Matty and I made.

"Daddy!" Angelique runs to him, stopping herself just short of throwing herself into his arms. We told her he'd have to take it easy.

But Jericho crouches down and opens his arms

wide. "What are you waiting for? Do I smell bad? I showered—"

"No, silly!" she throws her weight into his arms, and I see him wince. But he squeezes his eyes shut and hugs her so tight, I think the hug is worth the discomfort.

"My little Angel."

"I'm so happy you're home. I'm so happy we're all home," Angelique says.

He straightens, lifting her with him. When Zeke steps in to take her, he shakes his head. "I got her." He walks to me, kisses me and we hug as a family. Then he draws back, crouches down again, setting Angelique on her feet.

Angelique moves around him to take Matty's hand from his mouth and hold it.

"Daddy, this is Matty. He's my new friend. And Matty, this is my daddy. I told you about him. He's like your uncle. Right?" she turns her face up to me to ask.

"Um, yeah. That's right." Okay, that handles that.

"It's very nice to meet you, Matty."

Angelique nudges her dad. "Shake his hand," she whispers loudly.

"Oh. Of course." Jericho extends his hand and Angelique places Matty's tiny one inside. Jericho smiles and Matty attempts to. "Which room did you get, buddy?"

"The one next to Angelique," he says quietly.

"Oh, that's a good one," he says, then leans in close. "She's not making you play with her princess dolls, is she?"

Matty's smile widens. "Only a little. I told her I'm not dressing up like one though."

"That's a smart decision," Jericho says and stands, ruffling his hair.

Angelique takes both of Matty's hands. She's so sweet with him and although he's only a year younger than her, she treats him like he's a baby and wants to take care of him. "Should we go get cake, Matty? I think since it's a special occasion they'll let us eat cake for lunch. Come on."

"Okay," Matty answers and allows himself be led along.

We all watch them disappear into the dining room. Then I hear Megs's voice. So does Jericho and he turns to me. Dex and Zeke make themselves scarce.

"I have another surprise for you!" I move closer to him, set my hands on his shoulders and kiss his cheek. "Megs is here! And she brought cake."

"I'm going to have some words with Megs outside of the dining room." He tries to take a step around me, but I move to block him.

"It wasn't her fault. She didn't want me to go. I made her cover for me. It was all my fault."

He raises his eyebrows and just then, Megs comes into the hallway and clears her throat.

We both turn to watch her approach. She holds out a small gift box to Jericho. "A peace offering."

He grunts.

I nudge him. He takes the box and opens it. Inside is a Cotton Candy gift card. "What the hell is this?"

"Unlimited cake. Lifetime supply. For you and for your family." Megs smiles.

He reads the little card then looks up at her.

"Look," she says, the Megs I know back. "We both love Isabelle. I already love Matty and that little girl of yours is on that list now too, so I'm sorry for my part in this. I should never have let my stubborn friend," she casts a chastising look at me, "run with her stupid idea." Another look.

Jericho smiles.

"But I did and I'm so happy you're all safe. If a little worse for wear," she tells him.

He grunts.

"But we're going to be in each other's lives and weirdly, Jericho, I don't dislike you. Let bygones be bygones?"

He glances at the card again then back to Megs. "I don't suppose I dislike you either. You're pushy and are a poor decision maker, but I think you mean well."

"Wow," I say but they both shush me.

"Welcome to my home, Megs."

"Thank you, Jericho. Oh, and you have me to

thank for the balloons," she adds as we follow her into the dining room. It looks like a pastel color explosion as so many balloons bob along the ceiling, the kids jumping to try to catch the ribbons.

"Oh great," Jericho mutters.

"I'm glad you like it," Megs says. "And you're welcome."

They exchange a friendly smile and, for the first time since I've known Jericho St. James, we all come together almost like a normal family and have cake. Just cake.

## 51

# JERICHO

At Isabelle's insistence and with young Matty in mind, I step into Hildebrand's office and close the door. The Councilor is seated beside Judge on the leather couch in his office, paperwork spread out before them on the coffee table.

"Mr. St. James," he says and stands.

"Councilor. Thank you for seeing me. Judge. Thanks for coming." Over the last few weeks I've been consulting with Lawson Montgomery in dealing legally with the Matty-Julia issue. Given his knowledge of the legal system and his position within IVI, he's a good ally to have.

"Have a seat." He gestures to the glass of whiskey on his desk. "Would you like one? I think we may both need it."

"I think you're probably right."

He pours me a tumbler, refreshing his and Judge's then sits back down. "This is highly out of the ordinary."

"I realize that."

"Discretion will be of utmost importance as it always seems to be when it comes to my dealings with you."

It was how we started our talks about Isabelle. "I think we want the same thing. There is a child involved, after all."

"How is the boy?"

"Doing well. He's settled in nicely."

"Good. And your wife?"

I smile at the mention of her. "Also doing well." Her belly is rounding with the pregnancy and she's even more beautiful than she already was.

It's been four months since the events at Gerald Gibson's home. Matty has settled in and is not the scared little boy he was that first day I met him. He's sweet and outgoing and between him and Angelique, the house is always full of laughter and joy. It's more wonderful than I could ever have imagined.

He still asks about his mother but there's nothing we can do about that. We've told him she needs to go away for awhile, and he seems to accept that although I can see he's confused. Thanks to Hildebrand, we've at least been able to let him see her twice.

And that's one of the reasons I'm here.

"Let's get the easy one out of the way first," Hildebrand starts. "Mr. Jones has been reprimanded for his role in destroying evidence as far as the cremation of Carlton Bishop's body is concerned. He was threatened and I believe him. I've dealt with Ms. Bishop and I know how she operates."

"That's fine. I trust Dr. Rosseau's expertise and reputation would stand against Jones's should it come that."

"It won't. That chapter is closed. But the matter of Ms. Bishop."

I draw in a deep breath.

"I certainly wouldn't have thought that you, Jericho St. James, would be here on her behalf to plead for her life to be spared."

Plead. I don't like that word. "Neither did I, Councilor. And I'm only here for the sake of the boy." And Isabelle because her heart is too kind to want to take an eye for an eye. She is too forgiving. But Hildebrand won't be moved by Isabelle's kind nature. A Sovereign Son, however? He'll bend over backwards for Matty Bishop.

"And that is the only reason I have agreed," he says, but I wonder if that's true. Julia used him, too. And he knows it. Bringing her before The Tribunal will not shed him in a good light. As a Councilor, he is immune from punishment, but his name would be dragged through the mud. He'd likely have to resign his position. The humiliation would be too great and we both know it.

Judge clears his throat. "I think we have come to a resolution that would best serve the child." He opens the folder on the desk and lays out the paperwork. I already know what it says so I sit back and sip my whiskey as Judge goes through it.

"Ms. Bishop has agreed to give up her rights to the child. Matthew Bishop will be adopted by his cousin, Isabelle, and Jericho. He'll be raised with his own last name and seeing how the houses are now united, it makes the most sense for both families."

"And who will control the inheritance until he comes of age."

I smile, hold my glass up in a toast. "Well, as Head of Household, that would, of course, be me."

"Ah. Of course," Hildebrand says.

"Don't look like that, Hildebrand. I have no intention of dismantling the boy's future. The feud between the Bishops and the St. James's is over. I think we've all paid a high enough price. The wall between our properties will be torn down, the houses united. You have to agree, it will be good for all, including The Society."

He studies the paperwork, nods. "And The Tribunal's part in this..." he trails off.

Judge speaks. "You'll spare Julia Bishop's life. She will live in exile from the child and The Society under perpetual house arrest in a place of your choosing, Councilor."

"At IVI's expense?" he asks, eyebrows raised.

"At my expense," I say.

"And the location will be secret if I'm understanding this correctly?" Hildebrand asks.

"You are. No one can or will know. She will simply disappear from all of our lives while living her own in isolation. She won't infect anyone else with her poison."

He looks up at me, grins. Here it comes. His revenge on Julia Bishop. "I know a perfect place. She'll hate it."

"Excellent."

We spend another hour hammering out details and, after signing the forms, I take my leave to return home to my wife and family.

# EPILOGUE 1
## ISABELLE

Christian St. James arrives two weeks after his due date. He's beautiful. Perfect. And as I sit in my hospital bed watching him drift off to sleep as he's nursing, I think about how happy I am. I hadn't realized how long it had been since I've felt happy. It's strange how you forget something like that or don't realize it's missing until you feel it again.

A soft knock draws my attention. Jericho pushes the door open and peers inside, smiling when he sees us.

"Are they awake?" comes Angelique's loud whisper as she scoots under his arm and into the room. "Belle!" she calls out excitedly when she sees me, startling the baby.

"Angelique," Jericho starts. "We talked about being quiet, remember?"

"Oops!" She hurries toward us, bringing with her about a dozen balloons that bounce against the door. She pushes her way inside and behind her, his little hand in hers, follows Matty, holding onto one balloon.

"Sorry about that," Jericho says as he closes the door and pushes the helium balloons out of the way. "Damn Megs and her damn balloons," he mutters. I see he's also carrying a box from Cotton Candy which he sets on a nearby table.

"No, it's fine. The baby needs to eat anyway, and he just keeps drifting off to sleep," I say as Angelique and Matty both peer at him.

"What's he doing?" Matty asks.

"Drinking milk," Angelique says. "It's how babies eat," she explains, turning to him and letting go of his hand.

"Let's give Isabelle and the baby some space," Jericho says, placing his hands on their heads and nudging them aside as he nears me. He kisses me then kisses Christian's little head.

I look up at him, look at the two little ones, Matty sucking his thumb, Angelique smiling so wide as they watch Christian in awe. It's only the second time they've seen him.

"Would you two like to hold him?" I ask once Christian unlatches. I cradle him to rub his back.

"Yes please!" Angelique says with a jump just as Christian lets out a little burp.

"Come here then you two," Jericho says, lifting Matty up into the seat and helping them both settle into the large armchair side by side. Matty rarely leaves Angelique's side. He loves her like a big sister, and she adores him.

"Ready!" Angelique says, arms outstretched.

Jericho turns to me. "I'll keep hold of him," he tells me.

I nod, hand the little bundle over and watch him, this giant of a man, a big teddy bear as he cradles his son and carefully places him in his daughter's arms. He crouches close to them, talking to them both in whispers. Matty peers at Christian's face while Angelique adjusts his little hat.

"There, that's better, baby," she whispers.

Jericho looks over at me and smiles. We're a family now. A real family. Angelique has started to go to a proper school and Matty attends day care at the same school three times a week for a few hours. It's made a world of difference for Angelique. She's learning so much but not only that, she's come out of her shell. She's less shy, more confident, and less afraid. More curious. Like every little girl her age should be.

Matty is doing well, too. He asks for his mom every night but seems to accept that she's away. We'll take him to see her again in a few weeks. It's part of the agreement. She'll see him four times a year with supervision and she's accepted it. At least she seems to, but the alternative, what she'd face with The Tribunal didn't leave her much choice. I feel sorry for her at times, but then I remember the things she's done. All the people she's hurt and worse. I know to some extent she was protecting her son and herself. And I understand that she may have loved Carlton once but by the end, what she did to him, that's not love. And I don't excuse Carlton either. Not for any of it. Maybe one day I will but today is not that day.

About twenty minutes later Leontine comes to take the children. Jericho will spend the night here with Christian and I and tomorrow morning, we all go home.

Once we're alone and Christian is settled in his little basinet, he pulls the chair close to my bed, his expression serious.

"Everything okay?" I ask.

"Everything is fine. You were right, though. There was someone on our property."

I told him about the shovel standing against Nellie's grave and how I'd felt like someone was there, like I was being watched.

"How did you find out?"

"Hildebrand got it out of Julia."

Councilor Hildebrand is still having her interrogated and sharing information relevant to us with Jericho. She duped the older man and he's not one to cross.

"She'd hired someone but still claims he was there to help you. To be an ally," Jericho says.

"And the shovel against Nellie's grave?"

"She didn't know anything about it supposedly."

"I don't believe that." She was the one doing the things she accused Jericho of doing. Terrorizing me to divide us. "Who was it?"

"Some kid off the street. Paid him a few hundred dollars to scale the wall between our properties and scare you. That's it. I don't actually know if she had other plans for him, but the kid was just that, a kid. I'm not sure he'd have been able to do anything other than hide out honestly."

"You found him?"

"Zeke did."

"You didn't...hurt him?"

"No. She took advantage of him and he seemed pretty scared already."

"What happens now?"

"Now?" As if on cue, Christian begins to stir and Jericho gets to his feet, instantly scooping him up and carrying him over to sit on the bed beside me. We both smile down at our baby, our sweet little boy who looks so much like my brother that when he opens his eyes and smiles a gummy smile, I tear up.

"It's probably just gas you know," Jericho says with a chuckle.

"I know." I wipe my eyes, no less emotional. "Still."

Jericho hugs me to him, shaking his head a little but smiling. Christian settles back into sleep against Jericho's chest.

"As to what happens now, now we go home and we live. We raise our family and we enjoy every moment of it. I love you, Isabelle. I can't imagine life without you."

"I love you, too, Jericho. And it's a good thing you can't imagine life without me because I need you in mine. Now and forever."

## EPILOGUE 2
JERICHO

*One Year Later*

Isabelle's stomach is rounded with our second child. From inside the house, I watch her sitting at the edge of the pool in a bikini, her breasts fuller, long hair thick down her back. She takes off Christian's arm bands and wraps him in a towel. She's a wonderful mother and a radiant woman. More so when her stomach is swollen with my child.

I want a brood of kids. We've discussed it but she thinks I'm kidding. I'm not. Six is a good number. Maybe seven.

I strip off my suit jacket, set it over the back of a chair and head outside, rolling up my sleeves.

"Daddy!" Angelique calls out jumping up and down and splashing water everywhere.

"Look what I can do, Uncle Jericho!" Matty yells and disappears beneath the surface of the pool, the snorkel huge on his little face. He comes up a split second later about three inches from where he just was. "I can swim!"

"Wow, you really can," I say, trying to look amazed.

"But you're not allowed in the water alone, Matty, okay?" Angelique tells him very seriously.

He nods to her. "I know."

I get to Isabelle and kiss her before taking Christian whose arms are outstretched, his little face beaming up at me. He's got four tiny teeth now and looks like Isabelle with his big blue eyes.

"Is Angelique teaching you how to swim too?" I ask Christian.

Angelique comes up beside me, her little body soaking my shirt when I crouch down to hug her. "He's too young, daddy. I'll teach him when he's Matty's age."

I smile. She's become quite the big sister. "That's a good idea," I tell her.

Catherine walks over with ice cream and the kids run to her. She takes Christian from us to give him a snack and I wrap a towel around Isabelle's shoulders.

"You look amazing," I tell her, hugging her to me. "Pregnancy becomes you."

"I'm going to get you soaked," she says but doesn't pull away.

"Then we'd better take your suit off," I tell her and lead her into the house. "We'll be back," I tell Catherine as we disappear.

I take my wife upstairs to our bedroom and strip off her bikini. I then stand back and take her in, my beautiful wife. My beautiful, strong, incredible wife. I'm in awe of her every day.

"What are you doing?" she asks, her cheeks flushing red as she takes my hands.

"Looking at you." I turn her face up to kiss her mouth. She kisses me back. We walk into the bathroom where I run the shower and strip. We step into the stall together.

"You're a good mom and aunt, you know that? You're good for them. All of them."

"Thanks for saying that. And you're a good dad and uncle. They all love you, their big teddy bear. Even Matty."

I smile, kissing her as I lather her with soap. What I want to do is make love to her. What I want to do is carry her to our bed, lock our door and make love to my wife for days. But we have something to do today. So, a few minutes later, once we're finished with the shower and dressed, we head downstairs and out the back door. We pass the kids in the library where Leontine and Catherine are entertaining them.

"Ready?" I ask.

"Ready," she says. I take her hand and lead her through the path into the woods. It's wider now and paved with stone to the farthest point of the property where wildflowers grow thickest between Bishop and St. James land.

She squeezes my hand and when we reach the new clearing Isabelle's eyes widen as she takes it all in. It's the first time she's seeing it since the work began.

"Oh, Jericho," she says, looking all around. "This is incredible."

"You like it?" I ask.

Her eyes glisten and I follow her line of vision over the beautiful arched portico that was once a wall between our properties. It is now a grand gateway, something to connect rather than divide, the wide path planted with beautiful flowering bushes and trees, lit with lights that will glow golden into the night.

She turns to me, reaches her hands to my face. "It's perfect. Our families united now. Nothing to divide us again. Thank you for this. For taking Matty in. For doing this for us."

"It's for all of us. We're family."

"Thank you."

"I have one more thing I want to do." We walk hand in hand to the chapel where smoke is coming from the chimney, the scent of incense strong, as I open the door and we enter.

"What's going on?" she asks. She's never seen the fire lit here and the place is transformed. Warmer with the glow and the heat.

I lead her to the fireplace along the wall farthest from us and she stiffens when she sees the book there on the mantle.

I take it, Draca's diary, and hold it between us.

She drags her gaze from it to me and I see the shadow this book casts over her. I never want to see anything steal away my wife's happiness again.

"It should have been burned centuries ago, but I'm doing it now. And I swear to you no St. James will ever harm a Bishop again."

She smiles, puts her hand on my forearm. "Are you sure you want to burn it?"

"Yes," I say, turning to throw the book into the raging fire and watch as it's absorbed. The flames shoot higher momentarily, as if not accepting the food given them, throwing it back up for its foulness. But then as we watch, it burns, becomes ash like the man who wrote it. Who wrote his hate into words and gave that hate a life all its own. One that would long outlive him. "Rest in peace, Draca St. James."

I turn back to find Isabelle's eyes on me. She

takes my hands, stands on tiptoe and kisses me. I feel the loosening of a chain. A letting go of something dark. And I kiss her back. I kiss my wife, the woman I love, the woman who saw the devil I am and loved me in spite of it.

# WHAT TO READ NEXT
UNHOLY UNION

*Cristina*

Damian Di Santo.

I still remember his name.

I try to mask my expression. I won't let him see what him being this close is doing to me.

When he touched me a moment ago, I couldn't breathe. And even though there are three other men in the room with us, he's the only one I see.

The way he traced that scar, I know he knows what it's from. When it happened. How.

Does he know what I lost that night? What I've lost since?

My chest aches at the thought. It's familiar, that tenderness. And it never heals. Never gets easier no matter how many years pass. I still miss Scott and my parents so much. Still think of them whenever anything good or bad happens. Still catch myself thinking I can't wait to get home and tell them.

I shake my head to dislodge the thought.

"It's almost your birthday," Damian says, stepping to the side and gesturing to the coffin-like box on the table. It's the biggest one yet. I know without having to look inside that it holds eight roses.

The final delivery.

When I turn back to him, he's watching me with cold eyes. Icy like steel. And they seem to penetrate right through any defenses.

This man knows me, knows my past, even as he's a stranger to me.

"I brought your gift early."

"Why?"

"I was in the neighborhood," he says lightly. He's laughing at me.

"I don't want it." My throat is so dry I have to pause to swallow before continuing. "I don't want anything from you."

He simply studies me, expression unchanging, and I wish I could read past the barrier of his eyes. Wish I knew what he was thinking.

"Why don't you take your gift and your goons and get out," I say, sounding braver than I feel.

A smile stretches across his face. "That's not very gracious, is it? Considering all I've done for you."

"What have you done for me?"

Without changing position, he slides his gaze to

my uncle and raises an eyebrow. One corner of his mouth rises into a small grin, telling me how much he's enjoying this. He checks his watch and bends to pick up the box.

"You can ask your uncle after I'm gone. You have a few hours yet. I assume you'll want to spend them with your family."

"What does that mean?"

"Open your gift and I'll be on my way." He holds the box out to me.

"I don't accept your gift. I'm not interested in opening it. I want you to leave."

"Did I give you the impression this was a choice?"

"I already know what's inside, and I don't want it. I never wanted any of them." I shove at the box, hoping he'll step away because I need space. I don't want to be the one to back up. But he captures my wrist instead and I look down at his hand, big and powerful and damaged.

He'd held my hand in his that first night, too, but he'd been gentle then. He hadn't wanted to hurt me or scare me.

Now, it's different.

When I shift my gaze up again, I find him studying me.

"This one is special, Cristina. This is the most important one." He squeezes my wrist. "Don't make me ask again."

I tug myself free, knowing I only manage because he allows it. I look beyond him to the men standing over my uncle, then look at my uncle. I've never seen him like this. We've never been close, but he's always been a man I could lean on. I did a lot of leaning in the years following my family's deaths. Now, though, as much as he's seething, as much as he so obviously hates this man, he also appears smaller, weaker.

"You don't need his permission," Damian says.

I turn my gaze to his.

"Only mine," he adds. "Open the box, Cristina."

Damian. I remember thinking how much it sounded like demon that first night eight years ago.

I never told anyone that he was there that night. Never told anyone about the others in the study. But I knew all along that I'd see him again. This monster.

I've known I'd have a chance to look into his eyes. To know the evil that lies beneath the cool, handsome exterior.

The only ugliness is his hand.

And what's on the inside.

Taking the box, I move to sit down because my legs are beginning to tremble beneath me.

Damian watches as I set the box on my lap and undo the ribbon.

I pull the lid off and set it aside. The familiar smell makes my stomach turn. It grows stronger when I unwrap the tissue paper that blankets the dead roses. I take care not to prick my finger on a thorn because they always have thorns.

I peel the last layer away to see the lifeless flowers nestled in black paper. This time, there isn't a card with the number scrawled on it. In its place is a yellowed scroll of paper tucked between the flowers.

I look up at him, and his expression has gone deadly serious.

He meets my eyes, gesturing for me to go on.

I reach for the sheet, my hand trembling. I have to look. I don't have a choice.

The paper is old, and when I unroll it, it wants to curl back up.

I hold it open. My eyes fall instantly to my father's scrawled, drunk signature. He was drunk a lot after the accident. I think he may have been drunk during it. He and my mom had been fighting so much by the end.

I look up at him, confused.

"Read it," he commands, voice tight, eyes locked on that sheet of paper.

It's a contract of sorts. One that would hold up in no court of law. One that buys...No, this makes no sense.

I keep reading. The script it's written in is that of someone from another generation. But what it says, it can't be.

There's an exchange. My father's life for my childhood.

But that's not all. There's a promise that on my eighteenth birthday, the day I am no longer considered a child, I become fair game.

"This can't..."

I look up at Damian.

"Did you know it was my sister's wedding day?" he asks me.

I want to ask what the hell he's talking about. What this means. But my throat is as dry as a desert and I can't speak.

"A candlelit wedding. Her dream." His words sound sad, but then his face hardens, and his pupils become pinpoints as he focuses on me. "She never made it, though. None of us did." He turns his hand just a little, and I see the scarred flesh.

I think about the accident that stole my mother and brother from me. I don't remember it. I don't remember much, but the one thing I wish I could forget is my brother's face just before he went through the windshield.

I shake my head, momentarily close my eyes to block it. I can't think about that now. Not in front of him.

When I look up at Damian the sorrow I'd heard in his words doesn't show in his eyes. I get the feeling that sorrow has festered over time and turned into this. Because what I see is the monster he warned me about eight years ago.

I see hate inside him.

Hate for me.

The box and roses spill onto the marble floor when I rise, crushing the contract in my hand.

"This can't be," I whisper.

"But it is." He steps closer, looming over me, and all I can do is stare up at him. "Enjoy your last few hours of freedom, Cristina, because come midnight, you belong to me."

One-click Unholy Union!

# ALSO BY NATASHA KNIGHT

Unholy Intent

*Collateral Damage Duet*

Collateral: an Arranged Marriage Mafia Romance

Damage: an Arranged Marriage Mafia Romance

*Ties that Bind Duet*

Mine

His

*MacLeod Brothers*

Devil's Bargain

*Benedetti Mafia World*

Salvatore: a Dark Mafia Romance

Dominic: a Dark Mafia Romance

Sergio: a Dark Mafia Romance

The Benedetti Brothers Box Set (Contains Salvatore, Dominic and Sergio)

Killian: a Dark Mafia Romance

Giovanni: a Dark Mafia Romance

*The Amado Brothers*

Dishonorable

Disgraced

Unhinged

**Standalone Dark Romance**

Descent

Deviant

Beautiful Liar

Retribution

Theirs To Take

Captive, Mine

Alpha

Given to the Savage

Taken by the Beast

Claimed by the Beast

Captive's Desire

Protective Custody

Amy's Strict Doctor

Taming Emma

Taming Megan

Taming Naia

Reclaiming Sophie

The Firefighter's Girl

Dangerous Defiance

Her Rogue Knight

Taught To Kneel

Tamed: the Roark Brothers Trilogy

# ABOUT THE AUTHOR

Natasha Knight is the *USA Today* Bestselling author of Romantic Suspense and Dark Romance Novels. She has sold over half a million books and is translated into six languages. She currently lives in The Netherlands with her husband and two daughters and when she's not writing, she's walking in the woods listening to a book, sitting in a corner reading or off exploring the world as often as she can get away.

Write Natasha here: natasha@natasha-knight.com

NATASHA KNIGHT
*your dark romance with heart*

www.natasha-knight.com

## THANK YOU

Thank you for reading *The Devil's Pawn Duet*. I hope you love Isabelle and Jericho's story.

Made in the USA
Las Vegas, NV
02 December 2023

81999372R00254